Fleur McDonald lives on a large farm east of Esperance in Western Australia, where she and her husband Anthony produce prime lambs and cattle, run an Angus cattle and White Suffolk stud and produce a small amount of crops. They have two children, Rochelle and Hayden. Fleur snatches time for her writing in between helping on the farm. *Purple Roads* is her third novel.

www.fleurmcdonald.com

Also by Fleur McDonald
Red Dust
Blue Skies

Purple Roads

FLEUR McDONALD

ARENA
ALLEN&UNWIN

Arena Books, an imprint of
Allen & Unwin, Sydney, Melbourne, Auckland, London
83 Alexander Street
Crows Nest NSW 2065
Australia
Phone: (61 2) 8425 0100
Fax: (61 2) 9906 2218
Email: info@allenandunwin.com
Web: www.allenandunwin.com

Cataloguing-in-Publication details are available
from the National Library of Australia
www.trove.nla.gov.au

ISBN 978 1 74237 481 9

Typeset in 13/17.5 pt ITC Garamond by Midland Typesetters, Australia
Printed and bound in Australia by Griffin Press

10 9 8 7 6 5 4 3 2 1

*To my very own 'Road Train Man', my dad,
John Parnell, and the amazing woman behind
him, my mum June. Extraordinary parents.*

*To Anthony, Rochelle and Hayden: without you,
I would be nothing.*

Prologue

The streetlight threw a pale circle of light onto the road, but beyond its edge the night was dark. Sandy shrank deeper into the shadows to avoid the men chasing him.

He could hear their feet, pounding against the pavement, their panting breaths and urgent shouts.

'This way, I saw him go this way!'

'No! He ducked down the side street!'

A thorn was pushing into his thigh but he didn't dare shift position in case the movement alerted his pursuers to his hiding spot. He smiled as he thought he heard their footsteps start to fade. He knew the area better than anyone.

Six years on the streets had made him shrewd. At sixteen, he knew where the warmest doorways were, where he could get clothes from and the soup kitchens that would feed him without asking questions. He knew to trust no one.

The pain in his thigh worsened and he felt the thorn pierce his skin. Blood seeped through his flimsy tracksuit pants.

'I trusted you! How could you do that?' The words from years ago echoed from somewhere deep inside him. Confused, Sandy shook his head. Where had that come from? He couldn't allow those thoughts in.

He wouldn't allow them in.

But despite his determination, still they kept coming, softly at first, then louder and louder. Recollections as clear as yesterday forced their way back, making him forget the worrying foot-falls, as he absent-mindedly ran his fingers over the scar on his forehead. He squeezed his eyes shut, trying to stop the words.

Suddenly a hand firmly grasped his shoulder and yanked him out of the bush.

'I've been looking for you,' a voice from the past said.

As Sandy looked into the face of his captor, the memories weren't memories anymore. They were real.

'Uncle Jimmy,' he said without thinking. The walls he had built while living on the street crumbled. He was an eight-year-old boy again in *the arms of someone he loved. 'Uncle Jimmy.' The words came out as a sob.*

'Come on, lad; let's get you outta here, hey? We've got a business to run. Together.'

Chapter 1

The CD player changed to one of Matt's favourite songs and he sang along softly, glancing down at the speedometer and then across to check the temperature gauge. Everything was as it should be, but the truck didn't feel right. It was pulling too hard. The terrain wasn't steep, so what was the problem?

The song died on his lips as he looked in the rear-view mirror and saw a glow coming from the front trailer. Tapping his brakes, he watched in horror as sparks shot out from the drive wheels of the prime mover and a gush of flames from the tyres suddenly lit the darkness.

He needed to stop. He needed to stop *now*, but it took time for his big rumbling rig to slow – time Matt didn't have.

Reefing the handle open before the truck came to a halt, he jumped to the ground and ran to unhook the back trailer. Sprinting back to the cab, Matt revved the engine hard and tried to drag the front trailer away from the back, but the engine stalled.

'Please, no,' he begged, turning the key again, trying to control the fear and panic welling up inside him. As the engine roared to life, he floored the accelerator and the truck bunny-hopped forward. Finally, with the brakes locked on and the tyres burning, he managed to move the large machine, leaving deep skid marks in the gravel behind him.

Flames were spreading quickly, licking at the back of the cab. The heat was so intense he knew he wouldn't be able to unhook it – he just hoped he'd be able to save most of the sheep he was carting.

With smoke growing thicker with each passing moment, he took a deep breath, plunged into the haze and felt for the back of the trailer. Unpinning the door and lowering the ramp, he raced into the crate, trying to turn the heads of the startled ewes and push them out of harm's way. They were scared and uncooperative, but just when he thought he wouldn't be able to get any out, they took fright and started to bolt from the truck into the darkness, with Matt following behind the stragglers.

He ran down the ramp and once again assessed the situation, his stomach constricting as he glanced towards the cab and saw the fire creeping towards the fuel tanks. The oil from the diff would be fuelling it now. He thought briefly of the fire extinguisher, but there was no time.

A set of lights appeared down the road and

within seconds a rusty ute pulled up. An old man got out, grabbed a shovel from the tray and started throwing sand onto the flames. But it was too late. The flames had reached the diesel tanks.

Burning plastic, rubber and diesel hurled deep, black smoke into the night sky with a loud *whoomph*. Both men threw their hands up to protect their faces and backed away from the fire.

'All right, mate?' the older man asked after the explosion.

Matt could only nod, unable to speak around the lump in his throat. Then bile surged up into his mouth and he fell to his knees, vomiting and shaking.

The man pulled him up gently and led him to the ute.

'Sit here,' he instructed and Matt, dazed, did as he was told. Shortly after, he felt a blanket being draped over his shoulders. 'Not much we can do until daybreak,' the man said. 'I'll call for some more help,' and took a mobile from his pocket.

A while later with the calls made, the man reappeared and handed Matt a cup of sweet tea he'd poured from a flask. He urged him to drink. Matt's hands trembled so violently the tea slopped over the rim. The scald hardly registered but he let the man take the cup from him and hold it to his mouth.

'How am I going to tell her?' he kept saying, over and over. All he could think of was his future – and that of his family – lying in the charred ashes on the road. It took a little while before he realised that the guttural moans he could hear came from himself.

When the phone call came at 3.21 in the morning it didn't wake her. Anna was already awake, having just been up to the toddler. Alarmed at first, she had snatched up the receiver only to relax when she realised it was her husband. Frowning at his garbled words she said, 'Slow down, hon. I can't understand what you're saying. What's wrong?'

'Accident,' Matt gasped. 'I've had an accident. Truck fire. It's all gone.'

Shocked, Anna was still for a moment, before a hidden force made her shoot from the chair and pace around the living room, wildly combing her hands through her hair.

'Are you okay?' she managed. 'What about the sheep? The truck?' Questions tumbled from her mouth before she could stop them.

'It's all gone,' Matt whispered. 'All gone.'

'Where are you?' she asked.

'McKenna's Creek, north of Orroroo.'

'I'll be there as quickly as I can.' She went to hang up the phone, then added, 'Matt, I love you. It'll be okay. Everything will be fine, honey.' But she said it to dead air.

Quietly, so as not to wake Ella, she went into the kitchen to make a thermos of coffee and some sandwiches. She grabbed the last bar of chocolate, packed it all into a tin tuckerbox, carried it out to her beat-up dual cab, and threw it into the tray. Making sure the ute was out of gear she started the engine and flicked on the air conditioner.

Anna jogged back to the house for Ella. As she walked through the kitchen, the sleeping toddler over her shoulder, she glanced around, hoping that she had everything for the emergency. Then she walked out of the house, pulling the door shut behind her.

As Anna carefully laid Ella in the car seat, the child opened her eyes and took a breath, looking like she was about to cry. Grabbing a dummy from her back pocket, Anna popped it in Ella's mouth before she had a chance to let out a squeal and talked to her softly, stroking her cheek.

Ella sucked hard and her eyes began to close once more.

Pushing the door shut quietly, Anna breathed a sigh of relief. A long trip with a crying child didn't hold much appeal for her tonight. Ella should sleep now. The car's movement would see to that.

Looking over to Bindy, the old kelpie, watching from her hessian bag near the front door, she said: 'Keep an eye on things, old girl,' before getting into the ute and shoving it into gear. Switching the headlights to high beam, she followed the drive out onto the main road, swung the car to the right and headed north.

Music played softly as she drove past the darkened farmland; she pictured the scene in daylight: paddock after paddock of golden wheat and barley stubbles which weren't as thick as they needed to be to make money.

After five years of bad seasons, Matt's accident could be the last straw. For a moment the road blurred in front of her as hot tears welled in her eyes. She imagined the bank foreclosing, a clearing sale and the loss of the farm. But just as quickly, she filed those thoughts in the back of her mind. The most important thing was that Matt wasn't hurt. Together they could make it through anything – they always had.

As the first light kissed the horizon, Anna slowed the car to a crawl, for the grey kangaroos were the same colour as the cassia bushes and to hit one would cause more problems than they already had.

She drove on until the farming land and bitumen gave way to the deep purple dirt roads of the mid-north of South Australia and the sun had risen high in the sky. The stony red ground which now surrounded her was dotted with small scrubby bushes and tall gum trees that lined the deep creeks crisscrossing the country.

Finally she spotted a wisp of smoke. A few kilometres further on, she saw several bewildered ewes wandering along the road. Rounding a corner, she saw a pile of dead sheep, blood oozing from their noses, and a cloud of black, buzzing flies crawling over the carcasses. A little further on were the burnt-out remains of a truck, surrounded by lots of utes and cars.

As she pulled up in a cloud of dust Anna saw that the men in the distance and scrub land were mustering the surviving sheep. Other helpers were dragging the dead ones off the trailers and throwing them onto piles. The only man not moving was Matt, who was watching, silent and still.

Chapter 2

Three months later

The gentle sound of drizzle on the tin roof woke Anna. At first she lay still, wondering what the noise was, and then listened with relief as it grew heavier.

Even though it had been forecast, she'd tried not to get her hopes up. Both she and Matt were sick of listening to weather predictions which were so often proved wrong. Whenever the forecast rain failed to eventuate, Matt would stomp around the house, cursing the weathermen, the country and anyone who was close by.

And no matter how many requests Anna sent to her mother, who she was sure was watching over them, the skies had remained a steadfast blue.

But tonight, judging by the slow, steady drumming on the roof, the opening rains had arrived. She turned over, snuggled into Matt and lay there with her eyes closed, enjoying the sound. 'Thanks, Mum,' she thought. 'This is just what we need.'

After about five minutes, she woke Matt so he could listen too.

Together, they lay silently, their arms wrapped around each other, their bodies tingling with anticipation and their minds full of hope and churning with the jobs there'd be to do in the morning.

Matt and Anna's farm, 'Manna', was about ten kilometres to the north of Spalding and in the heart of crop-growing country. The road frontage land was flat and open, but as you went deeper into the farm, it backed onto undulating hills. The Broughton River ran around the base of these hills and had brought life to dry and parched land. When the rains had been constant the river had flowed freely. Reeds and grasses had grown in abundance. But now it was a dirty trickle and, in some places, it didn't even flow; it was just a series of stagnant puddles.

Gum trees grew sparsely, and even though the country lacked anything in the way of bushes and trees, in a few places the native pines had put down roots. In the broad-acre paddocks that didn't have crops sown in, deep stock pads cut through the paddock to watering and feeding points.

Matt had been servicing his seeding machinery in hope of a good opening break, and with the rains which had come over the past days, it now seemed his optimism had been rewarded.

'It's one of the best opening rains we've had in years, Bill,' said Matt. 'We've already had three days of rain, four inches, and according to the long-range forecast, there's more to come.' Matt paused. 'Could I make an appointment to see you today and work through another budget? I'd like to add in a bit more cropping.'

Anna couldn't hear the bank manager's voice on the other end of the phone so she watched her husband's face for a reaction. When he grinned and punched the air with a clenched fist, relief washed through her. Smiling, she turned away to tend to Ella, who was lying in front of the fire, her chubby legs waving in the air.

'Let's get this nappy on before you have an accident all over the carpet,' Anna cooed, gently pulling her little girl towards her. Ella grinned and tried to crawl away, all the time gurgling in toddler language as Anna stroked her downy hair. It was strawberry-blonde; in this she took after her mother and grandmother.

Anna expertly finished fastening the nappy, savouring her husband's voice, which sounded alive, full of expectancy and hope.

'No worries, Bill. I'll see you at twelve then.'

Matt put the phone down and whooped, then ran over and grabbed Anna around the waist, pulled her up and danced her around the room. Laughing, Anna felt a buzz of excitement course through her, enjoying seeing him so happy. This rain meant there would be lush green crops, the heads of wheat full and plump – and, most importantly, they finally had the chance to build up a healthy bank balance. That would mean Matt could give up driving his dad's borrowed truck; he wouldn't have to work nights and she would have her happy, fun-loving husband back – not the shell of a man he'd been since the accident three months earlier.

She knew she really shouldn't be thinking so far ahead. After all, they still needed many more inches of rain to achieve their goal. But after five bad seasons her sense of optimism was all that was keeping her going.

Five years of heartbreak. Late breaks, false breaks and the rain just drying up when it was needed most. Too many times they'd had to watch their crops wither, their souls crumbling a little more with every rain front that passed them by. Year after year, Matt had turned the sheep onto their crops in the hope of at least getting some small return out of their investment.

Their bank balance had dwindled until their savings were all but gone, the overdraft was sky high and the interest kept accruing with each passing day. Every year, however, even though it meant going deeper and deeper into debt, they fronted up to the starting line again. This year, the bank had made clear, was their last chance.

The truck fire had been devastating to them

both, even more so when, a few days after the fire, they realised the insurance on the truck had lapsed. There just hadn't been the money to insure it, a fact Matt had kept hidden from his father. Now there was no way of buying a new one or making any extra money. It had been Matt's trucking wage which had been keeping food on their table.

Anna had long since become an expert at scrimping and saving, but sometimes when she dressed Ella in hand-me-downs from one of her friends, she had to push aside a feeling of resentment at their bad luck. One day, she promised herself, her little girl would have beautiful clothes that were bought straight from the shops, not the threadbare ones she wore now.

'I'd better have a shower and get going,' Matt said, breaking into her thoughts. 'He's going to see me at twelve so I haven't got long.'

'Maybe Ella and I could come too,' Anna suggested. 'I can do the shopping while you're at the bank. It would save on petrol.' Their small local town of Spalding had lost its only bank when the powers-that-be had decided they needed to be centralised, and there weren't enough people to support a large supermarket.

'Yeah, good idea,' Matt agreed. 'We can talk figures and plans on the way there.'

Anna scooped up Ella, smiling. 'Sure.'

Although the cold, grey day was punctuated with heavy showers and the clouds sat so low they touched the peaks of the hills, the drive from Spalding to Clare was enjoyable. Anna and Matt relished the wet landscape, the creeks that had begun to trickle then flow with a force not seen in years and the puddles which had formed on both sides of the road. There were tractors in the paddocks, pulling seeding rigs across the rich ochre-coloured soil; the hum of the engines raced across the landscape.

Anna was aware of Matt's face darkening as he watched the machinery work; no doubt he was wishing he didn't have to go cap in hand to the bank because he wanted to put in more hectares of crop. But the fertiliser was such a large investment; he couldn't just book it up without talking to Bill about what he wanted to do. Already struggling to pay the interest and monthly accounts, it was a huge deal to add another fifty or sixty thousand to their overdraft.

Anna squeezed her husband's hand, and he turned to her with a smile.

'Look at all this water,' he said. 'Can you remember when you last saw it like this?'

'Not for ages, honey,' she said. 'The last year the Broughton River ran a banker was the year I left school. What's that, ten years ago?'

'At least! This season will get us out of the mire, I'm sure of it.'

His optimism reminded her of the first few years of their relationship.

Having both caught the same bus across to Clare every day to attend high school, she had known who Matt was, but never dreamed he could be interested in her.

She'd been just fifteen when Matt had asked her if she wanted to go to the school social with him. She still remembered how the large footy club rooms had been decorated with coloured streamers and balloons; the school principal's personal stereo had belted out tunes from the eighties. The whole school had taken great pleasure in singing 'Am I Ever Gonna See Your Face Again?' and adding their own lyrics to the chorus.

But it was when she thought of Matt clumsily putting his arms around her, as The Police sang 'Every Breath You Take' that she got goose bumps. Even after all this time, whenever the song came on the radio she relived their dance.

Stunned that a boy two years older had noticed her, she'd taken special care when dressing that evening. Her brothers, Nick and Rob, had ribbed her endlessly, although they too had been very attentive to their appearance, since they were taking the Timer sisters to the social.

Matt's mum had agreed to drive Matt and Anna to the dance, and as she pulled up in the quiet street just on dusk Matt tumbled from the car. From her bedroom window Anna watched him walk nervously up the path and knock on the door. Nick answered and, being in the same year as Matt, talked local and AFL footy until Anna walked through the door. Both boys fell silent as they looked at her.

Anna would say the moment she fell in love with Matt was when she walked into the sitting room and he looked at her with a glorious, shy smile. He was dressed in denim jeans and a red shirt, the sleeves rolled up. His strong arms and tousled brown hair had had a tingling effect on her she'd never felt before. Sensing a change in the mood, Nick had punched Matt on the shoulder and told him to behave himself – he'd be watching!

The social had been sparsely attended. It was seeding time and many of the farms' kids hadn't been able to get back to Clare. When they weren't dancing Anna and Matt had sat on some of the plastic chairs that lined the walls and talked.

Matt confided to her his dreams of owning a farm, being his own boss and feeling the freedom the land offered. He told her he was working on a local farm at weekends to save up enough money to buy a ute and a few sheep he had been told he could agist there. 'It's my start,' he told her. 'I'll get where I want to, I just know it.'

Anna recounted the difficulties of being a bank manager's daughter and constantly on the move. It seemed that as soon as she started to make friends they'd leave for a new town, a new school. Eventually she'd decided it was easier to hang out by herself.

'We'll have to change that,' Matt said as he slipped an arm around her shoulders.

From then on, they were inseparable. Anna, who had only ever been to friends' farms before, braved sheep poo and flies to visit the farm where Matt was working. Over the following years she became well versed in agriculture and began to understand Matt's craving to acquire land of his own. In the end it had become her dream, too.

After Matt left school, his father gave him part-time work driving for his truck company and, within time, Matt was able to buy the truck he was driving. This part-time job gave them a steady income and was the only way his parents had been able to help him financially. Still, Ian and Laura encouraged their son's hard work and aspirations. Matt's maturity and determination also impressed Anna's parents, even though they insisted she only see Matt at the weekends, so as not to disrupt her studies. It was clear to everyone these two young people were destined to be together.

Once Matt had left school and got a full-time job on a farm, he and Anna fell into an easy routine of Matt driving to town and picking up Anna on Saturday mornings. They would drive to footy or cricket, have Saturday together, and then spend Sunday at the farm. He taught Anna everything he was learning about farming.

Two years later and with the closure of the bank, Anna's family eventually moved to another town, but Anna stayed. Being from a close family, she found it lonely without her parents and noisy brothers, but the pull to be with Matt was too strong for her to even consider leaving.

A year earlier, her brother Rob had gone to Adelaide to study hospitality; he occasionally made the trip back to Spalding for a weekend, as did her parents, from Port Augusta, the town they had been transferred to. Nick moved to Port Pirie and got a job carting fuel all across South Australia. If he was passing through Spalding he would stop and call in on her or ring to see how she was, and it was those visits that eased the gap left by her family moving.

Anna was proud of Matt as he gradually bought more sheep, then a tractor. He raised some capital, started a contract seeding business, and after a busy seeding season, bought a header, which he contracted out at harvest time. While Matt was busy with the cropping, Anna would look after the sheep, all the while studying agribusiness at the University of Adelaide's Roseworthy campus.

Finally, six years after he'd left school and two years after her parents' terrible accident that killed her mother and left her father a paraplegic, Matt had enough money for a deposit on a farm. The accident caused grief to filter throughout Anna's family and for some time she wasn't able to even think about buying a farm. She was away from Spalding for weeks at a time. There had been the funeral to get through, organising her father's care and treatment, finding somewhere for him to live and helping him with his own heartbreak. It had been a highly emotional and draining time and she had been so thankful for Nick and Rob's support. Matt had been incredible; more than once she had told him that she was sure she wouldn't have been able to get through it without his constant support. Finally she managed to come through the hellish spell and they started to search for the perfect property.

Within a year they had found it: three thousand, three hundred and forty hectares to the north of Spalding. The older couple who sold it to them told Matt and Anna they were thrilled to be passing it on to such an enthusiastic couple.

Matt negotiated a bargain price for the rundown farm, but it still left them strapped for cash and very much dependent on some good seasons in order to hang on to it and improve it. For two years the seasons were mostly with them – good opening rains, follow-up rains at the right time and high sheep prices.

But then came the five consecutive years which weren't so good. Some of those years it hadn't rained until it was too late and too cold to seed the crops. During that time, sheep prices were low, wool was in the doldrums and as for cattle ... well, as much as Matt had desperately wanted to buy some cows, they had only been able to afford an old Friesian that Anna milked every morning.

Anna grinned as Matt squeezed her hand and smiled at her. This year would be different, she hoped, glancing over her shoulder at their beautiful sleeping daughter.

Chapter 3

Matt gulped down scalding coffee and savoured the bacon and eggs Anna had cooked for him.

He had planned this seeding down to the minute and he didn't have time to waste by eating, although he knew he had to. He wanted to be on the tractor from midnight until nine in the morning. That gave him the rest of the day to fix any breakdowns, deal with trucks or quickly do a stock check around the farm, before snatching four or five hours' sleep and then heading back out to the tractor. Anna could keep an eye on the stock, he knew, but it was more difficult for her now she had a toddler to look after. Her world revolved around Ella's feed and nap times.

Everything had gone according to plan today but the few hours' sleep he'd grabbed early in the night hadn't been enough. He had the first thousand hectares in and today the next two road trains of fertiliser were arriving. That meant around one hundred and twenty tonnes of fertiliser! He was worried though. Rain had been forecast and he hadn't yet been able to afford to build a fertiliser shed and so he had made the decision to pile it on the ground. If it rained while it was still out in the open, it would be ruined.

Matt rubbed his eyes. He was worn out and cranky, and there was no option but to keep going. There was so much riding on this season. Every time he thought about the crop failing or something going wrong – the tractor breaking down, a crop disease they couldn't afford to spray for or anything similar – he felt physically ill. The size of the debt they'd accumulated during the bad seasons was huge. He *had* to turn things around this year. So far the season was going really well and it was up to him to make the most of it.

Anna had tried to ease the pressure by offering to find work in town – maybe pulling beers at the pub or cooking in the kitchen of the local roadhouse – but Matt knew the little she would earn really wouldn't make any difference to the farm finances, only the house. And really he needed her to help on the farm.

Matt sighed as he finished his breakfast.

Anna glanced at her scowling husband. 'Can I do anything to help?' she asked, as she moved across to a grizzling Ella.

'Nope,' he said, his voice short. Distracted.

Anna had to steel herself to ask the question. 'Matt?'

'What?' he said testily.

'It's the rams – they're still in the yards. Where do you want me to put them?'

Matt threw down his knife and fork. 'Anna, I don't care. Just keep them away from the ewes. Bloody hell, I've got enough to think about without you hassling me about minor things. You know as much about what's going on as I do. *You* make the decision. And shut that kid up. I'm going to unload the fertiliser trucks then get back on the tractor.'

Ella's crying intensified, becoming shrill as Matt stomped out the door.

Anna picked her up, whispering, 'Shh, shh. It's okay. Daddy can't help it, it's just a busy, stressful time of year.'

Matt had become difficult to live with over the past few weeks; worse than he'd ever been. She'd tried to be understanding when he boiled over but he wasn't the only one who had pressure on him. Anna would look at all the bills before Matt and she knew as well as he did there wasn't the money in the bank to pay them. Even with the bridging finance Matt had negotiated to buy the fertiliser with, they were still sailing too close to the wind. She needed to talk to him about it, but it wasn't the time.

'There's never a good time at the moment,' she

murmured against Ella's soft skin, feeling increasingly uneasy. She hoped once seeding was finished it would get better. She tried to calculate how many hectares there were left to seed. All going well, perhaps another week would see them finished. Well, the bills would have to wait until then.

Putting Ella back in her play pen, Anna cleared the dishes from the table and went to find her rubber boots. It was a welcome change to have yards muddy enough to warrant them.

Matt watched as the white-gold fertiliser tipped from the truck onto the ground. White gold, he called it. It was certainly as expensive as the precious metal. He was driving the front-end loader, the bucket ready to scoop some of the fertiliser up and empty it into the seed and super bin. Once he filled it to the brim he would spread a tarp over the rest of the pile to keep it dry. Heavy logs sat nearby, ready to secure the tarp to the ground.

A trickle of anticipation ran through him; he was excited to be heading back to the tractor, but it was quickly followed by a feeling of guilt. He'd been horrible to Anna and he knew it – he hadn't meant to be. He should phone her and apologise.

He pulled out his mobile and punched in their home number, all the while watching the white pellets flow from the truck. No answer. That's right, he remembered, she would be putting the rams back in their paddock. He thought briefly how lucky he was to have her before switching his mind back to the job at hand.

Finally the truckie pulled the lever to lower the bins then gave Matt the thumbs-up. Matt responded in kind, then watched as the truck rumbled out of the gateway and back onto the road.

It wasn't until the last trailer was out of sight that Matt realised his heart was beating way too fast. It was an after-effect of the accident, he knew. The memory of the tyres bursting into flames and the loud explosions would be with him forever.

'When will I get over this?' he muttered, annoyed at his weakness. He jammed the tractor into gear and tidied up the edges of the pile then jumped down from the cab to spread out the tarp, making sure it was held down tightly with the logs.

'Shouldn't get wet now!' He grinned, his hands on his hips as he admired his handiwork, confident that it was as safe as it could be.

The next twelve hours passed in a blur of diesel and soil. He headed home for a nap and before he was ready, it was midnight again.

Matt woke and, bleary-eyed, forced himself to get up. Taking care not to wake Anna or Ella, he went to the kitchen to fill his thermos. Anna had packed sandwiches and thick chunks of chocolate cake into an esky before she went to bed.

He let himself out of the house and headed towards his ute. It was raining gently and even though he had the fertiliser on the ground, he was grateful that the rain wasn't showing any signs of stopping.

Matt was about to shift the ute into gear when he heard a tap on his door and looked up to see Anna. He wound down his window and smiled at her.

'I hope it goes okay tonight,' she said, touching his face gently.

Matt grabbed her hand and held it to his cheek. 'Only about another week and I'll be able to sleep again,' he said. 'I'm sorry I've been so tetchy. I shouldn't have yelled at you this morning.'

Anna shook her head. 'It's forgotten! I know how important this crop is.'

'Yeah, but I still shouldn't have reacted the way I did. Anyway, I'd better get going. No point in getting up at this hour and wasting time.'

Anna leaned down to kiss him and he felt a burst of love for her. She was the constant in his life, the person who made everything worthwhile.

It was quicker to take the dirt road bordering his farm to the paddock he was seeding in, so he headed out the driveway, dodging the puddles.

Matt was concentrating on the wet road when he swung into the paddock and his lights flashed over the tractor, and at first he didn't register what was wrong, just that the front-end loader had moved and some of the logs had rolled off the tarp. Then he saw the tarp was lying flat on the ground, its edges lifting in the wind.

He stared at it for a moment, trying to work out what was going on. Then he realised: there was no pile.

Their precious fertiliser was gone.

Chapter 4

The man driving the truck was apprehensive. It had been a while since he had done a long night run. He couldn't wait until he crossed the border into New South Wales. At least then he could disappear into the back tracks and dirt roads until he reached his destination. Unfortunately, until then, he had to stick to the main highway.

Every time he saw lights through the raindrop-stained windscreen, his stomach lurched.

'You're being bloody stupid,' he told himself. 'Why would anyone pull you over? You've got every right to be on the road.'

Glancing at his watch he saw it was it 2.39 am. At this stage the adrenalin racing through his veins was keeping him alert. He knew the hardest time would be just before and just after dawn. And he'd be driving into the sun, which would make it more difficult. Often the warmth on the windscreen would make him sleepy.

The CB crackled to life with his call sign.

'Nine Papa Zulu, mobile three to mobile nine, got a copy?'

He reached for the receiver.

'Got a copy, mobile three,' he answered.

'Got the goods?'

'Affirmative.'

'Roger that. See you in five hours at the designated area.'

'Roger. Over and out.'

The man clicked the handpiece back into its holder. Anyone who was listening could have thought the exchange odd, but there wouldn't be too many people listening to the CB this time of night. After many years in the truck industry, he knew most of the blokes on the road would be listening to late-night radio or audio books. If anyone had heard their conversation, the call signs wouldn't be recognised. They were only ever used on jobs like this.

The white lines disappeared under his rig, like they were being gobbled by a huge mouth, and he held the truck steady. He glanced in the rear-view mirror to make sure the other truck was still with him. He could see the lights.

He imagined what they looked like from the air. Two trucks hauling grain bins with a load of stolen fertiliser on board. Their lights stretched out in front of the truck, picking up the road, many metres ahead. Two men in different trucks, alone with their own thoughts. Each with their reasons for doing this. Driving, steadily eating up the kilometres across the country.

He thought of their destination. A Bachelors and Spinsters Ball seemed a strange place to be arriving with two trucks, but he was sure his boss had everything in hand.

As a set of lights appeared in the distance and slowly grew closer, he sighed, trying not to consider what would happen if they were caught. If he weren't in need of the extra money, there was no way he would be involved in something like this.

As the car whizzed past on its way to an unknown destination, he decided there was no point in even thinking along those lines. He wasn't going to get caught. Ever.

He emptied his mind, focused on the road and kept on driving.

Five hours later, the two trucks pulled over in a parking bay just inside the borderline. Both men got out and stretched but hardly acknowledged each other. Minutes later, a black sports car pulled up and a thin, lanky man with sharp eyes jumped out.

'Here,' he said, handing them each a hot paper cup filled with coffee and a packaged egg and bacon sandwich.

The first man didn't answer; he just unwrapped his sandwich and took a huge bite before slugging a mouthful of coffee. He didn't want to chat; he wanted to get the truck unloaded. His mate took his food back to the cab of the truck, leaving him to find out the details.

'Change of plans. The B&S ball is too risky. Plus the boss has found another buyer. You've got about another hour's drive,' the man with the sharp eyes said. He held out a map. 'Follow this and you won't have any problems. As you go in, there is a fertiliser shed on your left, near the shearing shed. No one will be home. Got it?'

'Yep.'

'Don't stuff it up.'

'Have I ever?' Glaring at the lanky man, the truck driver snatched the map and headed back to his rig. He disliked it when the boss sent his gopher. He didn't like him one bit.

'I haven't finished giving you your instructions yet.'

He stopped and turned. 'Well get on with it. We haven't got time for games.'

'When you've finished here, go on to Sydney and pick up a load from the depot there. This is a legit load that needs to be brought back to the depot in Adelaide.'

'Right.' By the time he had climbed into his truck the sports car had quietly disappeared down the road.

He finished off the sandwich and licked his fingers, then turned the key.

Grabbing the CB mike, he pressed the button. 'Let's move out,' he said and the radio was silent again.

One hour later, he flicked on his blinker and turned into a driveway. Seeing the super shed, he drove towards it, backed in and emptied his load, then watched as his mate did the same. Forty minutes later, without speaking, he gave the signal to leave and they were on the road to Sydney.

He couldn't help but breathe a sigh of relief.

Chapter 5

Six months later

Unable to sleep and not wanting to wake Ella, Matt had taken himself outside and squeezed into the old tyre that had been moulded into a swing.

Swing sway, swing sway. His feet touched the ground as he moved; it was dark and warm. Lost in thoughts of the past six months, he was oblivious to anything except the movement of the swing and the beer he held.

Embarrassment flooded through him as he remembered how he had torn down to a local truck yard in Clare the morning after he'd discovered the fertiliser missing, demanding to know who had been out on the road that night. Accusations flew, Matt insisting that someone must have seen something.

After all, truckies were on the roads often when others weren't. They talked to each other continually on the two-way and this company knew he had fertiliser on the ground. They had carted it.

Oh, he could still hear it all in his head. He wished he couldn't.

'Who else knew you'd carted it to my place, Frankie? Who?' Matt had yelled. 'Someone must have known 'cos it's gone. Someone who has a truck and knew it was there!'

'Mate, you'd better not be accusing me,' Frankie had warned, his eyes like slits. 'I know nothin' about you and your bloody fertiliser. I'm sorry I carted it to you. Now piss off, before you get hurt.'

Matt hadn't backed down – too angry, upset and fearful to notice he had pushed Frankie too far – a fist had flown through the air and connected with his chin, knocking Matt out.

He'd been hauled unceremoniously into the owner's office and left there until Anna had arrived to collect him.

They had both slunk from the yard, Anna humiliated that Matt had caused such a scene and so sad that he had been pushed to this. Matt had had his pride dinted beyond repair.

They had argued on the way to the police station, Anna questioning why he had been so stupid.

'What were you thinking, Matt? Some of them are your friends. Why would they know who did it? Why would you think they had done it?' Matt had remained mute, sure that someone, somewhere, must know something. They stopped at the station.

Not waiting for the car to come to a stop, Matt got out and slammed the door, stomping inside. He didn't wait to see if Anna was following.

A detective had ushered them into a windowless room and asked questions.

'Who knew it was there?'

'Only the company who carted it and the fertiliser company themselves,' Matt had replied.

'Do you know who could have taken it?'

Matt had sprung up, his fists against his sides, ignoring Anna's calming hand on his arm. 'If I knew that, I wouldn't be in here talking to you. I'd be out there getting it back. Do you know what this could do to me? To us? I could lose my farm!'

The detective had suggested that he sit down then said: 'Something like this is going to be hard to investigate. There won't really be any evidence left behind and if we do find it, how can we prove it's yours? I'm sure whoever has bought it will have mocked up the paperwork. It's probably just easier if we give you a report number and you claim it on your insurance.'

Matt and Anna gaped at the man. 'But it's not insured,' Anna managed to say. 'We don't really have any sort of insurance to cover something like this. It's too expensive.'

'Well of course we'll look into it, but I'm just telling you, it is going to be hard to investigate.'

They hadn't talked on the way home. The reality of what could happen paralysed them both and, really, there seemed to be nothing left to say.

The police hadn't come. They didn't return Matt's many phone calls and when he visited the station the answer he kept getting was: 'I'm sorry, there's not much we can do.'

His anger at the police and the system which had so clearly failed him simply served as fodder for his desire to find out who had wrecked his life.

From then on, he'd spent hours pouring over country newspapers, googling 'fertiliser theft' or questioning locals if they had heard of any other farm burglaries. His attempts at investigation had revealed nothing.

No one knew anything or at least nothing they were willing to tell him about, and it seemed to Matt he and only he had been targeted. Whether that was realistic or not, he didn't know, but the result was he was now obsessed with why it had happened to him.

'Why me?' was the question that he asked over and over. 'Why me?'

Matt had tried to move on since then. He'd dare anyone to say he hadn't. He'd helped Anna plant a veggie garden in the backyard, doing his best to hide his humiliation when he had to ask his best friend, Sam, for manure – yet another reminder of his failure. He'd tried to find work. Sam had offered him a tractor-driving job on his farm, but he wouldn't take charity from his friend and no one else needed a worker.

In between all of this, he still scanned newspapers, looking for a reason behind what happened. But it was over now – all gone and he felt empty. Every time he closed his eyes he saw all his worldly possessions lined up in rows ready for sale. Every piece of equipment had a history; a history *he* had created. The portable sheep yards he'd bought after contract seeding for a farmer on the other side of town, the tractor he'd been able to buy through hire purchase because he finally had enough assets behind him to take out a loan – all gone at the auction; it had felt like he was selling his soul. Matt swallowed hard at the memory of the auctioneer yelling out prices and the throng of people bidding or just milling around laughing and talking to each other, oblivious to his pain as he slowly and methodically lost everything he'd worked so hard to accumulate.

Tonight, when he'd woken and his eyes had adjusted to the darkness, he could see the cracks in the walls of the old house they had shifted into after the farm had been sold. Anna had looked for a farmhouse to rent, but the only habitable place she'd been able to find was a stone house in Spalding. It was on a corner in the main street, with a shop opposite and a pub on the other corner.

Matt had felt sick when she'd told him – not only had he lost his farm, he was going to be living in the main street, evidence of his failure there for all to see whenever people drove by. He could imagine the locals talking as they pulled up at the pub: 'Oh, have you heard? Matt and Anna Butler have moved into the house over there. Yeah, he lost the farm. Poor bugger.' Then they wouldn't give him a second thought as they drank their first beer and laughed at the jokes Joe the publican told.

Anna had tried to turn the house into a home. She had made bright yellow curtains for the kitchen and blue and white striped ones for their bedroom. She had used some of the Centrelink money they received to buy paint; duck-egg blue for the kitchen and for Ella's room a pale pink. But no matter what she did, she couldn't hide the decay, or rising damp or the fact the house had been built over a hundred years ago. It didn't feel like much maintenance had been done since. Tonight he had been able to hear the hot north wind whistling through the cracks around the windowpanes and see the streetlight shining around the thin curtains.

Swing sway, swing sway. Matt tried to ignore the ache building in his chest by giving himself up to the movement of the swing.

The night before the clearing sale, Sam and Kate had come over to help them load their final boxes into the trailer and Nick and Rob had both come to help shift the furniture from the farm into the house in Spalding. As the flat bed truck, driven by Nick and borrowed from Ian, had driven out of the drive for the last time, Matt stood looking at the disappearing trailer. Sam had appeared holding a beer.

He handed it to Matt, who took it, ripped the

top off it and swallowed the whole bottle in a couple of gulps. Then they had gone to sit in the empty shearing shed, swigging on more beer and rum, almost talking. But not quite. Matt had things he wanted to tell his friend, but he couldn't find the words. He wished he could describe the huge balloon of pain, hurt and frustration which sat inside him. The *helplessness*. He wanted to ask Sam how to get over this, how to face the future – but if he couldn't think of any answers, what chance would Sam have? Sam had never been in Matt's place and was unlikely ever to be, since he came from the oldest farming family in the district. From money. He couldn't possibly understand the way Matt had struggled to buy the farm. It didn't matter. Sam had stood alongside Matt every step of the way.

He and Sam had been friends since primary school, played footy together, drunk their first beers together and been each other's best man. Matt understood Sam was trying to be the best friend he could be, but he couldn't bear the pitying glances, the gaps in their conversations. They had gone from being the greatest of mates to having nothing in common.

In the long pauses, Matt had known Sam was searching for something to say. The noise of a chain clanking against the tin seemed so loud in the awkward silence. Then Sam had brought up the subject of Jasper, trying to convince Matt, as Anna had, that selling his faithful companion and working dog was a bad idea.

'Don't sell Jasper, mate. You'll need him. He's your friend.' Anna had insisted on taking her old kelpie, Bindy, with them but Matt had been adamant. If he wasn't farming he wouldn't be keeping anything that reminded him of all he had lost – he'd even sold his ute and bought a third-hand rust bucket of a ute, but at least it wouldn't remind him of the farm. And there was no way he was keeping the dog, even though Jasper had been his constant companion for the last few years.

Matt flashed back to the auctioneer's voice.

'Here's a dog who knows what he's about. He's a yard dog with brilliance. I've worked with him many times. He's a backer and barker. What am I bid for Jasper?'

As Alec Harper had raised his hand in the final bid, something inside Matt had broken.

Alec Harper now owned his mate. *Alec Harper!* Matt almost spat the name out loud as the swing creaked in the darkness. His neighbour, who was known for his lack of compassion towards animals. God only knew what his old mate was enduring now. Matt felt the ache of regret every single day.

Without warning, the air was filled with laughter as the patrons from the pub over the road spilled out onto the street. It must be midnight.

Listening to the young blokes talking and car doors slamming, Matt realised how far removed he'd become from what had been his life. He'd been happy, doing what he'd always dreamed of. Sure, they'd struggled financially, but that was normal and, besides, he'd always believed the hard times wouldn't last long. A couple of years ago it would have been him leaving the pub, Anna at his side, after dinner with Sam and Kate. A few laughs, a drink or two and a life.

But not now.

The rough rope scratched his cheek as he leaned against it. He sighed, and tried to shut out the noise. He wasn't the same; his life wasn't the same. Would it ever be? he wondered.

He drank the last of the beer and hurled the can angrily at the fence.

Consumed by memories, he couldn't stop the one he feared the most. The bank. In his mind, he watched himself entering the bank for the final time. Matt had refused to take Anna with him that day. He had still held on to the hope they would offer him another temporary limit, allowing him to buy more fertiliser and still get the rest of his crop in. Or at least some sort of a lifeline.

But just in case it wasn't to be, he had told Anna to stay home. He couldn't bare the thought of the woman he loved hearing that he'd failed. She'd argued with him that it was her hard work and her farm too – that he was her husband and she wanted to support him. But Matt was stubborn in his refusal, knowing it would be a tough meeting.

Bill had shaken his head.

'I'm sorry, Matt, I can't lend you any more money.

Maybe if you had insured the fertiliser you could have claimed and had another go, but I'm really not prepared to extend your overdraft any further. My advice is you need to seriously consider selling.'

Although he'd half expected this response, it still felt to Matt like someone had punched him in the stomach. He couldn't breathe and a roaring sound had filled his ears. Bill was still talking, but Matt couldn't hear what he was saying.

Surely this man didn't understand what he had just done. With a slash of his red pen and some careless words, he had destroyed everything Matt and Anna had worked for.

Chapter 6

In the darkness, Anna had heard Matt get out of bed and open the flyscreen door. She knew where he was going - the swing. She'd lost count of the number of times she'd gazed out the kitchen window, watching him on the swing, his head bowed in defeat.

Anna was just as devastated as Matt by the turn their lives had taken. They had adjustments to make, loss to deal with and a whole change of lifestyle. They both felt confined by the small country town, the boundaries of the tiny backyard. Chores which had once filled their days were gone. There was no stock needing attention, no fences in need of fixing, nothing to drive either of them out of the house. And neither of them wanted to go.

Anna knew Matt was too mortified to show his face on the streets of Spalding. Thankfully, for the first month or so she'd been too busy unpacking, painting, sewing or keeping Ella occupied to go any further than the front yard or corner shop. Even then, she tried to do the shopping first thing in the morning, avoiding any well-meaning but inquisitive people. Sympathy and questions about the future made the sting of failure all the more sharp and, anyway, Matt and Anna didn't have answers for most of their questions.

Maggie Butcher, who ran the corner store, seemed to understand how she felt. When Anna went in Maggie would just smile, ask how Ella was and ring up her purchases. She didn't push or pry, which Anna appreciated. And it wasn't just the gossips Anna wanted to avoid; it was her own mother-in-law as well.

Laura had complained about the front door being locked. 'I want to pop in and cuddle my gorgeous granddaughter,' she'd said.

Anna had looked at her incredulously. Laura couldn't understand that the theft had left Anna feeling violated, if not downright scared of leaving the doors unlocked. Still, reluctant to show any weakness, she'd tried to leave the front door unlocked, but she couldn't stop herself from walking through each and every room before it got dark, checking that no one had entered without her hearing. Oh, she knew that the thieves hadn't entered her house on the farm, but the fear that they might come back for more haunted her. Not that she and Matt had much left except each other.

The first time Anna was alone in the house and heard the squeak of the front door opening she'd frozen automatically, thinking it was a burglar, and looked for a weapon to protect herself. Then she chided herself for being so silly, knowing it would be Matt, and walked into the lounge to greet him with a smile and a hug. Instead it was her mother-in-law Laura, and Anna wondered why she hadn't knocked or at least called out, as most people in country towns would have done. Not Laura.

The overzealous Grandma thing had really got on Anna's nerves, especially the day she found Laura standing over Ella's cot, stroking her face as the child slept.

'Tell me you're here!' Anna shouted in her head.

'You don't mind do you, love?' Laura had asked her a few weeks after they had moved to town. 'It's so nice having Ella just around the corner. I never really saw her that much when you lived on the farm.'

Anna opened her mouth, then looked at Laura's expectant face. Even though she found it intrusive, how could she crush a woman who just wanted to spend time with her grandchild, especially at a time when Anna and Matt needed space to heal. So she had shaken her head.

'No, not at all! Ella loves it when you're here.'

Anna was rewarded with a bright smile.

If Laura had offered a sympathetic ear or words of comfort, Anna perhaps wouldn't have been so annoyed at her silent entries. But there was nothing like that. Laura didn't even seem to understand the trauma her son and his family had gone through. She came for Ella and Ella only.

Anna ached for her own mother, but she'd been stripped of her mum's support a long time ago. Her Dad was always on the end of the phone, but she was loath to worry him. He certainly had enough problems of his own.

Rob and Nick called more regularly than they had done before, just to check on them, but after time even their calls dwindled. They were like everyone else. Busy. Everyone, that was, except Matt and Anna, who had more time on their hands than they could deal with.

The compassion and support she craved came, unexpectedly, from Matt's father, Ian. In his short but comforting visits he reassured her that Matt would come through this blackness and encouraged her to hang in there. He would squeeze her shoulder, tickle Ella to make her laugh and head to the backyard to sit with his son.

Kate was the only person who wasn't family whom Anna was always pleased to see. She would come laden with freshly laid eggs or a bag of home-grown chops, but it was her hugs and kind words that kept Anna sane. She'd needed them and she sure hadn't got them from Matt, even though she'd offered plenty of sympathy to him.

As the months passed and Matt hadn't shown

any sign of coming out of his hermit-like state, Anna had begun to feel the strain of trying to handle everything herself. Running the house and, as ever, the lack of money became too much for her some days. Matt was in the house all the time. On the farm she would have loved having him around; they would have talked and laughed or snuck away during Ella's sleep to make love. But the dark mood he seemed permanently shrouded in made having him around every waking moment very difficult.

Tonight, however, she tried to take Matt's father's advice and fight the annoyance rising within her. Hopefully Matt would realise he wasn't the only one who was finding their change in circumstances hard. She didn't like town much either, but what she missed most was the relationship she and Matt once had.

In the past, they had talked about everything, sharing what had happened during their day over a beer at night, while they did the dishes together and when they went to bed. They were as close as two people could be. Their relationship worked because they were friends as well as lovers. Indeed, she knew their relationship was the envy of many in the district. Kate had once told her: 'If you and Matt ever break up, I'll stop believing in love!'

Anna had laughed. 'Break up?' she'd responded. 'Never!'

'Oh good, I hate to think of a world without love.' Though Kate had grinned, Anna knew she'd meant every word.

Now, uneasily, she had wondered if they might separate after all. She felt like it had been years since Matt had talked about his feelings, what he was thinking. Actually, he'd just about stopped talking at all, save minimal conversation when he couldn't get away with grunts. She couldn't understand why he'd turned away from her when they'd always looked to each other for comfort.

Recently, if she ever did ask how he felt, he just snapped, 'How do you *think* I feel?' Eventually she'd stopped asking.

She rolled over in bed, wiping away a stray tear. Their life had been so great. Hard financially, granted, but money wasn't everything. They'd had the farm, a beautiful child and, best of all, they'd had each other. Now the 'each other' part was slipping away.

Anna had tried to carry on as normal, but they couldn't go on like this. The sombre mood enveloping the house had to lift. There had to be laughter and fun again. Surely the only way to achieve that was to get back some semblance of normal life.

Anna felt Matt needed to get a job. He needed a purpose, a reason to get out of bed in the morning, since obviously she and Ella weren't enough to help get him moving.

She'd mentioned the idea to Ian of Matt finding employment, but he just shook his head. 'More time, Anna, give him more time.'

That had been a while ago though. Surely it was time now.

Hearing the Saturday night crowd starting to leave the pub, she got up, put on her dressing gown and went to find Matt.

He was sitting on the swing with his head bowed, the moonlight reflecting off the crown of his head like a halo. Anna knew that underneath all the grief there was a cheeky, fun-loving man. She had to find a way to bring that man back to the surface, to help him break through the bleakness engulfing him.

She opened the back door and went out to sit with him. They stayed silent, listening to the night sounds of the small town: front doors slamming, faraway voices cutting through the air, dogs barking and, even further in the distance, the rumbling sounds of late-night harvesting.

After a while, Anna reached up to slip her hand into Matt's. For a moment she thought he was going to pull away, as he had done so often over the past few months, but his warm fingers curled around hers, hanging on tight. Anna squeezed his hand and smiled into the darkness.

'Going okay?' she asked, squeezing his hand again.

'Not really,' Matt answered after a moment's silence.

'Is there something I can do to make things easier for you? You know I would if I could.'

He sighed and turned to her. 'I don't think so, hon. I guess it's something I'll just have to work through by myself.'

Sitting on the ground, she could feel his legs moving against her side as the swing gently swayed. Her heart ached at the pain in his voice, but there was good in what he'd just said. He'd finally spoken, out loud, about his feelings.

They sat there, hands entwined, until at last Anna unwillingly took her hand from Matt's and stood. 'My knees are aching and my bum has gone to sleep!' she said, wiggling her hips, to try to get the circulation flowing. 'I must be too old for sitting on the ground these days. Are you ready to go inside?'

'Not yet,' said Matt. 'But you go. I'll be in soon.'

Her reaction to his low, gravelly voice surprised her. Desire ran through her body. How long it had been, how she ached to hold him, feel close to him again. It had been so long since they'd touched. Since they had loved.

Tentatively, she reached out her hand to him.

'Come with me, Matt,' she said softly, leaning down to kiss him.

When he jerked away Anna didn't move. She just waited, her eyes pinned on his face, her arm outstretched, willing him to take her hand and follow.

Matt looked up at her and she could see the moonlight reflected in his eyes. She looked again. Yes, she was sure he wanted her too.

She touched his shoulder and whispered again, 'Come with me.'

Slowly he reached up and took her hand.

Anna's heart was singing as she led him back into the house, down the passageway and into their bedroom.

The next morning, when Anna woke, she was relieved to see Matt still lying next to her. She smiled as she relived the night in her mind. Wonderful!

She felt like the weight had lifted off her shoulders and hoped her Matt of old was back. All her doubts about their relationship had evaporated last night. They were back on track, she was sure of it.

She ran her hands over his back and gently coaxed him awake.

'Morning, gorgeous,' she said softly.

'Morning,' he said quietly. Anna's heart sank as she saw the distance had returned to his eyes.

'Coffee?' she asked. 'I could bring it to you in bed? Ella hasn't woken yet. We could ... You know!' She gave him a shy smile.

Matt was silent as Anna got out of bed to put the kettle on and then he got up too.

'I'll pass on the coffee in bed,' he said.

Trying to hide her disappointment, Anna nodded. Maybe he wanted to talk. Hopefully.

By the time Matt sat at the table, there was a steaming cup of coffee in his regular spot and Anna was slipping into her chair.

'Last night was wonderful,' she said.

'Yeah.' Matt stared into his coffee. Clearly he had nothing further to say.

'I can't bear walking on eggshells anymore,' she thought, and the realisation she was running out of patience with him shocked her. 'No,' she told herself. 'It won't be like this forever. You need to support him for as long as it takes. He did it for you.'

Anna's mother Lacey had been driving when an aneurysm claimed her. Her father, Peter, was in the passenger's seat when his wife had suddenly slumped forward, causing the car to career off the road. His legs and hips had been trapped under the dashboard and his spinal cord severed, leaving him a paraplegic.

Through the cloud of grief that had overwhelmed Anna as she dealt with her mother's death and her father's injury, Matt had been her constant support. He'd driven her wherever she'd needed to go, talked to the doctors and broken the news to her that her father would be confined to a wheelchair forever. And all that time, he'd still run the farm, never once complaining about the long stints she'd spent with her dad in Adelaide, until her brother Rob had taken over his care.

She often thought of the night that Matt had driven the two hours to the city just to give her a hug after a long, stressful day.

Yes, he had more than supported her. Now it was her turn to do the same for him.

Chapter 7

A week later

Matt was angry but was trying hard not to show it. He had made himself go into the backyard and breathe deeply, with his eyes shut, not wanting to think about the loss of the farm and the emotions swirling inside him.

It wasn't just anger, either. It was hurt, sadness, a sense of failure and every other bloody emotion he could imagine. He had looked for something he could enjoy doing around the house today, something that would make him feel worthwhile, useful. But he hadn't found it.

Firstly he'd decided to fix the sheet of tin that had woken him last night by banging in the wind. The constant clanging had driven him mad and, at first light, he'd headed out to the back of his ute where he kept his toolbox, and grabbed his hammer. He fossicked around in the garage, trying to find some nails, but he couldn't find them anywhere he looked. Angrily, he'd thrown the hammer onto the cement and strode inside. If he'd been on the farm he would have known exactly where to look, in fact he would have had the choice of using nails, screws, tech screws or even pop-rivets. But he didn't here. It had all been sold.

'Stuffed if I'm going to buy any more,' he thought as he slumped in the kitchen chair and gave up on fixing it.

The second thing he'd tried to do was to clean out the chook shed. He raked the manure out and gathered it into the wheelbarrow to throw in the corner of the yard for Anna to use later. Then he went to change the hay in the nesting boxes. No hay. He couldn't get any hay without borrowing some from Sam or another farmer. As he looked despairingly at the ground, he realised that in the feed tray were Layers Pellets. Layers Pellets bought from a *store*. Why was Anna feeding them Layers Pellets? She should be giving them grain.

Then he understood. There was no grain. It was all still on the farm.

Matt shut his eyes. He couldn't do a simple job without the loss of the farm being rubbed in his face. Finally, not wanting to go out, he had sent Anna to the merchandise store for a bag of sawdust and feed.

Coming out of the dim chook house, Matt was blinded by the sun and tripped over Bindy, Anna's old dog. She yelped in surprise as Matt tumbled down on top of her and it took all of his self-control not to yell and lash out at her.

By the time he'd gone back inside the house it was after lunch, so he flopped in front of the TV while Anna made a cup of tea and a sandwich. Then he heard it: the strains of *Landline* and the dulcet tones of Pip Courtney reporting on a new variety of barley that would be perfect for this area. He hadn't realised the show was repeated on a Monday.

His fists clenched as he fumbled for the remote control. In his haste to turn off the weekly farming show that he had watched every Sunday, he accidentally hit the wrong button and Pip's voice was amplified throughout the house. Cursing at not only the noise but his overreaction to something so small, he flung the remote to the floor and stalked across to the TV to turn it off manually. Not before he heard Ella cry and realised the noise had woken her.

For a moment chaos reigned. Ella screamed, Anna ran to her and the man Pip was interviewing droned on about why this was the barley to end all barley. Matt wanted to throw his hands over his ears and curl up in a ball.

Finally he found the off switch and there was quiet once more.

He found Anna in the kitchen, quickly finishing off making the sandwich, juggling Ella on her hip.

'I'll take her,' he said, reaching out for her.

'Here, Ella, go to Daddy,' Anna said as she leaned towards Matt.

Ella, her face still red from sleep, wasn't in the mood to be passed from one parent to another. She opened her mouth and started to yell, a high, ear-piercing shriek. Matt blinked in surprise and backed away for a moment, then frowned.

'I'll finish the sandwich,' he muttered and was thankful as Anna disappeared down the passage to settle Ella.

While eating his lunch, he flicked through the paper, searching for articles that could be related to his fertiliser or any other farm theft. Nothing. He had been targeted he was sure. But why? And by whom? Whoever had taken it had to have had inside knowledge that there would be fertiliser on the ground that night. There was no way it could be just pot luck.

He tried to quell the anger, to think about something else, but it was all-consuming. 'Stop it,' he told himself sternly. 'Stop it, now. You're making everything worse by dwelling on it.'

All the emotions were there, fudging the edge of his thoughts, his sights, his actions. There was something else there too. Denial. It wasn't *his* fault the farm had been sold. If the fertiliser hadn't been taken he would have had a great year. No. The blame lay squarely on the shoulders of the thief. And with all these feelings inside of him he couldn't quell the frustration he felt as scene by scene, the last six months replayed themselves in his mind.

Finally he knew he had to leave the house, even though it was almost dark and the day seemed to have disappeared in a haze of bad temper. 'I'm off for a drive,' he called to Anna, who was bathing Ella. Without waiting for a response, he let the door bang behind him, as he walked to his ute. Automatically he whistled and looked around for Jasper, but there was only Bindy, smiling, her tongue hanging out and looking wistfully at the back of the ute.

'Fuck it,' he swore. 'Just fuck it,' and almost ran to his ute, the need to get away was so strong.

As he drove around aimlessly he realised running wouldn't help. After all, his thoughts and feelings came with him wherever he was. He groaned and thumped the steering wheel.

Matt stopped on the edge of a dirt road to watch the sun set, drawn to the shadows that were long and dark. The sun slipped further below the hills. A warm breeze stirred and he listened to the birds calling to their mates that it was time to roost. He relaxed a little.

At least out here he could breathe.

He sat on the bonnet of the ute for some time, listening to the sounds of nature. Then he heard something odd, something that made his hair stand on end. Matt didn't move but strained to listen. All was silent again. He must have imagined the noise that sounded like a scream. Maybe it was a bird cry.

Or maybe it was the screech of a hydraulic ram needing oil. As he listened for a while longer, he was sure he could hear a machine working. That must have been it; a hydraulic ram.

Climbing back into his ute, Matt saw that it was well and truly dark. For a moment he gazed at the sky hoping to see a falling star. Maybe he could make a wish. He started the engine and flicked on his lights, before checking to his left and right. Over the crest of the hill, he could see the glow of car lights coming. He still had time to pull out, so he swung the ute onto the road and weaved his way back from the gravel roads he had driven seeking peace, to the bitumen, and reluctantly followed the highway back to Spalding.

Behind him, Matt saw lights appear in his rearvision mirror. He gripped the steering wheel a little tighter, checked all the gauges and determined where he was on the road – a hangover from his truck-driving days. 'Always know exactly what your rig is doing and where you are,' he could hear his father repeating again and again.

The lights moved quickly towards him and he cursed the driver who didn't seem to feel the need to dip them from high beam. Matt reached forward, his eyes not moving from the long straight stretch of road. He flicked up the mirror, so the lights weren't in his eyes, then waited for the vehicle to pass him.

It didn't.

Matt frowned and slowed slightly to give the other car every opportunity to pass, but it sat behind him.

It moved closer to the rear of his ute and as Matt glanced in the rear-view mirror, he wondered how on earth it wasn't touching him. He pushed up the speed.

So did the vehicle.

He slowed down.

So did the car behind.

It tailed him the whole way to Spalding, mimicking his moves and pace until Matt began to feel unsettled. Whoever it was was acting very strangely.

As Matt flicked on his blinker to turn into his street, the car followed. Anxiety turned to fear.

Was this car tailing him?

Instead of pulling into his driveway, he kept driving, turning aimlessly down deserted streets. First left, then right, right, left. Finally he wound his way through the back streets of the town towards Adelaide and still the vehicle was on his bumper, its lights glaring through the back window and into the front of the car. Occasionally, the other driver even flicked on the spotlights to try to blind Matt. He realised from the position of the lights that they were very low to the ground. He wracked his brains to think of a car that had those sort of lights and all he could come up with was a really flash, new, low-to-the-ground car. Maybe a sports car.

Matt shook his head, wondering what on earth was going on. He tried to see the vehicle, but the darkness and bright lights prevented him. All he knew was the car was only centimetres from his tail and had mirrored every one of his moves for more than twenty minutes.

Then he felt it, a slight tap and his head jerked back, hitting the headrest.

Bastard! They'd hit the back of the ute.

Matt could hear the rumbling of a V8 engine now and knew the vehicle behind him was very powerful.

Bump! And again.

What the hell? With his hands sweaty and heart pounding, Matt once more indicated that he was turning left down a dirt road and slowed, his foot on the brake. The car behind him slowed too, waited until he had turned off the bitumen and then shot on towards the city.

Pulling the ute onto the side of the road, Matt ran from the cab so quickly that his feet slipped on the gravel as he tried to reach the bitumen. He peered into the darkness and watched the red tail-lights disappearing further into the blackness. They taunted him. There was no way he could tell what sort of vehicle it was, what colour, or even read the number plate.

'Why?' he wondered. 'Why do something like that?' Whoever it was and whatever the reason, it had certainly scared the living daylights out of him and left him wondering what he really had heard up in the isolated hills. There was no doubting the car had come from the direction of the noise.

Chapter 8

Two weeks later

'I've been thinking, Matt. We really need to find some work,' Anna said one morning after breakfast. She watched his face carefully for a reaction. As she'd expected, the shutters came down but she persevered, determined to get through to him. 'And I know you'd prefer I stayed at home, but I'd like to help out, somehow. Would you mind if I tried to get some work? Kate and I have come up with an idea about a childminding business. It's something I could do from here.'

Matt put his plate on the sink and turned away from her. 'Do whatever you want to do,' he said. 'Sounds like it's been decided.'

There was a silence and then Anna angrily said, 'Far out, Matt! That's unfair. I'm *trying* to talk to you about it now!' She slammed her coffee cup onto the bench and took a deep breath. 'I've just about had enough of you and your silence or snide comments. All I do is tiptoe around you, scared to say anything in case you bite my head off. I can't talk to you. Don't you *care* about anything anymore? This is *ridiculous*! When are you going to get over it?'

Matt looked startled by her outburst, then his surprise turned to anger.

'Get over it?' he yelled, his fists clenched by his side. 'I've just lost my farm, everything I've worked for and you're telling me to move on? And what about you? All you do is rub my face in it. "How're you feeling? Do you want to talk? Do you still love me?" What sort of stupid bloody questions are they?'

'We've been here for eight months, Matt,' Anna reminded him. 'For eight whole months I couldn't get you out of the house but now you've decided to walk across the road to the pub and drink coffee or run away to some remote spot. All you do is mope around and feel sorry for yourself. I'd love to be able to drop all responsibility and sit in the pub doing nothing for hours on end. You're not the only one who's been affected here. You need something else in your life. I'm obviously not enough for you and neither is Ella. When was the last time you picked her up and gave her a cuddle?' Anna sighed. 'Matt, you're alive, and you've still got a family who loves you. Was the farm worth more to you than us?'

Matt said nothing, and a flicker of hope flared in Anna's chest.

But his voice was shaking with fury when he finally said, 'Don't you want to know who did this to us? Who actually sent us to the wall? This is someone's *fault*. We were targeted. Someone stole that fertiliser and that's the whole reason we lost the farm. I want to know who did it, even if you don't.'

Anna was shocked by the vehemence in his voice but she forced herself to press on. 'We have to put it behind us, Matt - look to the future. We need to work. We need money. We've got a child who depends on us. Knowing who did it isn't going to change the situation we're in right now.'

'Don't you miss working for ourselves, the farm, the smell of the dew in the morning? How can you *enjoy* living here? Don't you want to get out? Go back to life as it was before?'

'Matt, honey, we *can't* go back to how it was.' Anna could hear her own despair etched in her voice. 'No, I don't like the way things are now, but the farm is finished. We have to accept that. It wasn't just the fertiliser. The bad seasons were the start of it. Then the truck fire. Bloody hell, the only reason that was such a disaster was because we couldn't afford the insurance. You may not want to hear this, but it's the truth: we were struggling even before the fertiliser was taken. I know you thought we might get out of jail if we had a good crop, but it was a big if. We would have faced the same problems when we fronted up again next year.'

Matt let out a strangled cry and spun around blindly, as if trying to escape the barrage of words. Lashing out, his fist collided with the flimsy cladding that coated the kitchen wall, leaving a gaping dark hole that exposed the stone work underneath.

Then, without a word, he stormed out, nursing his sore hand.

Matt didn't have to order when he went to the pub. The bartender, Joe, knew what he wanted by now and brought the strong black coffee to Matt without being asked. Today, when Joe put the coffee down, Matt didn't even lift his head to thank him.

Matt had always thought Anna had believed in him; that she loved the farm as much as he did. But now ... He banged his fist on the table and felt it rock. The movement was enough to jolt him out of the mist of anger he felt. When he looked around he caught one of the regulars staring at him. He flushed, embarrassed to have let his emotions show to anyone outside the walls of his home.

He'd started coming to the pub a few months before, needing to get out of the house. He'd sat at the back of the room, facing the wall, and invited neither conversation nor interaction. The few locals who had approached him had received nothing but a nod in response to their questions. They had soon left him alone.

Occasionally his father would come to sit with

him, but Matt refused to acknowledge even Ian's undemanding presence. Ian would sip his coffee until his cup was empty, then rest his hand on Matt's shoulder and leave.

Over the following weeks, Matt had gradually shifted his position so that he was no longer facing the wall but the door instead. Though his sense of failure still felt too raw to talk to anyone, he found himself wanting to see life going on around him, even if he wasn't participating in it. It was at the pub and through his father that he met a truck driver called Shane Lyons.

One day Shane had pulled in at the rear of the pub in a green truck hauling a white tautliner with a week's supply of beer. A honk of the air horn had attracted Ian's attention, so when Shane entered the dining room carrying the counter meal Joe had given him, Ian was already waiting with his hand outstretched.

'Shane! Shane bloody Lyons! How are you, old mate?' The pair had shaken hands and chatted while Matt, only half listening, stared at the tabletop. Then he heard them mention the names of a couple he knew, Joel Cornell and Janey Sharp. He had raised his head to listen and, when his father glanced at him, he nodded ever so slightly.

'Shane, this is my son, Matt. Shane and I met when he was still driving stock trucks for my competition. He's hauling general freight now.'

Matt had enjoyed talking to someone who didn't

know him or his history, and he and Shane quickly found common ground in trucks and drivers they knew. It had been good to catch up on the news of Joel and Janey, too. He and Anna had received an invitation to their engagement party during the nightmarish final days on the farm, but they'd been too busy and stressed to attend.

Perhaps the biggest relief for Matt, though, had come when he'd blurted out the story of the truck accident. He'd never really talked to anyone about that night, but Shane had nodded his understanding and related a similar experience of his own; the back trailer of a truck he'd been driving had tipped as he drove through a winding valley. He hadn't been hurt, but most of the stock he'd been carting had been killed. He didn't drive road trains, B-doubles or long distances anymore. He wasn't saying he never would, but he wanted to wait until he felt ready. He'd forced himself back in the cab, though, carting general freight on short runs. 'After all,' he said, 'I have to keep some money coming in. I've got four young sons and a wife – they depend on me.'

They depend on me. Shane's words echoed in Matt's head as he left the pub and crossed the street to climb into his ute.

Anna's anger today had floored Matt. She so rarely lost her temper that it had shocked him to see her red-faced and seething. And reluctant though he was to admit it, he knew he deserved it.

They depend on me.

He'd ignored Anna when she'd waved the bank statement in front of him. He'd pretended not to hear when she told him there wasn't even enough money to buy Ella a dummy. He'd turned his back on her when she'd tried to hug him or offered support.

They depend on me.

Matt pushed his empty cup of coffee away and got up from the table. He had to get out. Get away. Try to get his thoughts in order. He certainly had never meant to hurt Anna, and by her backlash today, he knew his actions had wounded her.

He walked across the road, but as he was not quite ready to face his wife yet, he jumped into his ute and headed out of town.

Matt drove towards their old farm and when he saw the driveway he slowed to a stop and looked across the land.

Their old home.

He ignored the heat of the sun and the flies trying to cluster around his eyes, nose and mouth as he stared across the country, his arms crossed.

As much as it hurt him, he could see some positive changes had been made to the farm – some changes he had wanted to make himself but had never had the money for, like the new boundary fence he now walked across to and leaned on. If he was being sour, he would say the farm looked like a tax deduction, but he'd run out of energy to even be upset today.

The sheep in the paddock next to him were due

for shearing and he could see even from a distance that their fleeces would yield well.

There were two sealed silos towering above the shearing shed and what looked like a new header in the shed.

He was aware the new owner had money and, despite disliking him, he could put the bitterness he felt aside, knowing his farm was well cared for.

For the first time, as he looked at his lost dream, he realised there was nothing more he could do. It *was* finished.

He stood there until the sun began to sink, gazing longingly at what was once his. Then, as the flies disappeared and the stock made their way to the troughs for their nightly drink, he got up and strode towards his ute with a new sense of purpose. He *hated* what had happened to his family, but he knew what he was going to do now.

'They depend on me,' he whispered.

Chapter 9

Two months later

Matt swung the large rig into the depot on the edge of Adelaide and pulled up on the gravel pad. After letting the truck idle down he gathered the few belongings he had taken with him on the round trip to Ceduna.

His CDs were his closest friends at the moment. When he was driving he turned the music up loud and sang along, and sometimes he could almost forget about the permanent ache in his chest.

Before his accident, driving had been just a means to make some extra money. Now he did it for the money but also because he could lose himself in the driving. He didn't have to think; all he was aware of was the pull of the truck and the white lines of the road ahead. With drums and guitar riffs reverberating around the cab, he felt like he could cope with what the world had thrown at him. But only when the music pounded.

The truck shuddered and Matt's ears began to ring as he adjusted to the silence.

'G'day, mate. Good trip?' Shane thumped on the door and kept walking.

Matt gave him the thumbs-up, then yanked open the door and jumped down from the cab. He walked over to the throng of other drivers who'd also just returned from long trips.

It had been Shane who had suggested Matt apply for the driver's position that had become available at Jimmy Marshall's 'East-West Haulage'. Matt had been excited at the thought, but he knew Anna had been apprehensive about all the extra driving that it would involve.

The depot was situated on the outskirts of Adelaide and Spalding was two hours' drive away, through a mixture of wide open plains and paddocks seeded with a variety of crops and dotted with stock. Closer to Clare the country changed to high hills and deep valleys all covered with tall gum trees that gave the land a time-worn feel. There were winding roads and tight corners, all of which worried Anna.

'It will be another two hours' driving on top of what you've just done. Won't you be too tired after days on end at the wheel?' she'd asked. 'What if you have an accident on the way home?'

'That won't happen. If I'm too tired, I'll bunk

down on the side of the road or stay in the truck. It'll be fine.'

'Why can't you drive for your dad again, Matt?' Anna had tried to change his mind once more.

'I can't, Anna.' He looked despairingly at her. 'I just can't face people who know me at the moment.' He hadn't added that he hoped the drive home would give him opportunities to track down who had stolen their fertiliser.

Recently stories had begun to filter through. Small things had gone missing; a bloke had had a pencil auger taken and two weeks later a lamb weighing crate had been snatched from the back of a ute while parked in the pub car park. Maybe he hadn't been targeted. Maybe he was just the first one. Matt had thought if he heard about another theft he could check out the location. It would give him more time on the road at odd hours and maybe, just maybe, something would fall his way and he might be able to track down the culprit.

And it had worked.

Not a week after he had started, he'd heard of a farmer to the east of Spalding who had had three of his electric fence units taken. Matt had decided to see if he could find the farm. Following the road map, and after twisting and turning down many dirt roads, he found an out-of-the-way farmhouse nestled in between two hills.

Matt shut off the engine and got out.

Silence.

He leaned against his ute, his arms crossed, and breathed the night air. Still not a sound. He glanced around, and although it was dark, he could make out the shadow of a fence and hear the rhythmic clicking of the electric fence. *Click . . . click . . . click*.

The lone light from the farmhouse was a speck in the distance and, as he watched, it went out. Whoever had taken the units would need nothing but a torch.

As he thought hard, Matt realised that if anyone saw him here, he would have a lot of explaining to do.

His eyes flicked over to the green glowing numbers of the clock on the dashboard and he took notice of the time. He pushed himself off the car, ran across to the fence, quickly disconnected the unit and brought it back to the car. He checked the time again. Two minutes.

How easy it would be if you knew what you were after and how to find it.

He had replaced the fence unit and continued on his way back to Spalding, excitement building. He was sure he could find out who the culprit was and his truck-driving job was the key.

Matt really enjoyed the camaraderie of this tight-knit group where nobody really cared what his history was. Shane, Joel and Janey knew why he was back driving again, but to the others he was just Matt, who drove trucks and had a wife and child at home.

He nodded to the group and listened to them exchanging news of their trips.

'The sun was sinking and there was a fair bit of dust from the car in front of me,' Zack was saying. 'You know how it hangs in the air and sorta becomes a haze?'

Matt and the other blokes who had carted in the north nodded. It was one of the most dangerous times of night – especially when dirt roads and bull dust were involved.

'Well they came out of nowhere, these two fricking camels wandering across the road. I couldn't pull up in time, so I just kept going. They went right under the truck.'

'Shit.' Joel winced at the thought. 'How's the belly?' he asked, referring to the engine and underside of the truck.

'Pulled a couple of fuel lines out, but I fixed them up best I could and kept going. Blokes in the next town cleaned up what I'd done, but our grease monkeys will still have their work cut out for them, I reckon.'

'How'd your trip go, Matt?' Shane asked.

'Fine, mate, nothing but a few roos and a flat tyre. But I was driving on bitumen, not like Zack. Those dirt roads, they can be killers, especially at dawn and dusk.'

There was a chorus of 'Yeah, you're right' as all the blokes nodded in agreement.

'Well,' said Shane. 'I'd better be off home.'

'Yeah, me too,' Joel said. 'See if Janey's got any more wedding plans to discuss.' He smiled wryly. 'We used to talk diesel engines and trucks once ...'

'Only going to get worse from here, mate,' Shane said, clapping him on the back. 'Wait till she starts talking kids! All you'll hear about then is teething, nappies and sleepless nights. You won't be getting her back in a truck for years!'

'Yeah, well, thanks for the encouragement. Catch you all next run,' Joel said, waving over his shoulder.

The boys all started to drift off in different directions. Matt headed to the office where his boss, Jimmy Marshall, would be waiting for a report on the trip and the condition of the truck.

'Ella, stop it. You can't hit Kylie, it's just not nice.'

Matt heard Anna's voice above Kylie's screams before he opened the car door. He closed his eyes and leaned his head on the steering wheel, craving the silence of the car on the drive home. This bloody childminding business was fine while he was away, but he wanted it to end the minute he got home. Of course he knew that wasn't fair or possible, but he wished for it. He wanted to run in and scoop up Ella in a big hug without another child around. He also craved peace and quiet. He needed to unwind, a thing all truckies understood.

After days of listening to a loud, rumbling engine –
not to mention loud music – the best thing was to
get in the car and drive home slowly. The car engine
was almost inaudible compared to the sound of the
truck.

Today, Kylie's screams put Matt on edge before
he'd even pushed open the front door. He took a
deep breath then stepped inside.

'I'm home,' he yelled above the crying toddler.

A harassed Anna came out of the lounge room
holding Kylie, Ella toddling behind her.

'Dada!' Ella smiled and tried to move quickly
towards him.

Matt, his heart melting, got down on the floor
and crawled towards her. 'Ella!' he replied in the
same tone.

'Dada!'

Anna smiled as she watched her husband nuzzle
their daughter's cheek, stand and swing her into his
arms.

'Hello,' she said, kissing him on the cheek. 'Good
trip?'

'Yeah, not too bad. How's things here other than
being pretty noisy?'

'I'll phone Kylie's mum and see if she can come
and get her.'

As Anna headed for the phone Matt hugged Ella
to him, enjoying her baby smell and velvety soft
skin. Ella put her hand to his face and said 'Dada!' in
the same excited tone she had first used. As she ran

her fingers down his face he knew he'd be forever grateful to Shane for saying, 'They depend on me.' It had reminded him what was really important.

Two hours later Kylie's mother still hadn't arrived, and the alternating tired squeals and sobs were more than Matt could bear.

'I'm off,' he said to Anna.

'Where are you going?' she asked, pushing her hair back off her face to reveal a fraught expression.

'Just out and about.'

Her eyes darkened briefly with anger, then she smiled. 'Okay, see you when you get back.'

He drove out of town to a parking bay by the creek. He loved coming here. Its banks were lined with reeds, frogs croaked when there was water and crickets could be heard chirping on warm summer evenings. Gum trees towered above the park benches and barbecues, swaying gently.

He lay on the bench, his hands under his head, mesmerised by the waving leaves, the sound of birds calling, the wind rustling in the grass.

After a while, he got up and went for a walk along the creek. It was ironic, he thought, that the seasons had turned out for the better since he had got out of farming. One season had come and gone and it had rained on time, with good follow-up rains right when they were needed.

He skipped a couple of stones across the water's

surface then glanced at his watch. It was time to head home if he wanted to bath Ella. Even though the truce between him and Anna was still uneasy, he had begun to enjoy spending time with his family again.

Matt saw the blue flowers of Salvation Jane growing on the side of the creek and stared at them for a while, eventually reaching down and picking a handful. A plan in place, he scoured the bank looking for some other sort of flowers, it didn't matter if they were weeds. After picking Sour Sobs and some Doc, he bunched them all together. The bouquet would be an apology to Anna when he returned home; he knew he should have stayed and helped out with the screaming Kylie.

Matt had just started to head back to his car when his mobile phone rang. Looking at the screen, he saw it was Sam. Anna had probably rung Kate to tell them he was home. He rejected the call and put the phone back in his pocket. Sam would be full of farming news and he wasn't up to listening to it tonight. He knew that it was Sam's way of being supportive, but he just didn't get it. Matt didn't want to talk about farming. He didn't listen to *The Country Hour* or *Bush Telegraph* on ABC radio anymore either. Everything was still too much of a reminder of all he had lost.

He was surprised when the phone started to ring again – Sam. He let it go to the message bank this time, but when it rang for the third time he decided he should answer.

'How's it going, mate?'

'Matt! I'm glad you answered!' Sam sounded breathless.

'You all right?' Matt asked, a feeling of dread spreading through him.

'Yeah, yeah, we're all fine. Are you driving? I've just heard something on the grapevine you need to know about. Daniel MacIntosh from over Burra way has just had his whole knockdown chemical taken from his shed – all two thousand litres of it.'

Matt felt himself grow cold. It was happening again. Running to the ute he yanked open the door and reached into the glove box, taking out a small black notebook and opening it to a blank page. 'What else do you know?' he asked, trying to find a pen.

'Not much really. Dan called the cops but they weren't terribly interested.'

Matt snorted. 'Sounds about right. They didn't give a shit when it happened to me. Just said, "Here's your report number for insurance." They're not likely to do anything this time either.'

'But isn't this the fourth one since you were hit?' said Sam. 'Surely the cops will have to start taking some notice.'

'No, he's the fifth if you don't count the two small incidents, with the fence units and lamb crate about five months ago. Whoever it is practised on me then went back to small things. Must be happy to take on bigger and better things again.

What I can't understand is how they keep getting away with it.' Matt flicked through the notes he'd taken about the previous thefts. 'They're nicking big loads – Dan's chemical order would've been in big enviro-drums. Fertiliser needs a bin on the back of a truck. Fencing gear needs a forklift and at least a ute. It would take a fair bit of planning. I mean, how are they getting on to the farms and not being noticed?'

'Stuffed if I know,' said Sam. 'I guess if there were two blokes they could probably lift the drums and fencing gear together, but it would take a while and the longer they spent on a farm the more chance they'd have of being noticed. There'd be lights of the vehicles and we've all got dogs that bark at anything unusual.'

Matt was quiet, thinking about how badly he wanted to find out who had done this to him and Anna. He'd tried to come to terms with the fact the theft had happened, that they'd lost their farm and he'd had to give up his life dream and take a different path. But with each new theft he heard about, his determination to find out who was doing this increased. He knew Anna thought he should look forward and stop obsessing over the past; to a point she was probably right, but finding the thief was the one thing which might make him feel whole again. He knew he wouldn't find closure or be rid of his sense of failure until that happened.

Sam's phone call had just made the desire to find the perpetrator even stronger.

'I don't know who's behind this, mate. But I'll find out,' Matt said softly staring out of the window.

The flowers gathered with good intentions now lay wilting and forgotten on the passenger's seat.

Chapter 10

Anna glanced up at the clock, wondering what time Matt would be home. Kylie had been picked up a little while ago and the house was finally quiet. Ella was curled up in a ball on her little foam Barbie couch, fighting to keep her eyes open; the day of babysitting had left both her and Anna exhausted. Anna was only keeping Ella up so she could see Matt when he came home.

Kate's idea of the babysitting business had been a great one and Anna loved doing it. When she'd placed a notice in the local school newsletter she'd quickly been inundated. There were plenty of mums who preferred not to drag their young kids around the supermarket, and farmers' wives who jumped at the opportunity to have a coffee with friends without the interference of little hands and voices.

Babysitting wasn't hard for Anna because she liked children, and Ella loved the company. Anna enjoyed watching her daughter interact with other children. It gave her the social outlet she had been lacking as an only child, and goodness knew they could do with the sound of children's laughter around the house.

Relations between Anna and Matt were still awkward since their dreadful fight, though Matt's apology had helped.

'I'm sorry,' he'd said. 'I know I've been hard to live with. I don't know how I'm going to get over this, but I'm going to try. I know you and Ella need me.'

Falling into his arms, Anna had tried to explain that she wanted to support him, but she didn't know how to anymore, despite loving him so very much. She would willingly take on all the hurt he was feeling if only she could get the old Matt back.

Even though they had made love that night and had wanted, *needed*, to be in each other's arms, the days and weeks that followed had been difficult. Anna had assumed they would talk about everything and work through it all, but Matt had declared that he wanted to put it all behind him and he didn't want to reopen old wounds.

Matt was still angry much of the time, though, and Anna was wary of provoking him, in case it caused another outburst, so she didn't press him. If only he could let it go! Although he had told her he was getting on with their life, he was still obsessed with finding out who had stolen their fertiliser. And the more he concentrated on this fixation the less likely it seemed they would be able to fully reconcile and rebuild their relationship.

After a conversation with Kate, and desperate for advice, Anna had taken the phone number Kate had given her and rung Kate's cousin, Dave Burrows, who worked as a detective in Western Australia's Rural Crime Squad. He'd explained that most rural crime was opportunistic and that what had happened to them 'was just one of those things'. Dave had agreed with the local Clare detective that something like fertiliser would be very hard to investigate, though Dave had wondered out loud if he could help the bloke with his personal skills.

'I'm sorry he was like that, Anna. It could have been handled better, especially since there was so much at stake for you.'

She repeated this to Matt, but with little effect. As more farm thefts were reported his focus had only grown more intense.

But to her mind, trying to take things into his own hands wasn't only hopeless – it could be dangerous.

Since Matt had started his new job, Anna had met some of the other truckies and their families, Shane and his wife Belinda and their children, and enjoyed their company. Belinda had even called a few times when their husbands were away at the same time. It had been nice to chat to someone who understood the difficulties of having a husband who was absent for long periods of time. Especially when they both had young children. They had commiserated over coffee and laughed when they realised they had the same routines in place for their kids.

As time passed, Matt had said less and less about finding out who had stolen their fertiliser, though Anna suspected he hadn't really let go of the issue; it was just he was saying less about everything. There were times when he withdrew into himself and hardly spoke at all. At other times he disappeared for hours and Anna didn't know where he was. He didn't answer his mobile and when he came home he offered no explanation about where he'd been. Not wanting to upset the delicate balance they'd achieved in their relationship, she decided not to try to force answers from him. Naive maybe, but she didn't have the strength for any more confrontations at the moment.

'Mama!' she heard Ella cry. With a start Anna realised she had been so locked in her memories she hadn't noticed her daughter trying to get her attention.

'What's up, bub?' she asked. 'Must almost be time for your bath. I wonder where your dad is?'

'Mama!'

'And what mischief he might be up to,' Anna added, dropping to her knees to tickle Ella's tummy, laughing as the little girl squealed with delight.

Bindy barked as there was a rap on the door;

Anna heard Kate's voice. 'Hello? I'm here bearing gifts!'

'Kate!' Anna scooped up Ella and headed to the kitchen, where her friend was unpacking a brown paper bag full of food. 'I didn't know you were going to call in!'

'Aha! There you are!' Kate said, reaching to take Ella, who had stretched her arms out for a cuddle. 'Look what I brought for you.' Kate produced a toy cow from the bag and Ella lunged for it, only to drop it in fright when it emitted a loud moo. Kate laughed. 'It's okay, sweetie, it's meant to do that.' She set Ella on the floor with the cow. 'It moos when you squeeze it. See?'

Anna felt a pang; it was sad that Kate was having trouble falling pregnant when she loved children so much.

'I didn't forget us,' Kate said, standing up to show Anna a bottle of wine she'd brought. 'And I'm here with news – there's a new clothes store opening in Clare and they're having a grand opening! Champers, cheese and biscuits, the lot. We're going!'

'Really? Who's opening it?' Anna asked as she reached for the wine glasses.

'A couple of newbies from Adelaide. They're planning to bring all the high-fashion brands to Clare. We really should support them if we want gorgeous things to wear on Melbourne Cup day!'

'Melbourne Cup day? What about on Friday night to the pub? Reckon old Joe and the rest would appreciate us in our finery!' She felt a twinge of sadness remembering how she used to say, 'Do you think the sheep will appreciate my new haircut?'

'Absolutely! He won't be able to contain himself! So can you come? I don't want to go by myself.' Kate poured the wine with a flourish and held up her glass. 'Cheers!'

'Cheers.' They clinked glasses and took a sip. 'When is it?'

'Two weeks from tomorrow.'

Anna got up to check Matt's roster on the fridge then shook her head slowly. 'Sorry, no can do. Matt gets back from a few days away.'

'C'mon, Anna! What time does he get back? Night time? We could be back by then.'

'No, I'd better not, Kate. I want to be here when he gets back. I'd hate to think of him coming home to an empty house after being away for such a long time. And after all the roadhouse food, I like to give him a good dinner.' Anna took another sip of wine.

'Ah bugger. But fair enough, Anna – I'd do the same for Sam.'

They continued chatting while Ella played happily on the floor, and Anna felt the tensions of the day fade.

'So which kids did you have here today?'

'Just Kylie – she was still here when Matt came home, which was a bit of a disaster. He couldn't handle the noise, so he took off for some peace and quiet. Then again, that's not so unusual. He's been taking off quite a bit lately – and I'm not always sure where he's going.'

'But you think he's getting better, don't you?'

'I'm not sure.' Anna paused. 'I *hope* so.'

They were silent for a while then Kate said, 'Well, I'd better go. I need to get dinner on before Sam gets home. He's been to Burra today, picking up a new seeding rig.' She drained her glass and put it on the sink.

'And I'd better get this little one to bed, she's exhausted! Thanks for all the goodies.' Anna looked at the cakes and biscuits Kate had piled on the bench.

The two friends hugged goodbye and Kate gave Ella a kiss, then Anna followed Kate to the front door to see her off.

The sun was sinking as Kate drove away; Anna watched her car until it had disappeared from view. The main street was quiet and empty, and Anna felt a rush of loneliness at the sound of laughter coming from the pub. Where was Matt? she wondered for the umpteenth time as she closed the door.

Going through the motions, she bathed Ella, fed her and put her to bed. Then she got the dinner on and sipped the remaining wine while she waited for Matt to appear, the only sound in the house the ticking clock which seemed to move slower the more she watched it.

Seven pm came and went, eight, nine then ten. Anna began pacing the floor. Matt had never been gone this long before. She wasn't sure if she should call the police or just keep waiting. If there had been a car accident surely someone would have rung or come and got her. Had it been six months ago, she would have been worried he'd tried to commit suicide, but now she couldn't think of one damn reason why he hadn't come home.

By the time 11.30 pm came and went, panic was churning in her stomach. When she couldn't bear the waiting any longer, she gently picked up the sleeping Ella and strapped her into the car seat. Leaving a note on the table for Matt saying to ring her if he came home, she went looking.

Cruising the lonely, deserted country streets only to find nothing, she turned left and headed out of town towards a parking bay she knew he sometimes went to. But as she drove in and swung the car around to sweep the lights over the whole park, she could see no sign of his white Rodeo ute.

Next she drove to his father's depot, but he wasn't there. With a heavy heart, she drove out past the old farm, sure she would find him sitting in the moonlight, staring over what had been his land. But he wasn't there either.

Driving back into town, the roads were empty except for a couple of kangaroos, a stock truck loaded with sheep and two passenger cars.

On a whim, she left the car running so Ella wouldn't wake up and ducked across the road to the pub. Peering in the windows, she tried to see if Joe had taken pity on Matt, letting him stay while his staff cleared up from the night's trade.

She looked over the whole bar, hoping to see Matt sitting against a wall, drinking coffee. Nothing.

She ran around to the car park at the back of the building. The parking lot was empty.

Finally she headed home. Pulling into their street, her heart sank to see there was still no ute in the driveway.

Inside, Anna put Ella in her cot and then threw herself onto her own bed, staring into the darkness, her ears straining to hear his rattling ute turn into the drive. But it didn't. Where on earth was he? Was it so hard for him to call her?

When six am came and he still wasn't home, she picked up the phone and rang Kate, bursting into tears as soon as her friend answered.

'Anna, what is it?' Kate asked, her voice full of concern.

'Matt hasn't come home. I don't know where he is.'

'What? Hold on, I'll ask Sam if he knows.'

Anna could hear muffled voices in the background then her friend came back on the line.

'Sam said he talked to him yesterday afternoon, told him about a bloke who had some chemical stolen over near Burra, but he doesn't know where he was when they were talking. Hang in there, we're coming over.'

But when a ute pulled into the drive ten minutes

later it wasn't Kate and Sam, but Matt himself. Anna ran out and threw herself into his arms.

'Oh, Matt! Are you okay? I've been so worried. Where've you been?'

'Just driving around,' he answered, detangling himself from her.

'Just driving around? Why didn't you ring? I've been worried sick all night! I didn't know whether I should call the cops, if you'd been in an accident . . . Matt, tell me what's going on!'

'Nothing is going on, Anna. Leave me alone. I'm tired. I'm going to bed, all right?'

Angry now, Anna grabbed his arm. 'No it's not all right!' she shouted. In the silent morning, her voice carried and curtains shifted in the studio above Maggie's shop. Matt tried to steer Anna inside but she shook off his hand.

'Tell me where you've been,' she demanded. 'What was so important that you couldn't call me? Have you been trying to find out who took the fertiliser?'

'So what if I have?' he hissed at her. His eyes were red with tiredness and the shadow around his jaw had flecks of grey just beginning to show. 'I'm going to do something about it, even if you won't.'

Anna stared at him as everything fell into place. He'd been driving around, looking, watching. Waiting. 'Oh, Matt, really?' The heaviness in her voice betrayed her sadness.

They both turned as a diesel engine rumbled

around the corner and drove down their empty street, turning into their driveway.

'What the hell are they doing here?' Matt asked, recognising Sam's ute. He looked at Anna accusingly.

'I called them when you didn't come home. I thought you might have been wrapped around a tree!'

Kate bounded from the car. 'Matt, where on earth have you been? We've been worried sick since Anna rang us.'

'No need to be worried,' Matt said, his voice flat. 'I'm fine.'

'You might be, but Anna wasn't,' Sam said, with a hard edge to his voice, 'and neither were we. We had no idea where you were, what could have happened to you.'

'It's not actually any of your business,' Matt said, his eyes cold.

'It became our business the minute Anna rang us and, believe it or not, you're our friend. Anna was worried and so were we. This has gone on long enough, Matt.' Sam's voice was low and angry. 'We've all been patient but you can't do this.'

Matt stared at Sam. 'Look, *mate*,' he said, raising his voice. 'I'm fine and, like I told you, it's got nothing to do with you. Now if you'll excuse me, I'm buggered and I'm going to bed.'

Anna gasped at Matt's tone. She couldn't believe he was talking to his best friend like this.

'Hey, let me tell you something, Matt,' Kate jumped in, her face set. 'You're being an arsehole and you want to be careful. You keep on treating everyone the way you are now, you're going to end up really lonely. There might even come a day when Anna won't be bothered to hang around.'

'You know what?' Matt fired back. 'None of you, not a single bloody one of you, knows what I'm feeling, so just piss off home and mind your own business.' He stalked inside, slamming the door shut behind him. They could hear his angry footsteps echoing on the wooden floorboards and a few seconds later Ella started to cry.

Anna stood staring after him and then took a step towards the door. 'I'm sorry,' she whispered, looking over her shoulder at Kate and Sam. 'I'm so sorry, but thank you.'

'Anna, I'm sorry. This might have been my fault. I told him about another theft,' said Sam, reaching out to touch her shoulder.

'I'm sorry,' Anna repeated as she shook her head, then rushed inside to soothe Ella.

Chapter 11

The mobile phone rang. Picking it up, the man hit the answer button without speaking.

'Tonight, ten o'clock,' a female voice said. 'Same pickup as last time, second left on the marked trailer. Use the back doors. Understood?'

'Got it,' the man answered, then hung up.

'Hey, mate!' called Shane, waving at Matt as he pulled up in the depot. 'How were your days off?'

'Good, Shane, and yours?'

'Fine – other than a quick trip to the hospital. Daniel, the cheeky bugger, managed to plough his scooter into the garage door and split his chin open. He's okay, thankfully.'

'I'm glad I've got a girl,' Matt said. 'And that she's not old enough to ride a scooter!'

'Oh, it's all still coming your way,' laughed Shane. 'So, ready for your long run? First one, isn't it?'

'Yeah it is and I am!' Matt was just pleased to be out of the house. Anna's reproachful looks were annoying the hell out of him. 'Jimmy said I'll have a co-driver. Do you know who it might be?'

Shane grinned and pointed at his chest. 'That would be me!'

'You? Didn't think you did long runs.'

'Nah, don't usually, but the boss says you've got to be trained right, so it'll be you, me, white lines and the long paddock.'

The 'long paddock' was the Nullarbor, which he was looking forward to crossing. A long straight run, music up loud and nothing but the rig and the road. He reached into the ute and pulled out his overnight bag. 'Well, then,' he said, swinging it up over his shoulder, 'we'd better go and see the boss and get ready. What are we carting?'

'I'm off to the office to get all the paperwork, so I'll let you know. Reckon we should aim to be outta here by five at the latest. It's the Dublin sale tomorrow and we want to avoid all those farmers bringing their sheep into the sale yards.'

'Righto, I'll go and see Jimmy, find out if there's anything we need to know about the truck or the road condition.'

They went their separate ways. Matt was glad to have a mate as his co-driver. Living in a two-metre cab with someone for four or five days without a break could be a strain, but Shane was a great bloke and Matt knew they'd get on fine. He trusted Shane's driving ability – and as a co-driver that was the most important thing of all.

Matt knocked on the boss's door. 'G'day, Jimmy.'

Jimmy looked up and a grin spread across his face. 'Matt, me lad, come in. Ready for the drive?'

'Sure am, boss.'

'Got Shane teed up to go with you, Matt. He's the best bloke to show you the ropes. He understands this job well, even though it's been a while since he's done it. He knows the road and the good places to stop, have a feed and a shower. Plus he's thinking he'd like to do a few more stints like this – money's better doing these sorts of runs and his kids seem to cost him the earth. A run with you will be a good way for him to ease back into it.'

'I'm looking forward to it,' Matt assured him.

'So, when you gonna roll?'

'Shane said he wanted to be out of here by five to avoid the farmers coming to market day.'

'Good idea. Some of those farmers bring their five lambs or three steers down in the most clapped-out trailers or old trucks held together by baling twine and wire. Scariest crew on the road, let me tell you. Last year, there was an old farmer bringing in his pigs – knew them all by name, mind! Got onto the Port Wakefield highway and his tailgate came unlatched. Good thing his ute didn't go above fifty clicks 'cos those pigs fell straight out the back. Oh

Lord, the CB was busy that day. Farmers, truckies and all sorts were calling in with reports of pigs on the loose.

'Took a while, but they were all found. Few had a bit of gravel rash, but none were badly hurt.' Jimmy frowned and shook his head. 'Yep, best to avoid those farmers.'

Matt decided not to tell Jimmy *he* used to be a farmer and *he* used to cart his lambs to the Dublin sale yards in a truck.

'It's really only the hobby farmers who are a problem – not got the right equipment,' Jimmy added, as if reading Matt's mind. 'Safe travels, Matt. If you need to talk to the office or check in with the mechanic, stop at the nearest roadhouse or parking bay and phone them, or call in on the CB. Make sure you don't pick up the mobile phone while you're driving or the cops'll be all over you.'

Matt nodded and left the office, smiling to himself. Jimmy was the kindest, most eccentric bloke he knew. He was in his late sixties, Matt guessed, with wispy grey hair combed across his broad forehead. He lived in a small two-room transport hut in the depot and East-West Haulage was his life. Without a wife or children, his drivers were his family and he treated them as such. Other drivers had told Matt about the bonuses at Christmas, the long chats and fatherly advice when things weren't going so well. It didn't matter what time you pulled into the depot – it could be three in the morning – Jimmy would get out of bed to find out if your trip had gone well and whether the truck was in good nick. He liked to know his men were happy. Happy men meant happy families and all of this created a harmonious workplace.

In among the line of ten prime movers parked silent and still, Matt found his truck. A young boy who was employed after school as a detailer was giving the windshield one last buff. He said g'day, shoved the rag in the back pocket of his overalls and moved on to the next one. Matt did a quick run over the engine, checked the tyres and climbed into the cabin. He turned the key and the engine rumbled to life. Matt smiled. He was excited about this trip – he was the happiest he'd felt in what seemed like a lifetime.

Shane appeared a few minutes later with paperwork, and hoisted himself into the passenger seat.

'To the satellite depot!' he said jovially.

Matt put the truck into gear and headed out of the yard. The satellite depot was only five minutes' drive but many streets away. It was where all the freight was delivered to and stored in large sheds. Men on forklifts zoomed around from one trailer to another, loading the goods. They were lined up next to each other, but in separate bays so there could be no confusion about which trailer went with which rig and driver.

'Bay three is ours,' said Shane, and jumped out as Matt swung towards their load.

Slowly reversing in, Matt watched Shane's hand movements in the mirror, directing him. When he felt the thump of the dolly connecting to the trailer he eased his foot onto the brake and slipped the truck into neutral.

The two men did a quick check of the trailers, kicking the tyres and making sure the locking straps of the tautliners were tight.

'Good to go,' said Shane. 'You want to take the first run while I have a bit of a kip? Then I can drive the night shift.'

'No problem. You like the night shift best?'

'Yeah, buddy. Much quieter than my house when the four ferals are squabbling and running around!'

They climbed back into the cab and got comfortable, then Matt stepped on the clutch and smoothly pushed the split-shift gearstick into low and they left the depot for the open highway.

As Matt drove towards the west the sun was sinking. It was a steady trip up the highway, passing the hobby farmers Jimmy had been so concerned about, to the open land of the farming area. Behind the wheel, Matt felt free, although he couldn't help but think about the way he had spoken to Sam and Kate. He supposed he should apologise, but damn it, he wasn't ready to and he was right when he'd said they didn't understand. How could they?

Shane sat in the front for the first couple of hours and then climbed through into the sleeper cab. Before closing the thick vinyl curtains he said, 'Wake me just before Ceduna.'

Several hours later, Matt pulled up at a twenty-four hour roadhouse in Ceduna. He and Shane got out, ordered a late dinner of steak, chips and salad and headed for the showers.

By the time they got back to the truck it was the early hours of the morning and Matt was looking forward to the bunk. The small bunk was like a cave, he thought, as he settled into his sleeping bag: pitch black and warm.

He lay awake, staring blindly at the roof, thinking of Anna and how he missed their closeness before they lost the farm. Then, to dispel the gloom settling over him, he thought of Ella and her trusting smile, her chubby fingers reaching out for his.

With this happy image in mind he let himself be lulled to sleep by the rhythm of the truck.

When he opened his eyes next, it was still dark and the truck had stopped.

He waited for Shane to call out and say it was time to swap drivers, but he heard the door open and Shane settle back into the driver's seat. There was a clunk of gears and the truck started to move. Obviously Shane had stopped for a leak, he thought, as he slipped back into slumber.

Chapter 12

The panicked shouts echoed through his dreams, overlaid with the thumping of chopper blades, the burst of gunfire. And then there were the screams – and the bodies.

No matter how hard he tried to escape the horrors of the Vietnam War, the images were embedded in his soul to be relived nightly in his dreams.

The sound of the siren grew louder and louder until he awoke with a start. His breathing came in shallow gasps as he took in his surrounds, realising the siren he had heard was actually his mobile phone. He snatched it up.

'What?' he growled, still tense.

'Jimmy, it's Janey here, mate.'

In a split second, Jimmy's mind catapulted back to the here and now. He looked at the clock – 3.42 am.

'What's up, Janey?' he asked. 'Got a problem?'

'Yeah, I'm about two hundred k north of you and popped a turbo charger. Any chance of getting one of the mechanics up here?'

'No problems, girlie. I'll get on to Frank. I think he took the service vehicle home. Whereabouts are you exactly?'

Janey explained where she was and Jimmy said, 'Hang tight. I'll give you a call back when I know what time he'll be there.'

'Thanks, Jimmy. Sorry to wake you.'

'I'm glad you did,' Jimmy replied, meaning it. 'Do you need me to let Joel know?'

'Nah, I'll give him a ring when I know what time I'll be home. Talk to you soon.'

They hung up and Jimmy dialled Frank's phone number. Apologising for waking him, he passed on all the details and said he'd help him load up the new turbo charger.

Jimmy hit the disconnect button and went to make himself a coffee while awaiting Frank's arrival. He wouldn't sleep again tonight. As the kettle boiled, he stared at the kitchen counter, his mind crowded with memories. So many memories . . .

'Mum! Hey, Mum? Uncle Jimmy's here!'

'How're you doing, young Sandy?' Jimmy asked as he got out of his Valiant. 'Look at your face! Anyone would think you hadn't had a bath in a week!' Jimmy pulled out his hanky to wipe the boy's snotty nose.

'Uncle Jimmy!' Sandy whined and twisted away, instead wiping his grimy face with the hem of his threadbare T-shirt.

Jimmy shook his head, but laughed. 'So why aren't you in school?' he asked.

Sandy shrugged. 'Didn't wanna go.'

'That's no excuse! Bloody hell, how do you think you'll make a dollar when you get older if you don't go and learn things?'

'I just wanna drive trucks like you,' Sandy said.

'Do you now? Well you still need to be able to read and write to do what I do. What happens if you get lost and you can't read the street signs?'

'I wouldn't get lost – I bet you never do, Uncle Jimmy.' Sandy looked at Jimmy with admiring eyes and Jimmy felt love flood through him. He never could understand why he was so taken with this little kid, but he had been from the first time he'd held him in the hospital.

'Have you been driving trucks again, Uncle Jimmy? Can I come on your next run?' Keen eyes stared up at him.

'Well, it's up to your mother. But I got no problems with it as long as it's during school holidays – 'cos you have to go to school, that's the deal. You wanna take it?' He held out his hand. 'If you shake on it, you have to keep your word, lad. A handshake seals the deal.'

Sandy screwed up his nose. 'I guess. But school's boring.'

Jimmy ruffled his hair. 'Course it is, but it's good for you. I didn't get the opportunity you've got to go to school. Grandma needed my help on the farm. School's real important. Now let's go and see your mum.'

'Mum's got a new boyfriend,' Sandy whispered.

Jimmy raised his eyebrows. 'Has she now?'

Sandy nodded vigorously.

'Is he here at the moment?'

'Nup, he's at work.'

'What's his name?'

'Charlie.'

'What's he like?'

Sandy shrugged. 'He's all right.'

Jimmy nodded. 'Well, let's go in.'

At that moment his sister came out, a cigarette in her hand. Jimmy could see she'd made a special effort with her hair and bought a new dress. Her lips were painted ruby red.

'How are you, Margo?' he asked.

'Fine, Jimmy. You?'

'Fine.'

There was a silence, then Jimmy asked, 'Can I come in?'

'I guess,' Margo said ungraciously. 'But you stay out here,' she said to Sandy. 'Don't want you dragging mud into the house. Charlie doesn't like it.'

Jimmy winked at his nephew while fighting down anger at Margo not wanting her own child in the house. 'Who's Charlie?' he asked as he followed his sister into the house. On the kitchen bench there was a loaf of dry bread, margarine and a jar of Vegemite. There was also a bottle of beer. Before she had a chance to answer, Jimmy grabbed her arm. 'You drinking again, Margo?'

'Special occasion,' she said defensively.

'Oh yeah, and what's that?'

'Charlie got a job.'

'And who's Charlie again?'

'He's me boyfriend. He's a good bloke.' Margo crossed her arms and glared at Jimmy as if daring him to contradict her.

'Well I hope he's better than the last one,' snorted Jimmy. 'If he so much as touches the boy out there, I'll have the social services on to him as quick as a flash. Goes for you too, Margo.' It was a conversation they had at least once a year.

Margo's spiral down would start slowly. Cigarettes, then a few beers at night. Then came the angry words from Jimmy and denial that anything was wrong from Margo. The beers would be on the table at lunchtime and, not long after, she'd be leaving Sandy at home by himself at night, while she was at the pub picking up blokes.

Jimmy wished he could take the boy to live with him, but Margo wouldn't have it. He knew she loved Sandy, in her own strange way, but she couldn't handle the responsibility. Margo'd never been one for conforming, never done things the way they should be done. A single mother and proud of it,

Jimmy wasn't sure whether she even knew who the boy's real father was.

'You're starting again, Margo,' he warned, seeing the signs before him.

'I am bloody not. If yer haven't got anything good to say, then you can nick off.'

Jimmy grabbed her arms. 'You've got to think of that lad out there. He needs a proper mum, he needs to go to school and he needs someone to make sure he has a bath and good food at night. Hell's bells, Margo, how can you do this to your own flesh and blood?'

'I ain't doing nothin'. Now if the lecture is over, I have things I need to do.' She flounced out of the kitchen and Jimmy sighed. He would hustle Sandy through the shower, get him into some fresh clothes and take him to get fish and chips. At least that way he'd know the boy had eaten today.

The whistling of the kettle drew Jimmy out of his reverie and, swearing quietly, he flicked the switch, before sloshing the boiling water into his cracked cup.

He looked around the room sadly, wondering if his life would have been different had his number not come up. He could've cared for the boy. His gaze rested on the faded photo of the six-year-old Sandy that he kept in the kitchen above the sink.

He looked at it every day, as a reminder of what he had lost.

The bright smile and eager eyes that grinned back at him always tore at his heart.

Chapter 13

Anna struggled to walk across the uneven ground in her high heels. Tottering alongside her, Kate giggled.

'You'd think we were drunk already!'

'Speak for yourself,' retorted Anna. 'But I'd be much better off in my work boots. I don't know why you wouldn't let me wear them. What if I step in horseshit? I'll wreck your shoes.'

'I'd like to see you in work boots wearing that dress!'

Anna couldn't help but laugh at the image. She was wearing a strapless satin gown that was a cast-off of Kate's sister's.

She'd been reluctant to try it on, being self-conscious about her body since Ella was born; the pregnancy had changed her shape. And without the physical activity of the farm, she'd gained weight.

But Kate had insisted.

'This will fit you perfectly!' she'd said when she'd brought it round to Anna's house.

'I don't think so, Kate. You'll be able to see my bum jiggle.' Anna held it out in front of her. 'Oh no,' she said throwing it on the bed. 'No way! It's strapless. My boobs will fall out. And what about my jelly belly?' She grabbed the excess flesh on her stomach and shook it for Kate to see.

'Try it on anyway,' Kate had been adamant.

'Oh, just for a laugh, then.' But Kate had been right: it had fitted perfectly and the dark green fabric was perfect against her light skin and strawberry-blonde hair. Anna had gone from feeling like a frumpy mum, to beautiful in the space of minutes. Kate had lent her a green clutch and strappy high heels and, for the finishing touch, clipped a green peacock feather into her hair.

A voice over the PA announced that the horses for the first race were about to gate up and Kate grinned. The atmosphere at the Clare races was always electric and today was no different.

'Giddy-up, you old mare,' Anna said to her friend, pretending to slap her on the rump. 'We'll miss the first race.'

'Old mare my arse!' said Kate feigning annoyance. 'You're the mare, I'm still a filly!' They linked arms and headed past all the utes, four-wheel drives and horse floats to the front gate, paid their entrance fee and entered the racecourse.

It was a beautiful course, set amid rolling hills planted with rows of grapevines, and Anna was glad she'd come. Even though the paddocks were golden brown now, waiting for rain, the grapevines still held a vivid green, smattered with the vibrant blue of Salvation Jane.

When Kate had suggested the day out, her first impulse had been to say no again.

'I haven't got a babysitter,' she'd said.

Kate had shaken her head. 'Not good enough – you know Laura would do it in a flash.'

Anna sighed. 'It's not just that. We haven't got the money, Kate. Please don't ask me to do something I can't.'

But Kate was undeterred. 'Well how about this? If you drive us to Clare, I'll pick up the rest of the bill.'

'It's an incredibly generous offer, Kate, but I can't accept it. I –'

Kate held up her hand. 'I won't take no for an answer, Anna. I want a day out and I want a friend to come with me. You're it!'

Anna wavered. 'When is it? If Matt's home, I really can't do it, Kate.'

Kate gave her a stern look. 'Anna, I know you love him, but after the all-nighter stunt he pulled a while back, I think you're owed a day out, don't you?'

Anna bowed her head and looked at the table. Kate just didn't understand. Yes, she'd been angry with Matt, worried out of her mind. But she wasn't interested in revenge. She just desperately wanted her husband back, and that meant giving him every opportunity to open up to her. She needed to be there for him. What if he wanted to talk and she wasn't there?

Then she remembered what Matt had been like when he'd come home after his first trip across the Nullarbor. She'd made sure she'd been home, bustled around fixing him a nice dinner, but he had barely acknowledged her presence and when she'd asked about his trip he'd just answered in monosyllables. She'd been angry when they'd gone to bed, but still she had reached for him.

He'd turned away.

At the memory, some of Anna's defiance returned and she lifted her head.

'Okay, Kate, that sounds like heaps of fun.'

'Fantastic!'

So here they were now, smelling the sweat from the horses' warm bodies, eavesdropping on the chatter around them and listening to the clinking of glasses.

The women were all dolled up, but many had a dusty line across their rears, from leaning against the railings. The men's attire ranged from smart suits right down to blue singlets and thongs.

'Shall we get a glass of champers or find a bookie?'

Kate took out her glasses and slipped them on; as she opened the racing guide they had been given as they came in through the gate. 'I don't know a thing about horses and betting,' she said. 'Do you?' She looked at Anna.

Anna felt a giggle erupt from her at the absurdity of it all. 'I can't think how I would know anything about it. I've only been to the races twice in my life. Matt brought me to the New Year's Day races the year I turned twenty-one. We had a fantastic time – but we didn't win a cent!' She smiled, recalling their pleasure. 'That was the year we finished harvest early.' Her smile dimmed, to be replaced by a spasm of sadness, but she tossed her head, refusing to give in to it. 'C'mon, I think a drink is the go, then how about we find somewhere to sit and study the form guide. Surely one of us can win some money!'

They found a shady tree and sipped their drinks while waiting for the next race.

'Hey,' said Kate, peering at the guide. 'I know this guy, Andrew Natter – he went to school with my brother. Maybe we should bet on his horse?'

'What's its name?' asked Anna. 'I'll only place a bet if I like the name.'

'Golden Boy. Hmm, not particularly imaginative.'

Anna leaned over to read over her friend's shoulder. 'There's got to be something better … What about this one, Nabisco? Isn't that the name of a biscuit company?' She flipped to the back of the guide where there was information on all the horses, owners and trainers. 'Oh, here's a good one: Alzan – it sounds like something out of Harry Potter!'

Kate laughed.

'And here's one for Matt,' Anna continued, the champagne making her reckless. 'Madalena. It means bitter!'

'Anna!' Kate giggled and punched her on the arm. 'The drink has gone to your head!'

Anna smiled guiltily and looked back down at the racing guide. Now that she was laughing and joking it felt like forever since she had enjoyed herself. And it felt good. She was actually having fun for a change. It was time she started living her life again, she decided. She couldn't let herself be dictated to by Matt's moods. She would go places when she was invited and she would hold her head high. There was no reason not to.

'Thanks, Kate,' she said as she took another sip of champagne, her voice laden with meaning.

'You're welcome,' Kate answered breezily.

'We'd better place a bet – the race starts in ten minutes. Have you chosen one?'

'I'm going for October Wind. Let's hope he runs like it.'

Kate went to place the bet while Anna made her way to the toilets. Looking out across the car park, she saw a white ute pull up close to the fence and park under a tree. The man who got out looked vaguely familiar but she couldn't place him. She knew the dog, though – it was Jasper. The man must be Alec Harper.

Turning quickly, she walked away. She didn't

want to have any reminders of their old life. Not on the day she had decided to live again.

She found Kate and they pushed their way through the crowd to the rails; they watched with bated breath as the horses made their way into the barriers. As soon as the last horse was settled the gate flew open and they were racing. The crowd erupted, cheering so loudly Anna couldn't hear Kate yelling, despite the fact she was standing right next to her!

The horses galloped past at full stretch, their muscled shoulders and silky coats flashing by. As their hooves thundered down the track Anna could feel the rhythm through her feet. It vibrated through her body, making her feel strangely euphoric.

As she caught sight of October Wind she began to jump up and down with excitement. 'Go, October Wind!' she screamed. 'C'mon, you can do it!'

Kate grabbed her arm. 'Carn, Octy!' she shouted, the rest of the crowd yelling in a frenzy of encouragement.

Then it was over.

The horses slowed from a gallop to a canter, from a trot to a walk. The jockeys were slapping each other on the back but only one had his fist raised in triumph.

'Who won? Who won?' gasped Kate, still breathless.

'The one who's got his fist in the air,' Anna replied, straining to see. 'But I've got no idea who it is!'

Then the announcer called, 'First Carlotta, second Adonia and in third place, October Wind.'

Anna and Kate looked at each other and shrieked with laughter.

They collected their winnings and, in high spirits, reclaimed their position under the tree to study the form guide for their next flutter.

After much light-hearted banter about horse names, they came to their decision. 'Okay,' said Anna. 'We'll try for Believe in Miracles. I think it's pretty apt, don't you?'

'Absolutely. You place the bet this time and I'll go to the loo.'

'I'll meet you back here.'

Anna took her place in line behind a man who was flashing fifty-dollar notes around. He'd obviously had a good win. As he turned, he bumped into her.

'Excuse me,' he said gruffly. It was Alec Harper.

'Sorry,' she muttered, feeling her face turn red. She stepped to the left just as he did and they bumped into each other again. 'Oh, I'm so sorry,' she said, ready to sink into the ground with embarrassment.

Alec looked at her, frowned, and finally stepped around her.

'You right, love? Can I help you?' the bookie asked, holding out his hand for her money.

'Oh, yes please. Twenty dollars on Believe in Miracles.'

'I can't believe we won so much money!' Anna crowed. 'Two hundred and fifty dollars!'

'Well it's yours. Just give me back the twenty we put on and you can have the rest.' Kate was beaming as they walked out of the gates in bare feet, holding their ridiculous heels in their hands. 'You can buy that gorgeous daughter of yours a new dress for her birthday. What a fantastic day! Thanks for coming with me, Anna – I wouldn't have had nearly as much fun without you.' She threw her arm around her friend and then looked over as Anna tensed. 'What?' she asked. 'Oh ...'

Chained in the back of the ute that Anna had seen earlier was Jasper. But it wasn't Jasper as she'd last seen him. Now he was skin and bones with weeping sores over his feet.

Anna felt such distress and anger as she rushed to pat him. 'Oh, Jasper, mate. Hey, Jas,' she said softly. 'Remember me? Oh look, he does.'

Jasper had leapt up at the sound of Anna's voice. He strained at the chain. 'Oh you poor bugger,' she said tenderly, as she felt him wince at her touch. 'The bastard is in there throwing his money around while this poor dog is suffering. Can we report him to the RSPCA?'

'We can do better than that,' said Kate, glancing around. She reached into the ute's tray and unclipped Jasper's chain. 'Grab him.'

In one swift movement, Anna had Jasper on the ground. 'Let's go,' said Anna, and with the dog limping between them they walked as quickly as they could back to the car.

Chapter 14

Matt weaved his way through the steep hills, just before Spalding, passing the golf club and little bridges that crossed the Broughton River. The reeds grew high on the banks of the river and the hills were lined with granite reefs. The paddocks of dry grass gleamed golden in the evening sun before the sun slipped behind the hills and long dark shadows were cast across the land.

He smiled to himself. Five minutes until he could hug Ella.

As he rounded the corner the familiar sights unexpectedly caused a suffocating feeling to envelop him. Even though he knew it wouldn't be long before he'd be walking into a cool house where Anna waited with open arms, he felt trapped. Small town, small house, small backyard.

Ella, he must think about Ella.

The ute bounced slightly as Matt drove over the railway line and looked across to the service station. Feigning normality, he breathed deeply and waved to the owner who was outside locking up the bowsers. He continued on down the main street, passing the Town Hall, War Memorial and bowling club before pulling into his driveway.

It looked like Anna had mowed the lawn today; he could smell the scent of freshly cut grass, reminding him of the hundreds of hectares of hay he had cut in previous years. The cement path had been swept and Matt knew, even before he opened the door, that the house would be neat and tidy and his favourite meal would be in the oven.

It was a comfort knowing that Anna was so loyal to him and tried to do all the things that kept him happy. Matt struggled to remember when he told Anna last how much he appreciated her, even though her attitude towards his quest to find the thieves annoyed him. He couldn't remember the last time. He would have to do it tonight.

Forcing himself to get out of the car, he mustered a smile as he flung open the front door.

'Hi guys, I'm home!' he called.

Anna ran out from the laundry.

'Hi!' She reached up to give him a kiss. 'Good trip?'

Matt nodded as he dropped his bag. 'Where's Ella?'

'Asleep – she's had a big day at Grandma's house.'

'She's been at Mum's? Why?'

'Kate and I went to the races in Clare.'

Gazing at his wife in surprise, Matt realised that even though she was wearing shorts and a baggy old T-shirt, she had makeup on and her hair was up. How pretty and young she looked, he thought. How *untouched* by their misfortune.

'Matt.' Anna touched his arm and it took all his willpower not to draw away. She really had got on with her life, it seemed, while he was still hurting. Had they really grown so far apart?

'Matt, Kate and I saw Alec Harper at the races.'

Matt swallowed. 'So?' he asked. Turning away, he picked up his bag and headed towards the bedroom.

'He had Jasper with him.'

Matt stopped. Was she trying to hurt him with the reminder? Surely she wouldn't be that cruel. 'So what, Anna? He's not my dog anymore.'

'Well, actually, he is.'

'What?' He spun around to face her.

'Kate and I took him off the back of Alec Harper's ute.'

Matt stared at his wife as if she'd gone mad. 'You took him from Harper's ute? You mean you *stole* him?'

'Well, I wouldn't say stole, more like took him for his own good. Matt, you've got to come see him,' Anna said urgently. 'Alec was by the track flashing his money around while poor Jasper was tied up in the sun on the back of the ute. He's been hitting him, I'm sure of it – he cringed when I patted him. His feet have sores all over them. I took him to the vet and got some cream, but he needs lots of rest and –'

'Well he won't be getting it here. You have to take him back, Anna. What were you thinking, stealing someone else's dog?'

'Didn't you hear me?' Anna demanded. 'He's being mistreated. He needs us and he's in our laundry now. He knew me, Matt – as soon as he heard my voice his ears pricked up and he just about wagged his tail off.' Anna was pleading now, but Matt was having none of it.

'No, Anna. Take him back. Take him back now.' There was a pause as he looked at his wife and wondered if he really knew her. 'I'm going for a shower.' He went into the bathroom and closed the door behind him. Sinking onto the floor, he sat with his head in his hands. He half hoped Anna would follow him; he could start a fight then, yell at her, rant and scream. Maybe it would make him feel better.

Then he heard the front door slam, making the window above the basin rattle. Anna was gone.

Slowly he rose up and turned on the taps. Stripping down, he could see the change in his body. He'd gone from being trim and muscled to slightly flabby. Roadhouse food and lots of time spent sitting still would do that. The V-shaped tan on his neck had faded and instead of both arms being tanned now it was just his right, the one that rested on the door of the truck as he drove. He was a truckie not a farmer. It used to be that he was tired from the daily physical activity – the burn of his muscles when he lifted something too heavy or the fatigue after a hard day in the sheep yards. Now he was just tired; it was easier to sleep and not think than it was to live this half-life. He found himself missing the smallest things – his hand straying down to pat his loyal mate; running a wire along a fence and feeling the heaviness of the wire strainers in his hand; the smell of rain; driving to his favourite spot and watching the sun set.

Matt stood under the hot water and concentrated on the hard jets of burning water hitting his face and chest. But his thoughts kept straying to Jasper. Finally he couldn't stand it anymore. He dried himself, got dressed and went to the laundry door.

'Jasper?' he said quietly.

He heard the thump of a tail and pushed open the door.

Jasper whined with pleasure at the sight of his old master. He tried to jump up, but was hindered by his sore feet. Matt dropped to the floor, his arm around the warm body.

'Jasper,' he muttered, burying his face in the dog's rough coat. As he stroked Jasper's head and fondled his ears, Matt realised how much he'd missed him. How much he needed him.

'What's he done to you, hey?' Matt asked softly. 'Sit, boy. Let me look at you.' Matt ran his hands over Jasper's body. He could feel a lump over the rib cage, which hadn't been there before. When he probed the area, Jasper whimpered. Broken rib. Too skinny.

'Anna was right, wasn't she? He's been hitting you, old mate.'

Jasper thumped his tail. His tongue hung out of his mouth and he seemed to be smiling. Matt smiled. 'Yeah, buddy, I've missed you too. But I have to give you back. You were sold.'

As if Jasper understood Matt's words, he slumped to the ground. With a huge sigh, he put his head on his paws and moved his eyes to look up at Matt.

Master and dog sat together for a while, then Matt heaved himself up, went out to the hall and pulled out the phone book. He found Alec's phone number, dialled and listened to it ring and ring. He almost hung up; at least he could tell himself he'd tried to return Jasper.

'Hello?'

Caught off guard, Matt cleared his throat. 'Uh, hello? Is that Alec Harper?'

'Yes.' The voice was cold and unfriendly.

'Um, Alec, it's Matt Butler calling.'

'Yes?' He was impatient now.

'I've got my – uh, your dog here. He –'

'How the hell did you get him? He went missing at the races. I assumed someone had stolen him.' His anger crackled down the wire.

'I'm not sure how my wife came across him. I guess she found him on the road.'

'Bullshit. He was chained in the back of the ute. I saw your wife at the races today – she must have taken him. As far as I'm concerned, this is a matter for the police.'

Matt frowned. 'I don't think so, Alec,' he said evenly. 'If my wife did take him from the back of your ute – which I'm sure she didn't – I think Jasper's injuries speak for themselves. I will return him to you, because a deal's a deal, but let me tell you this: if I see Jasper in this condition again, I'll report you to the RSPCA.'

'Report me? Piss off. I expect you to return the mongrel today.' He hung up.

'Shit.' Matt slammed the receiver back into the cradle, breathing heavily. 'Why did I go and bloody ring him?' His hands clenched into fists.

The door opened and Anna came in, pushing Ella in her pram.

'Daddy!' The little girl clapped her hands.

'Hello, baby girl!' he said, then murmured to Anna in an undertone, 'Jasper is Alec's now. He bought him. You should have just let it be.'

'Let it be? He's your friend, Matt! You can't let him be treated like this.'

'I've already rung Alec.'

Anna's hands flew to her face. 'You haven't! Matt, why?'

'He has to go back.' Matt turned away. 'I don't like it any more than you do, but don't you see? If I don't give him back, it makes me no better than whoever stole our fertiliser.' Looking over his shoulder he saw the telltale redness in Anna's eyes. He sighed, put his arm around her and squeezed her gently. Then he went to the laundry and called Jasper, who followed him to the ute. 'I'll be gone a while,' he told her.

He left Jasper chained to his kennel near Alec's house without bothering to go in and make his presence known to the dog's owner. It was hard enough to be leaving his dog behind, but to be treading on soil that had once been his was messing with his head. Jasper watched him go, his tail drooping. Matt knew the dog wouldn't understand why his old boss was leaving him behind or that his tears had overflowed as he drove away.

Entering the pub, Matt walked straight up to the bar and ordered a Coke.

'One Coke coming up,' Joe said and pulled out a glass.

'Oh, make it a beer, Joe – a bitter, please. Only got to walk across the road, don't I?'

Matt sat at the end of the bar, his back against the wall, and sipped his beer slowly. Joe didn't try to talk to him, and neither did the two old blokes staring at the TV screen fixed to the wall.

As the pub started to fill, Matt ordered another

beer and tried not to think about Jasper, but the more he tried not to, the more memories of Jasper wormed their way into his mind. The good things they'd done together, the companionship.

He felt a hand on his shoulder and turned around to see Sam. His face coloured as he remembered the way he spoke to his friend the last time he saw him.

'G'day, Matt,' Sam said.

'Sam,' he said, nodding to hide his discomfort. 'Beer? I'm just about to get another one.'

'That would be great. How're Anna and Ella?'

'Fine. All good.' Matt held out a ten-dollar note to catch the publican's attention. When he did, he asked for two middies.

Joe lined them up, Matt took them and held one out to Sam. 'I'm sorry ...'

Sam held up his hand. 'Doesn't matter, mate. It's forgotten. All I want to say about that is try not to be too hard on Anna. She's a huge support, even if you don't realise it now. So tell me, what's been happening?'

Pleased not to have to dwell on their last meeting and trying to put Jasper to the back of his mind, Matt found himself telling Sam about his last trip away. When he had finished he knew there was no other way around it. He had to ask Sam about the farm.

'All good out there,' Sam replied. 'We're cleaning out a few dams and catchments while we're waiting for the opening rains. Anyway, look, I'd better make a move. Kate will string me up if I'm late home tonight.'

'No worries, mate.'

Sam clapped him on the shoulder. 'It's good to see you out and about again.'

'Nothing better than one off the wood,' Matt joked, raising his glass. He had to hide that he felt on the inside like crying. Matt ordered another beer and looked around for someone else to talk to. He needed to keep his mind busy and he didn't want to go home just yet. The pub was filled with raucous laughter and people lined up at the bar.

Mark Chambers, a merino stud breeder, brushed past him and accidentally spilled the beer onto Matt's shirt.

'Ah shit, sorry, mate,' said Mark. 'Oh, g'day, Matt. I've been thinking about ringing you.'

Matt couldn't think why so he just waited for him to continue talking.

'I know you had that fertiliser nicked a while back and I heard you didn't get much help from the cops.'

Matt stiffened and tried to move away. This was the whole reason he had avoided everyone for so long. Then Mark rushed on and Matt got the message that Mark was just as apprehensive about discussing the incident as he was.

'I wanted to let you know that I had ten bales of top-quality wool taken from my shearing shed about three weeks ago. The best wool I've ever grown! It left me feeling pretty crook, so I can only imagine how you'd be feeling. Ah, hell, I'm not saying this right.' Mark ran his fingers through his hair as words tumbled from his mouth. 'The cops haven't been that helpful to us and I thought you should know that you're not on your own. I'd better get going, looks like our crew are going in for tea.' Mark turned away.

'Wait a second, Mark.' Matt found his voice. 'When was this?' He felt in his back pocket for a little notebook and a pen.

Mark frowned a little. 'The exact date?'

'Yep.'

'Oh I think I noticed it on Australia Day. No, it was the day after. We'd spent Australia Day in Wallaroo with friends and two days later I had to go to Adelaide for a meeting, so I was going to take the bales down on my truck. I went to load them the day after Australia Day, but I was ten bales short.'

'Who else knew that you'd been shearing other than the contractor?'

Mark shrugged. 'Anyone could have known. Julie could have told her friends, I'd have told mine, the shearers could have told theirs!'

Matt thought for a moment. 'Did you notice anything strange around the farm before it happened? Like, oh I don't know, a car you didn't know or did any strangers knock on your door?'

Mark was shaking his head slowly. 'Nope, nothing like that.'

Matt scribbled in his notebook and out of the corner of his eye he saw Mark make a hand signal to someone across the room. He glanced up and realised that Mark needed to go. His wife wanted to order a meal.

'Thanks, Mark,' Matt said, shaking his hand.

'No problem, give me a call if I can help in any other way.'

Matt pondered on the information. The only time he felt truly alive was when he was thinking about investigating the thefts.

This was just what he needed to take his mind off Jasper.

Chapter 15

1968

Jimmy opened his eyes and realised he was at the base camp. He'd been here for two days and was due to head back out into the jungle tomorrow. He yawned and stretched, all the time listening for sounds of the war; sounds that might have changed overnight and could indicate danger. Nothing. It was quiet except for the shuffling of men around him.

He rolled out of his makeshift bed. What he wouldn't give to sleep in cool, crisp cotton sheets instead of this grimy sleeping bag thrown on top of a camp bed.

He was tired, tired of this bloody war, tired of living like an animal and just plain bone tired. He picked up the letter he'd been trying to write last night and looked at what he'd written so far.

G'day, young fella,

How are you going over there in Australia? How's your mum? Hope you're both doing well.

I'm back at base camp at the moment. I've had two days off and will be heading out again tomorrow.

Jimmy sighed. It wasn't much of a letter, he knew, but how could he tell Sandy about the fighting? How could he tell an eight-year-old that he had seen a boy of the same age lying on the ground, his mother leaning over his lifeless body, screaming? He was so sick of the screaming – screams of anguish, screams of pain, screams of torment. So many screams you'd swear you were in hell.

He picked up his pen only to throw it down straight away. He ran his hands over his face once again and swore softly. Snatching up his toiletries bag, he headed for the showers. A shower and shave would clear his head.

As he walked to the communal showers, Jimmy thought about tomorrow with a mixture of dread and excitement. He liked being with his mates, but it was injury and death which frightened him. He was scared of *not* being killed instantly. His dreams were haunted by things he'd already seen: the shrieks of men without legs, who'd walked through booby traps, men being shot, hurt and dying, but not yet dead. Men who had loved and would never be the same, wishing it was them who had died.

Then, there was Sandy. The thought of someone not looking out for the lad was what kept him awake at night and left a feeling of cold dread in the pit of his stomach.

As the water trickled over him, giving sweet relief from the humidity, he ran through his mental list of things he had to do that day. There was his washing, of course. And he had to restock his pack with rations and ammunition. He'd better test fire his gun, too. At the back of the base camp was a large, deep hole where the men went to test their weapons to make sure they were working properly – if they failed in the field, it could mean death.

On the last patrol Jimmy had been on, they were waiting on orders to move out when someone heard a cracking of sticks and a rustle behind them. The whole platoon had spun around, rifles raised, only to see a water buffalo. They'd all laughed quietly, not wanting to admit they'd had the bejesus scared out of them.

Ah! He could write about that for Sandy.

He turned off the shower, dried himself and headed back to the Hootchi he shared with one other soldier. The tent was surrounded by sandbags piled waist-high to absorb any stray bullets or a grenade attack. Of course, if bombs fell from above it was a different story . . .

When my platoon was out last week, we saw a water buffalo. It was really huge – a bit like a bull. We also saw three snakes. There are some funny-coloured ones; bright green ones that match the trees and bushes, and ... there's even a type that looks like my paisley shirt! There's also cobras over here, so we have to be pretty careful when we're out walking through the rice fields.

I'm going to have breakfast soon. Have I told you the food is crap? Not like the fish and chips we had the last week before I left. I dream about those fish and chips!

I can tell you today's menu without even going to the mess tent. We'll be having eggs; powdered eggs or eggs brought in from America. Can you believe they ship eggs such a long way? The army injects the fresh ones with ether, so they stay fresh. I know it works, but the eggs taste disgusting – like nothing but ether! And there will probably be baked beans. You'd be right if you were here, because I know you love baked beans.

Today I'm going to be restocking my pack ...

Jimmy trailed off there. He didn't want to talk about testing his weapons, or about how the medic would be coming by later to check his feet for tinea or blisters that could get infected. His crotch would be looked at too. There was no room for dignity with a war going on.

Anyway, I just wanted to say hi and let you know your Uncle Jimmy loves you.

Jimmy rolled the pen around in his fingers and recalled the day he'd told his nephew he was off for a second tour of duty. The dirty little face had lit up when he'd seen Jimmy pull up across the street, and Jimmy had dreaded breaking the news to this boy who was at once so fiercely independent yet still so reliant on his uncle's visits.

'Hi, Uncle Jimmy!' Sandy had called.

Jimmy had forced a smile. 'Hey there, young fella. You want to go up to the shop and get an ice-cream?'

'Oh, yeah!'

'Where's your mum?'

'Inside cleaning up the kitchen. Harry's coming over tonight.'

'Harry? I thought his name was Charlie.'

'Nah, he and Mum had a fight. She likes Harry now.'

Jimmy didn't say anything, just put his arm around the thin shoulders and propelled Sandy towards the house. 'Well, let's tell her where we're off to.'

At the shop they had chocolate ice-cream cones followed by strawberry milkshakes. The lad had kept his promise and had been going to school every day, so he had lots of schoolyard tales to tell. Jimmy laughed at his description of one of the teachers.

'She's a new teacher. The older kids say she's real pretty, but she just looks like a teacher to me.'

'What does she look like?'

Sandy shrugged.

'Is she tall or short? Skinny or fat? What colour is her hair?' he prompted.

'Well,' Sandy said slowly, 'she's tall and got brown hair. She's not fat and not skinny.' He pursed his mouth, trying to find the right words. 'She's ... healthy.'

On the way home, they stopped at the park and sat on the grass. It was here that Jimmy broke the news.

'So, me boy, you remember how I went over to the war a year or so back? To Vietnam?'

Sandy stopped picking at the grass and looked up, his eyes deep voids, without emotion. 'Yeah.'

'Well I've been called up for my second tour.'

'But you said you wouldn't go back!' The despair in his nephew's voice nearly broke Jimmy's heart.

'I know, lad, but if the army and the government say I have to go, I have to. It's called conscription. But, Sandy, I'll write every week and your mum will do her best to look out for you. You just need to promise me you'll keep going to school.'

'Why should I?' the boy said in a sullen voice. 'You won't be here to check.'

'But I'll be checking when I come home.'

Silence.

Jimmy said rashly, 'You need to get a good education so we can go into business together when I get back. I'll need you to help me drive trucks and stuff.'

'Really?' the boy asked hesitantly.

Jimmy was warming to the idea now. 'Yeah! We'll get a couple of trucks and cart freight to businesses, like cement to hardware stores and cans of food to grocery shops. Whaddya reckon?'

'Sounds great, Uncle Jimmy.' His voice was still quiet, but Jimmy detected a note of hopefulness.

When he delivered his nephew back to his mother, he told Margo he'd be leaving for his second tour of duty on Monday week. Margo just nodded as if the news didn't really affect her.

Jimmy had felt so despondent as he drove away from the shabby weatherboard house.

Now Jimmy signed the letter – *'Love, Uncle J'* – and scrounged around in his pack for some Australian money. Putting five dollars into the envelope, he addressed it and shoved it in his pocket. He'd drop it off at the Red Cross tent before he left the next morning.

'Hey, Jimmy! You free, mate?'

Jimmy recognised the friendly voice of company quartermaster, Alan Bridle.

'Yeah, skip.'

'I'll need to go to the laundry in Ba Ria shortly. Can you be my protection? I've spoken to your sergeant.'

'Yes, sir.'

Jimmy smiled to himself. What a stroke of luck. To accompany the company quartermaster meant he could see Min-Thu, talk to her once more before he left tomorrow.

If it wasn't the lad occupying his thoughts, it was Min-Thu, with her long-dark-brown hair and almond-shaped brown eyes. He'd noticed her the first time he'd gone to the laundry with the CQ.

The second time he went, he'd asked if anyone spoke English, hoping she could. He'd smiled broadly when she had shyly put her hand up without looking at him.

'Can you read English?'

'I try,' she said. 'I learn.'

'Can I help you? I could write you notes.'

'No, no. I learn. At lessons,' she had said, turning away to hide her embarrassment at being singled out.

Despite her demurral, the next time he returned he slipped her a note, as he did the time after and the time after that. On the fifth visit, she'd handed one back to him.

And so it started – the friendship between a soldier and a young laundry girl. A friendship which had brought him joy in a time of anxiety, sadness and fear. He just hoped the friendship might become something more.

Chapter 16

Anna took a deep breath, picked up the phone and dialled. It only rang twice before it was answered.

'Hello?'

'Mr Harper, it's Anna Butler. I'm ringing to make you an offer on your dog.'

'I'm sorry.'

'I'll give you two hundred and thirty dollars – that's more than you paid for him at the clearing sale.' Her hands were sweaty and her heart was pounding in her chest, but her voice was calm and steady.

The idea had come to her in the middle of the night: she could use the money from the races to buy Jasper back for Matt.

But Alec had other ideas. 'I don't think so.'

'Why not?' asked Anna, surprised.

'Because he's mine – I paid for him. And because

I don't like women interfering in my life – which is what you did when you stole him from me.'

There was a click as he hung up. Anna's eyes filled with tears. It had taken so much courage to pick up the phone; she'd never considered that Alec Harper might turn down her offer.

Before she could think any further she picked up the phone and pressed redial.

'Why do you want a dog you mistreat?' she asked before he'd even said hello. 'You could actually be doing someone some good by letting Jasper go. You could help heal my husband.'

'Mrs Butler,' Alec broke in, 'you seem to have mistaken me for some kind of do-gooder. Now listen: I bought the dog. He's mine. I can do what I like with him. I certainly won't be selling him back to you. And as for healing your husband, I don't believe that is my job. He was obviously an inept farmer, which is why you went bankrupt. Maybe he should just learn to deal with it.'

Anna gasped. 'You bastard! How dare you?'

'How dare *you*, Mrs Butler?' Alec's voice was cold. 'How dare you steal my dog then have the audacity to ring me and ask to buy him back? Please, don't call again.'

Anna burst into angry tears as she slammed the phone into the cradle and slid to the floor.

There was a corresponding cry from Ella's bedroom. Anna had to pull herself together for her daughter's sake. She went to the bathroom and hastily splashed her face, then went into Ella's room.

'Don't we have a birthday party to plan for you?' she asked brightly.

'My birfday, birfday!'

Anna hugged Ella to her, tears pricking her eyes once more. 'Sorry, Matt,' she whispered. 'I tried.'

Chapter 17

Anna threw open the door and grinned at her brother. 'Nick!'

She hugged him then looked over his shoulder to see his wife, Jodie, walking up the path carrying a huge birthday cake in the shape of a Barbie doll.

'Jodie, that cake looks amazing!' Anna said in awe. 'How long did it take you to make?'

'Oh, not long. Icing it was the hardest thing. I'm just hoping my favourite niece will like it!' She grinned.

'She's your only niece,' Anna said, rolling her eyes. 'Oh! It's so good to see you guys – it's been too long. Come on, Rob and Claire have brought Dad. They're all in the backyard with Laura and Ian. Matt's got the barbie going. Kate and Sam should be here soon.'

Excited squeals reached them as they stepped into the backyard and Anna could see her dad, Peter, was giving Ella a ride on his lap. He slapped the side of the wheelchair with one hand, pretending it was a horse while Bindy ran alongside barking. Laura was sitting on the lawn, her legs stretched out in front of her, chatting to Claire, and Matt and Ian were standing at the barbecue, Matt turning sausages and Ian trying to engage him in conversation, though Anna could tell Matt was lost in his own thoughts.

She looked at Rob, her heart full of love. She and Nick had been so grateful that he and Claire had offered to nurse their father back to health. And Claire, a physio, had achieved wonders with him.

Her father now lived independently in Adelaide and was back working at the bank, something they hadn't dreamed would be possible immediately after the accident.

Anna often thought about the terrible time they had been through then, comparing it to the difficulties she and Matt were going through now. She still thought losing her mum was so much worse than losing the farm. But they were thoughts she would never vocalise.

'Uncle Nick! Aunty Jodie!' called Ella. She slipped off Peter's lap and raced towards her uncle and aunt, then stopped dead, looking wide-eyed at the birthday cake. Jodie squatted down so her niece could get a better look. 'Do you like it?' she asked.

Ella breathed, 'Pretty, pretty!'

Jodie put the cake on the table and held out her arms for a hug, and then Uncle Nick had his turn.

Anna was glad Ella's third birthday was proving such a happy occasion. Her second birthday had been clouded in misery as they had not long moved to town and were still dealing with the aftermath of losing the farm. But now, with Matt's wage from driving and her babysitting business, they were finally getting back on top of things. Not having to worry about where the money was going to come from to buy the groceries and pay the power bills was a huge relief, and to have enough left over for a few little extras, well it was just pure bliss. There had been enough money to buy Ella a toy pram for her birthday and have a family party.

'Helloooo! Anyone home?' called Kate as she and Sam opened the back gate. 'I've got a delivery for a Miss Ella Butler!'

'Kate!' Ella ran over to her and Kate handed her a present, laughing as Ella sat on the ground and pulled at the paper.

Bindy nosed her way under Ella's arm, trying to see what was going on, but Kate shooed her away.

'Mummy! Look!' Ella held up a fairy costume complete with wings, shoes and a sparkly necklace. 'Put on, put on,' she cried as she jumped up and down excitedly.

Anna laughed. 'Sure, Ella, you can put it on.' With Kate's help, Ella struggled into the costume. She ran around the lawn waving her wand and pretending to fly.

'Grub's up!' called Matt a little time later. Ella was

the first one served. She carefully wrapped her bread around the sausage and grinned at Uncle Nick as he squirted some tomato sauce on top. Ella sat next to her cake and ate solemnly, while the adults served themselves sausages and salad, the men opened beers and the women replenished their glasses of white wine. The table pulsated with laughter and conversation; Anna felt very content.

After everyone had eaten, the whole family sang 'Happy Birthday' with gusto. This was how it was supposed to be, Anna thought – good times shared with your family around you. Who could wish for more?

She smiled broadly as Matt helped guide Ella's hand over the knife and into the cake and kissed her on the nose before serving a piece of cake to her.

A short time later, Ella was blowing kisses to everyone as Anna led her into the house for her afternoon nap.

'Had fun, darling?'

Ella nodded, almost too tired to talk.

Anna convinced her to take off the fairy costume and tucked her in, leaning down to give her a hug. As the little arms wrapped themselves around her neck, Anna breathed deeply, enjoying the smell and feel of her little girl.

'Sleep tight, sweetheart,' she whispered.

Anna went into the kitchen to turn the kettle on and stood near the open window, just watching everyone. Snatches of conversation floated in on the breeze.

'I can understand that, mate,' Nick was saying.

'Don't know how . . . any ideas?' said Matt.

Anna went outside to take orders for tea and coffee.

Nick and Matt were so deep in conversation they didn't hear her approach.

'Well I wouldn't expect her to understand. Women just don't think the way we do. But I reckon you're on the right track – we just need to work out how to do it properly, not aimlessly like you are now.'

'I know just driving around at night isn't going to find them, but . . .'

'What the hell are you two talking about?' Anna demanded, her voice low and angry.

Both men started.

'You'd better not be going on about who took the fertiliser again. It's done, finished – there's nothing we can do to change it.' Anna saw Matt raise his eyebrows at Nick as if to say 'I told you', but she continued on. 'And what if you do find something? What are you going to do then? Do you really think they're going to hold their hands out and say, "Here, Matt, come and handcuff me?" Of course they're not – they're probably dangerous blokes and you shouldn't go anywhere near them. There's only one thing to do. Look forward, look to what good things are going to happen in the next year. Know we're together as a family and we're supporting each other until it's just a distant memory.'

'I don't agree, Anna,' Nick began.

Anna held up her hand. 'Nick, I don't want to hear it. Now come join the others.'

It was not the time or place to argue, so the three of them rejoined the group, though Anna couldn't recapture her earlier sense of contentment. She was cross that her brother would encourage Matt and it disturbed her to know that Matt was still as obsessed as ever with the stolen fertiliser.

When the plates and cups were empty Ian and Laura got up to leave. Anna went out the front to see them off. As she re-entered the house she came face to face with Nick, who had come in to use the toilet.

'Nick,' she said, 'please don't do this.'

'Do what?' he asked. 'Help Matt find out who did it? Why not? He needs to know, Anna.'

Anna shook her head. 'No he doesn't. He needs to move on, Nick. I know him better than you. He's completely obsessed – he acts as if nothing else matters, not even Ella and me. For the sake of our family he needs to forget what happened. He has to look forward now.'

'Anna, think about it like this: what if someone took Ella and you found her dead?' Anna reared back. 'Listen to me,' Nick insisted. 'Imagine the police not doing anything, not answering your phone calls, not bothering to come and take fingerprints or try to track down the bastard who did it. Would you let it go? Would you say, "Oh, she'll be right, let's just look forward"? Of course you wouldn't. You'd be leading the pack of people trying to find who did it, why it happened, who was to blame.'

'It's a bit bloody different, Nick!'

'Not really. See, Matt feels like he's lost a member of his family. He's grieving the same way that you or any of us would if we lost Ella. The same way *we* did when Mum died. He worked and built the farm up with nothing but his own two hands and you. This fertiliser theft made his whole life crumble before his eyes. Why can't you see he needs to do this for closure?'

'Nick, I hate to burst your bubble, but we were struggling even before the fertiliser was stolen. We'd had five bad seasons, remember? And our only regular source of income taken away with the truck fire!' Anna was angry. 'You're interfering. Just leave him alone. He doesn't need to find out who did it.'

'But he does, Anna,' Nick said urgently. 'I understand things weren't going well before it all happened. You're probably right – this was just the straw that broke the camel's back. But if this is how he needs to deal with it, you should support him through thick and thin – it might be the only way to recover the bloke you married. I'm sorry if you think I'm interfering. I'm trying to help you understand from a bloke's perspective. And, don't forget how great he was when Mum died.' With that, he stepped into the bathroom and shut the door.

Anna stared after him, her thoughts whirling. Surely he couldn't be right? But she remembered what he'd said about Ella, about how she'd feel. He was definitely right about that.

Chapter 18

Matt walked out of the smoko room only to be accosted by a small barking bundle, its hackles raised. He laughed as Turna ran around his ankles, growling ferociously. An ear-piercing whistle echoed around the sheds and the bundle shot off.

The brown and white Jack Russell terrier appeared again a short time later as Matt was checking the tyres on the truck.

'You know, Turna, you've got a serious attitude problem,' Matt said as the dog lifted his leg on every wheel he could.

'Sorry, Matt, is he giving you the shits?' Janey was walking towards him. Like him she wore a green King Gee shirt, shorts and Rossi boots. Her hair was pulled back in a plait.

'You should muzzle that dog, Janey – I'm sure he thinks my ankles are his next feed!'

'Hell on wheels, aren't you, Turna? Come here, mate.' She squatted down and picked up the little dog, who seemed to become jelly in her arms.

Matt risked a snapping of teeth and reached over to fondle the soft ears, trying not to think about Jasper.

'You've got a dog, haven't you, Matt?' Janey asked, craning her face away from the dog as he tried to lick her chin.

'Not anymore.' Matt turned back to the tyres.

'You should get another one. They're such great company. I love having him with me when Joel and I aren't driving together. He almost talks back when I'm chatting away to him. You woulda had a good farm dog, hey?'

'Yep. I did. Anna has an old kelpie, but she's been retired for years. Just stays around the house now. How are the wedding plans going?' asked Matt, wanting to turn the conversation from dogs. He couldn't get another dog: it was Jasper he needed.

'Yeah, real good, mate. Tried me dress on a few days ago. Gawd, I look a bit strange in it. Can't remember the last time I was in a dress. And we've got the menu sorted now. The reception place is real nice. You and Anna'll be there, won't you?'

'You bet! Couldn't miss the opportunity to see you in a dress, could I?'

'Smart arse,' Janey grinned and whacked Matt on the arm as he finished checking the spare tyres were all chained. He stood up just as Shane walked around the front of the truck and called hello, which set Turna off again.

'Steady on there, little dog,' Shane said. 'I'm allowed to be here! Jeez, Janey, how'd you train that dog to be your personal bodyguard? I don't know how he doesn't get run over, running through the yard like he does!'

'I keep a bloody close eye on him and normally he doesn't go too far from my side. Matt here must smell good or something. It's the second time he's tried to round him up, today!'

Shane sniffed towards Matt, theatrically. 'Dog must have his senses stuffed up.'

Janey laughed. 'I think it's just from spending so much time with me in the truck,' she said seriously. Turna was tucked under her arm now and she tried to stop him from wriggling. 'Well, I'd better get going. I'm heading up to your neck of the woods today, Matt. Clare, Spalding, Jamestown, Orroroo, then home again.'

'Better keep the dog in the cab. Who knows what he'd do if you let him out!'

'Yeah, yeah, laugh all you like,' said Janey. 'But I'll tell you what, I was camped at a roadhouse in Port Augusta a few weeks back and some bastard tried to open the cab door. I'd locked it, of course, but Turna went apeshit. The lowlife must've taken off 'cos by the time I got the curtain unzipped and was outside I couldn't see anyone. Heard a car take off, though, so I guess he scarpered as soon as Turna barked. Couldn't ask for better protection, could I, mate?' She patted Turna.

Matt shook his head. It happened all too often.

'Funny thing was, you know how you get in the state just before you wake up when you're sorta aware, but you're not? Well I thought I could feel the truck shaking like someone was trying to unpin the back doors.' She shrugged. 'But when I walked around the anti-tamper cable tie was still in place, so nothing was taken. So it helps having Turna around. Oh, I know he wouldn't be much good if there was a serious bust-in, but he does a good job.'

'Some idiot wanting to pinch something and make a quick buck, I guess,' Matt said. 'Well, Turna, looks like you earned your keep that night.'

'G'day, you lot! What's goin' on?' Jimmy was limping towards them, a smile on his face.

'We're just discussing the virtues of Turna.' Shane grinned.

'Of which there are many, I'm sure,' Jimmy said dryly, reaching out to pat the dog. Turna couldn't decide if he wanted the pat or if he should be protecting his owner, so he accepted the pat while growling. Everyone laughed.

'Janey was just saying someone tried to get into the truck but Turna did his bit. How's your leg today?' Shane asked.

'No different to any other day. Old war wounds always stay with you. Janey, are you okay?' The older man's voice was concerned.

'It was all fine, Jimmy. Turna scared them off.'

'I've heard about a few problems around roadhouses and parking bays,' Jimmy said pensively. 'I was going to talk to everyone at the staff meeting on Thursday night.'

'I've heard of farm equipment being taken,' Shane said. 'A generator, fencing gear, even some wool. Those sorts of things. It all seems to be happening up north though – Port Pirie, Jamestown, those areas. But it's being taken from farms or from isolated houses, not out of trucks. Anyone else heard of anything?'

Matt felt his face flame red and looked down before replying. 'I know there was a bloke from over Burra way who had some chemical stolen recently.'

'Really?' Jimmy shifted his weight from his bad leg to the good. 'Poor bugger. I don't know what gets into people these days. Wouldn't have been like it when I was young!'

'What would happen if the freight was stolen out of a truck?' Janey asked.

'The insurance would cover it, and that's why we have anti-tamper devices. Not a lot of transport firms bother with them, but I think it's easier to have them on rather than not. It's your own insurance, if you like.' As he talked, he ran his fingers over a small brass plate with the initials MT welded onto the trailer.

Matt had asked Shane what it meant when he first started driving for Jimmy. Shane had told him Marshall Transport was the name of Jimmy's first

150

business. He'd started a trucking business in 1970, carting general freight around Adelaide. In 1987, things had started to go bad – the stock market had crashed and the ripple effects were everywhere. People weren't paying their bills. In 1988 Jimmy had made the decision to keep two trailers and one prime mover and sold the rest. For a while he worked as a sub-contractor and then he took a risk. He borrowed enough money to start this new business, which was now thriving.

Matt's respect for the man had grown after hearing this. He'd been knocked down, just like Matt had been, but he'd got back up again. There were times Matt thought he wanted to do something similar. Maybe he could save enough money to have another try. But then there were other times the fear of failure terrified him and he didn't think he could bear to try again.

Matt watched as his boss absent-mindedly rubbed the brass plate and wondered if Jimmy ever thought about having to shut the first business down. Did it leave a hole in his heart, like it had with Matt? Had it left him feeling so empty there was nothing more inside him?

Tuning back into the conversation, he saw Janey nod, agreeing with whatever Jimmy had just said.

'You know, there was a bloke up past Jamestown who had a gun stolen out of his gun cabinet. It's bloody amazing to think so many crimes happen in the country area. We expect to get broken into in the city, but not way out on farms!' she said.

'Absolutely.' Shane nodded. 'What about last year, when that farmhand took twenty lambs out of a feedlot and brought them to the Dublin sale yards? Do you remember that? It was all the talk over the CB. The cops got him, though, as he was unloading. Can't remember what happened to him.'

'Went to court and got two years for stealing as a servant,' Jimmy said. 'There seems to be more and more thieving going on. Maybe I should give you all Jack Russells! Anyway, I think we need to keep an eye on things.'

Everyone nodded their agreement and Jimmy limped away.

'Right, I'm off,' said Janey. 'Can't be late or I might get the sack!' She grinned broadly and winked at Jimmy on her way past. 'Catch you all later.'

'Yeah, I'd better get going too,' said Shane. 'Jack's got some swimming thing on later and I want to be there for it. Catch you, Matt, Janey.'

Matt went about tidying up the truck, reflecting on Jimmy's joking comment about getting them all Jack Russells. But Matt didn't need a new dog – his old mate Jasper would do him fine. He groaned. Jasper again.

He slammed the door of the truck, refusing to let Jasper any further into his thoughts.

Chapter 19

1968

Dear Min-Thu,

You'd like Australia, I'm sure. The sky is so big it looks like it never ends. The dirt is red – especially in the north.

It doesn't rain there like it does here. There are days you would get a whole year's worth of rain. Your land is so beautiful, with its clear water, green jungles, sheer cliffs and islands. It's such a shame all we are doing with this war is damaging it.

Jimmy was walking through rice paddies and doing his best not to think about the day ahead. Composing letters to Sandy or Min-Thu was how he kept himself calm, all the while scanning the terrain for signs of the enemy, his senses on high alert.

His boots, heavy with water, made for slow going

through the fields. He could hear his mate's laboured breathing behind him matching his own and his arms ached from holding his weapon above the water. Ten point four kilos of gun plus his pack and ammo – there were days he felt like a pack horse.

CQ Bridle had instructed them to double-check their ammunition before they left on patrol six weeks ago.

'Fire it into the hole forty times instead of twenty. We need to make sure it's all good. There are stories coming out of other camps that there's been a faulty batch of ammo come in from the US. Gazza told me about losing two of his lead men.'

'What happened?' Jimmy asked.

'They fired on Charlie Company comin' out of a rat hole. Apparently our blokes saw 'em get hit and they sorta jerked back like they had been, but then they kept coming towards the rest of the platoon. It sounded like something out of a movie.' CQ Bridle shook his head sadly. 'What a waste of good men, just because someone couldn't be bothered checking everything was okay.'

There's a huge rock in the middle of Australia: Ayers Rock. I'm hoping I'll climb it someday.

Jimmy had fallen for Min-Thu good and proper – and now he knew his feelings were reciprocated.

They had continued exchanging notes and, on his last visit to the laundry with CQ Bridle, Jimmy had steered Min-Thu behind a tree, away from the watchful eyes of the man in charge. Quickly, he had kissed her – and his heart had soared when she kissed him back.

Barely a minute later he had heard CQ Bridle bellowing his name.

Jimmy had slipped a note into Min-Thu's hand then gently pushed her back towards the wash house before casually striding out from behind the tree.

'Skip?'

'We've finished here. Back to base camp.'

Jimmy took his position on the back of the vehicle, rifle raised. As they drove off, Jimmy glanced over his shoulder and saw Min-Thu waving goodbye . . .

There was a burst of gunfire behind them and Jimmy whirled around, his gun dropping to his shoulder in readiness to react while his eyes raked their surrounds in search of whoever had shot at them.

He saw a red-faced digger at the end of the line looking sheepish.

'There was a great big fucking cobra,' the young man spluttered. 'Right beside my leg.' He pointed at the water with his gun.

'Bloody idiot,' muttered Jimmy. 'You'll get us all killed.'

They continued on their way, heading for base camp. The last six weeks had been tough.

After two weeks on patrol in some of the thickest jungle they had ever seen, Jimmy, his partner Kimbo and three other blokes had spent the last week at a mortar position, deep in the jungle.

The mortar pit was surrounded by sandbags and an automatic rifle sat on the edge, ready to fire. And it had fired. Jimmy could feel the vibration of the gun in his sleep. He was pleased it was his last assignment. He had three days of rest and convalescence and then he was off home to Australia.

The note he'd given to Min-Thu asked her to join him on his three days of leave. He was hoping that would be long enough to convince her to come home with him.

Two hours later, footsore, tired and filthy, the platoon passed through the checkpoints and entered base camp. They set down their packs and breathed a sigh of relief: they'd made it.

During their weeks in the field they'd stumbled upon rat holes and caves, swept areas for mines and booby traps, and walked or crawled on their stomachs through jungles and hundreds of hectares of rubber tree plantations. They'd been shot at, and they had fired back. They'd seen bombs dropped and rivers of smoke pouring into the atmosphere. They'd watched as a pod of helicopters flew at low altitude – there was nothing more sinister than seeing twenty or more, hovering only metres above the ground, with men streaming from them, their guns raised. Ready.

They'd seen other soldiers – their comrades – lying where they had fallen and had called in their positions, so their bodies could be recovered and taken home. They'd tended to the injured, including Vietnamese women and children. They'd also taken prisoners.

Oh yes, Jimmy was pleased to be going home. He'd had enough of war to last him ten lifetimes.

'Jimbo, mate! Good to see you back.' Jimmy turned to see CQ Bridle at his shoulder.

'Skip,' Jimmy answered in acknowledgement. 'Pleased to bloody be here. There were a couple of times I really didn't think we were going to make it.'

'You'd better go get yourself a drink then and thank your lucky stars you did. Jeez I've heard more horror stories in the last little while than the whole time I've been here. You're off on leave tomorrow, aren't you?'

'Yeah, then heading back home by the end of the week.' Jimmy knew that CQ Bridle probably wished it was him going home. His face was more lined and weary than it had been when he had marched out six weeks ago.

'Got a note here from your friend.' CQ Bridle pulled a crumpled envelope from his pocket and handed it to Jimmy. 'Be a bit careful, eh, mate? We've had problems with hand grenade attacks since you left.'

Jimmy knew what CQ Bridle was saying: no one was to be trusted, and that included women and children. But Min-Thu wasn't like that – and it had been Jimmy who had instigated the first move, anyway.

That night, sitting alone outside the boozer, listening to music and laughter, he opened the letter and smiled as he read it.

She would meet him.

Jimmy jumped off the truck to the jeers of his mates and went to meet Min-Thu. He saw her from a distance, waiting in line to buy a Goffer can from a girl surrounded by US soldiers. He grinned, realising Min-Thu was probably getting a Coke for him. In his last letter he had said how much he missed the sickly sweet taste when he was out patrolling. She had replied that she disliked the smell so much she could never bring herself to taste it.

As soon as they entered Vung Tau, the soldiers were carefee. They couldn't wait to jump into the crystal clear waters and sleep in a real bed.

The wide dirt streets were heavily littered, but that didn't detract from the beauty of the place.

Jimmy watched as Min-Thu paid the girl and turned towards him. He knew she hadn't seen him.

'On yer, Jimmy,' called Kimbo and let out another piercing whistle. The rest of the boys on the back of the truck egged him on.

Jimmy flicked the bird back at them and walked on towards her, a smile on his face. He heard the truck rev its engine and start to move off slowly down the street, tooting its horn at a group of children, who dispersed, chattering loudly as the men on leave drove past.

'G'day,' Jimmy called out and watched as Min-Thu turned towards his voice. A smile crossed her face.

'Hello!' she called back.

Jimmy was amazed at how her English had progressed in the two years he had been writing to her. From knowing only small, basic words, she was now able to read, write and speak fluently.

He loved their conversations, both written and spoken. They hardly talked of the war, but covered everything else, from their families to their favourite meals.

Min-Thu had written that she thought his favourite meal of steak, chips and tomato sauce sounded terrible. Especially the sauce. In his reply Jimmy had joked that her meals of sour fish head soup didn't sound much better.

And he told her about Sandy. He tried not to think too much about his nephew while he was over here, but he'd wanted Min-Thu to know how Sandy made his world seem right, how the boy made him laugh and how Margo's indifference to him saddened Jimmy more than he could say.

Min-Thu's next letter was filled with compassion. Family was the most important part of her life, she'd said. She hoped she would meet Sandy one day.

Jimmy had breathed out deeply and held the letter to his chest. With those words she'd dispelled any thoughts he'd had about two cultures, so different from one another, clashing. Yep, she was special.

He hurried towards her now.

Jimmy had to stop himself from running towards her. From the corner of his eye he saw the girl selling the drinks drop her tray and Jimmy glanced towards her to see if he could help.

He saw the grenade she was holding.

There was no time to react – *BANG!* Min-Thu disappeared behind a cloud of smoke. The air filled with dust and debris. People shrieked with fear. Jimmy screamed, crying out Min-Thu's name.

BOOM! Another explosion.

Jimmy dropped to the ground and covered his head with his arms to shield himself.

He was dimly aware of someone dragging him away from the blast site, yelling for a medic, but he paid them no heed. Confusion reigned as other voices asked for help. 'Min-Thu!' he called so loudly, his voice broke. 'Min-Thu!'

'Get down, get down, get down,' yelled another voice and there was yet another blast.

As the dust began to settle, Jimmy could see bodies lying mangled on the ground, thrown by the force of the explosions. He could see a leg about fifteen metres away and an arm within reaching distance.

He tried to stand but his legs didn't seem to be

working. Frantically he tried to drag himself back to where he had last seen Min-Thu.

'Mate, c'mon, you need a medic. They're on their way. How about you stay still?' A hand clamped down on Jimmy's shoulder.

It was Kimbo, who had ripped off his shirt and was trying to apply pressure to Jimmy's bleeding leg. His vision blurred at the edges as the pain filled his being. 'Min-Thu,' he croaked.

'Holy shit.' Kimbo was talking again, but Jimmy could hardly understand what he was saying. 'Stay there, mate, don't move. Listen to me, Jimmy – *don't move*. Keep your head down.'

Kimbo moved off and Jimmy, disregarding his mate's instructions, turned to see where he had gone. He was just in time to see his mate carrying a decapitated head away. With rising horror he recognised Min-Thu's bloodied face and sightless eyes, then he fell into the welcome abyss of darkness.

Chapter 20

Anna tried to open her eyes, but the sleepless night she'd just had was making her sluggish.

The phone rang.

Swearing, she sat up quickly and fumbled for the phone next to the bed.

'Hello?' she said, her voice croaky.

'You sound terrible,' said Kate. 'What's wrong?'

'Ah, Kate! Ella was sick last night. She woke up at about eleven and I don't think she went back to sleep until about four am.' She glanced at the clock. It was now eight o'clock.

'Poor little thing. What's wrong with her?'

Anna tried to get out of bed carefully so she didn't wake the sleeping girl. Ella let out a small cry then settled again. Cradling the phone to her ear, Anna reached out to touch Ella's forehead and was relieved to find it was cool. Obviously the Panadol, cool flannels and hours of rocking her gently had helped break Ella's fever.

'She had a very high temperature and was terribly clingy and sad. There wasn't really anything else wrong – it's probably just a twenty-four-hour thing. Hopefully she'll sleep for a while 'cos I'm exhausted!'

'Oh, what a bugger I have to go to Adelaide today. I'd come and help otherwise.'

'We'll be fine,' Anna said, yawning. 'What are you doing in Adelaide?'

'My cousin Dave and his family are coming over from Perth, so I'm heading down to catch up with them. It's been ages since I saw his family.'

'I hope you have a great time.' Anna was distracted by Ella, who had woken up and immediately started to cry. Anna shushed her and stroked her head, but it didn't make any difference. She felt hot again, too. Anna wondered how her temperature could have risen again so suddenly and tried to calculate when she had last given Ella some Panadol.

'I can't hear you, Kate,' Anna said as Ella's screams grew more frantic. 'I'd better go. Drive safely.' She hung up the phone and turned to Ella. 'Oh, you're all hot and bothered again, sweetie.'

Ella's large eyes were glassy and her cheeks were wet with tears.

'It's okay, I'm here.' Anna stroked her forehead and Ella's tears started to subside. Her breathing deepened and her eyes began to close. Finally she was asleep again. Anna sat on the edge of the bed for a moment, her head in her hands. Coffee. She needed coffee.

Out in the kitchen she switched on the kettle, threw heaped teaspoons of coffee and sugar into a mug and slumped over the bench, her head resting on the cool laminex. So this was what it was like to be a single mum. Exhaustion blurred her thoughts, her temper was frayed and still she had to keep going. She had to make sure there was food on the table, that Ella was bathed and played with, when all she wanted to do was curl up in a ball and sleep. Frustration coursed through her. She wasn't a single mum, damn it. She had a husband, but he was too busy on his long runs and too tired when he came home to help. Or he didn't want to.

As she poured boiling water into her mug, a sleepy Ella appeared in the doorway, a teddy bear tucked under her arm, thumb in her mouth and tears threatening. Anna briefly closed her eyes, wanting to scream, but took a deep breath.

'Hi there! Do you want some juice?'

Ella nodded and spoke around her thumb. 'I hot, Mummy.'

Anna leaned over and gently took the girl's thumb out of her mouth. 'Pardon?'

Ella frowned. 'I *hot*, Mummy.'

Anna brushed her fingers over Ella's forehead on the way to the fridge and realised she *was* hot. Very hot.

'Mummy has run out of juice. How about I just run across to the shop and get some more? Can you watch TV while I go?' She turned on the ABC and was distracted by Jay, who used to be on *Water Rats*, jumping around singing 'Five Fat Sausages Sizzling in a Pan'. She shook her head. He had been one of the sexiest men on TV and now here he was on *Play School*.

She grabbed her purse and slipped out while Ella was occupied. Running quickly across the road she pushed open the door.

The shop was always welcoming. Maggie had installed a potbelly stove near the back corner to dispel the winter's chill, and an air conditioner for when the summer heat got too stifling.

Anna loved coming in here. Maggie stocked things you just couldn't find these days – it was almost like stepping back in time. On the counter sat an old-fashioned cash register and large clear jars crammed with humbugs, liquorice allsorts and boiled sweets. The walls were lined with shelves stacked with tins of vegetables and long-life products. There was even a small display of local talent, with paintings and handicrafts from artists working in the region.

Maggie herself sat in the same spot every day – she had probably sat for decades on the tall stool with a cushioned top, her ankles hooked under the cross bar, her hands busily knitting.

Her smile was warm and, like any good shopkeeper, she was aware of most happenings in the small town, although she never partook in any gossip.

'Good mornin', Anna,' Maggie said in her soft Irish lilt. 'You're lookin' a wee bit peakish today.'

Anna tried to smile, as she walked towards the refrigerator at the back of the store to grab a bottle of orange juice. 'Ella's been sick most of the night and it's just me at home. I think I might have managed three hours' sleep.'

'Eh, ye poor love. It's difficult to cope with young 'uns on your own.'

Anna placed the juice on the counter and asked for a packet of Panadol – for herself. 'I'm probably coming down with it, too,' she grumbled.

'I know young Fiona Lay has been sick, as has the wee Contrall boy. So there is somethin' goin' around town. When is your fella due home?'

'Not for another a day or so. I think his run was to Sydney this time. I've begun to lose track of where he goes he's on the road so often.' She broke off, surprised by the bitterness in her voice.

Maggie rang up her purchases. 'Ah, pet,' she said sympathetically. 'Sometimes life with a man can be hard, but as you're seein' now, it can be harder without. Just know you're loved.' She reached across the counter and held Anna's hand in hers.

Mortified at the prick of tears, Anna snatched her hand away, gathered up her items and walked quickly out of the shop. She was angry with herself for letting her emotions show. It didn't matter what she did behind closed doors, didn't matter if she wept floods of tears, but she had to hold it together in public.

Running back to the house, she saw Sam's ute in the driveway. Inside, Sam was sitting on the floor next to Ella. When he saw Anna, he stood up, smiling. 'Ah, I thought you must have been at Maggie's,' he said he as nodded towards the empty container on the bench.

Anna held up the full bottle she was carrying and waved it about. 'Hi, Sam, what are you doing here?' she asked, grabbed a plastic cup out of the cupboard and poured some juice into it. She measured out some Children's Panadol, mixed it in the juice and handed it to Ella. 'I'd just run out of orange juice, so I ran across to get some. Ella won't take any medicine unless it's mixed in with the juice.'

'Kate said Ella was sick and asked me to bring round some soup she had in the freezer. I've put it in the fridge.'

Anna smiled at her friends' thoughtfulness. 'Thank you.' She pushed two white tablets out of the box of Panadol she'd bought for herself and washed them down with orange juice straight from the bottle.

Sam frowned. 'Hard night?'

'You could say that.'

'Do you want to have a shower while I'm here to look after Ella? I'm told it's the hardest thing to do when you're a mum.' Sam looked slightly embarrassed mentioning it, but Anna was flooded with gratitude.

'Did your sister tell you that?' she asked. 'Well, she's right. I haven't managed to have one yet. Are you sure you're okay with Ella?'

'Absolutely,' he said. 'We'll read some stories, won't we, Ella?' he said. 'My nephews love it when I read them stories when they're sick,' he told Anna.

Ella looked at Sam solemnly then disappeared into the lounge and came back with a book.

'Hmm, *Belinda*. I don't think I've heard of this one. It looks good! What's this on the front?'

'Cow,' said Ella.

'A cow? Are you sure? I thought it was a horse! Come on, let's go and find a chair, then we can read it.'

Anna bolted for the shower, thankful that Ella wasn't crying. There were times when her head felt like it was going to explode from Ella's screams.

In the bathroom she stared at her reflection. Her face was pale and she had large black rings under her eyes. She could honestly say she had never thought her life would pan out the way it had. She sighed and let her head fall gently onto the mirror and stayed like that for a very long time.

Later, emerging from the steaming shower, she found her headache gone and, amazingly, even with the lack of sleep, she felt as if she could handle the day on her own. Anna could hear noises from the kitchen, and remembered she hadn't given Ella her breakfast yet. When she went out, Ella was sitting at the table, her face smeared with Vegemite. Ella gave her a toothy grin as Anna dropped a kiss on her head.

'Thank you, Sam,' she said, then added guiltily, 'I should be looking after you! You're the guest.'

Sam held out a steaming cup to her. As she took it her fingers brushed his and she felt a rush of energy run through her. Her face flushed at her reaction and, embarrassed, she turned away, hoping he hadn't noticed. But Sam caught her shoulder and turned her around to face him.

'Anna,' he said, looking her straight in the eye, 'you don't have to be everything for everyone or do everything by yourself. You've got friends who will help.'

Chapter 21

Matt checked his rear-view mirror and noticed a car coming up behind. He looked ahead, knowing what he would see – a large hill with a corner at the top.

As the car drew closer, Matt frowned. He took his foot off the accelerator and started to brake; he wanted to hold this idiot up. Surely he wouldn't pass now. Not with a hill you couldn't see over.

The rig started to slow just as an insistent flashing caught his eye. Glancing in the mirror again he saw the black car was right on his tail, flashing its lights. Matt couldn't make out who was behind the wheel, but his first instinct was to pull over. There must be something wrong. He changed down a gear and watched in horror as the car pulled out, trying to pass, then pulled back.

Matt's eyes flicked from the road in front and back again to the mirror. 'You dickhead,' he muttered as he tried to work out what to do. Seventy-five kilometres per hour and dropping.

The man in the car was getting more agitated, his front bumper looked like it was nearly touching the back of the single trailer, and the next thing Matt knew the car was veering sharply into the right-hand lane.

Alarmed, Matt saw a glint of silver coming towards him. Another car. Bloody hell!

The black car shot past him, horn blaring, then swerved back into the left-hand lane just missing the nose of the truck. It accelerated away just as the car coming from the opposite direction ran off the road into the gravel.

With rising horror, Matt realised he recognised the silver car. He saw a flash of blonde hair and Kate's terrified face as her car hurtled off the road. Matt's eyes were pinned to the rear-vision mirror when he felt a bump. As he struggled to keep the truck on a straight path, he realised he'd knocked over a yellow sign and perhaps taken out a few of the white posts on the side of the road.

After what seemed like an age, he finally brought the truck to a standstill, flicked on the hazard lights and leapt out of the cab.

He ran along the bitumen, desperate to get to the car, which had come to rest on the side of road, somehow avoiding a tree and a fence. 'Kate? Hell, Kate?' The fear made his voice high. Yanking open the door, he saw she was conscious. Relief coursed through him. Her frightened eyes met his and he saw the terror leave her face to be replaced by recognition and relief.

'Kate, are you hurt?' He reached in to touch her shoulder.

'Um, no. I don't think so.' She unbuckled her seatbelt and with Matt's help struggled out of the car, shaking.

Matt watched as she raised her trembling hands to her mouth then suddenly sank to the ground. Matt squatted beside her. 'There now,' he said gently. 'It's okay. It's over now.' He tried to ignore the flashes from his own truck accident that had forced their way to the forefront of his mind.

'Who *was* that?' she gasped.

'A bloody idiot. He roared up behind me, started beeping his horn and trying to overtake. I don't think he even saw you coming.'

Kate took a few deep breaths then gave him a tremulous smile.

'I'm so glad it was you in the truck. Far out, what a maniac. What was he thinking?'

'I couldn't guess.' Matt shook his head grimly. 'Where are you going?'

'To Adelaide. My cousin Dave is over from Perth. We're having a bit of a family get-together.'

'Are you right to drive? Do you want me to ring Sam and get him to pick you up? Or you can come with me in the truck, if you want.'

'No.' Kate paused. 'No, I'll be fine. Sam's got a

meeting with the accountant. I'll just take it steady. I'm only an hour or so away.'

Matt said, 'I wish I could report the bastard, but I didn't catch the make of the car or the licence plate. It was something sporty though. Did you?'

Kate shook her head. 'No. It all happened too fast.' She reached out to Matt for a hug. 'Shit. Scary stuff.'

Matt gave her a tight squeeze then said, 'Let me check the car for you and get it back on the road.' He jumped into the driver's seat and turned the key. Carefully he manoeuvered the car back onto the bitumen and left it idling.

'Well it all looks okay, and I can't hear anything to worry about in the engine. Temperature seems fine.' He got out.

'Thanks, Matt. I'll see you soon.'

'Drive carefully, Kate.'

He watched as she got into the car and closed the door. She wound the window down and stuck her head out. 'Have you spoken to Anna today?' she asked.

'No, I've been away for a couple of days. I'm heading home tonight.'

'I rang her this morning and Ella was sick. She sounded exhausted.'

'I'll give her a call.'

'She loves you so much, Matt.'

Matt looked off into the distance. 'I know.'

Kate lifted her hand. 'See you.'

'Yep, see you later.'

Back in the truck Matt cursed the driver of the black car. What on earth would possess someone to pass on a bend and a hill? Could the man have been suicidal? A flashback of a car tailing him into Spalding hit him.

His fingers dialled Sam's mobile number and he listened to the dial tone on open speaker. When Sam answered, he told him Kate had already rung, but at least Matt could reassure his friend that his wife was fine.

He then tried his own home number and listened as a mechanical Anna asked him to leave a message. Matt hesitated for a moment, then pressed the disconnect button.

Matt parked the truck in the darkened depot and slowly climbed out. Glancing at his watch, he saw it was just after eight. He glanced towards Jimmy's ATCO hut, expecting to see the door open but, unusually, it was shut. He could hear Jimmy's voice, and he sounded angry. When there was no answering voice, Matt realised the boss must be on the phone. He shrugged. He could catch up with Jimmy when he returned from holidays. Collecting his gear from the truck, he made his way towards the car park where his ute was waiting.

He was just climbing in when he heard the hut

door slam and Jimmy call out his name. Matt sighed. It had been a long day and now he was heading home he really didn't feel like recounting it all.

But Jimmy was already crossing the car park to where Matt was standing under the bright spotlights.

'Matt, me lad, how did you go? Did everything run smoothly?'

'Yeah, all the deliveries were fine, truck purred along. But I did clean up a few of the white posts and a sign, and broke the spotties while I was at it.'

'I see. What happened?'

'An idiot in a black car is what happened.' Matt felt his anger return. 'You wouldn't bloody believe it, Jimmy. He roared up behind me, tailgated for a few k, then tried to pass on that bend just outside of Peak Town. You know, Jimmy, I've had something similar happen before. Not long after we lost the farm. Some clown in a powerful car – I could hear the engine – tailed me and even rammed into my old ute. It scared the shit out of me and I never understood why it happened.'

'Really? Oh shit.' Jimmy shut his eyes as Matt continued.

'Yeah, I slowed down, tried to get out of his way, but he passed me just as a car came around the corner. I was trying to get off the road so I wouldn't be involved in an accident when I took out the sign and posts. Sorry about that.'

'No, Matt, no. Not your fault. You did a good job.

175

What a bugger of a thing to happen. What happened to the other car?'

'She ran off the road and was fairly shaken, but otherwise she's okay. She's a friend of mine, as it happens. She's fine though.'

'Ah, that's good, that's good.' Jimmy's face was grim. 'Probably some young bloke who's just got a new car and is testing it out. Jeez, some people only exist to make your blood boil. Well, Matt, you'd best be off home. Drive safely, won't you?'

'Goodnight, Jimmy. See you again in a couple of weeks.'

'Oh you're off on holidays. Is it really twelve months since you started here? Well enjoy them, Matt!'

As Matt pulled out of the depot, he saw that Jimmy was still standing in the car park. He looked old and beaten.

Matt pushed open the front, door and was met with a blast of heat. He could smell what he thought was lamb stew and the house was quiet.

He smiled. This was what he liked to come home to.

Throwing his bag on the floor, he went in search of Anna. He'd thought of nothing but her arms around him tonight, knowing she would be able to banish any thoughts of the black car and fear he had felt earlier today.

Matt had been surprised when he realised how much he craved her comfort. It felt like a long time since he'd felt such a need for her, but he hadn't been able to get her out of his mind since the accident earlier in the day. He'd tried a couple more times to call but each time it was the answering machine that had picked up. A near accident wasn't the sort of message to leave.

The kitchen was empty so he called out, but there was no reply. He checked the lounge and saw Anna sleeping on the couch. Matt smiled gently and watched her for a while, wanting to reach out and stroke her face. He extended his hand then remembered what Kate had told him about Ella being sick. He decided to let Anna sleep.

Matt kissed his fingers and pressed them gently to his wife's forehead, then went in search of dinner.

Chapter 22

Royal Adelaide Hospital, 1970

There was a noise, an irritating noise. Almost like the mosquitoes from the jungles in Vietnam, persistent and annoying. It seemed to be coming from a long way away.

Jimmy lay there listening, trying to work out what it was. He preferred the darkness to the pain and memories. His recollections were kept at bay when he was heavily medicated, and the pain in his leg – a constant reminder of that dreadful day – was just a dull throb.

The guilt over Min-Thu's death had consumed Jimmy during his fever-filled months. He could vaguely remember calling her name. His brow was soaked with sweat as he tossed and turned in the small military hospital. His dreams had been filled with her; her smile, her hair, her mouth, as she tried to produce words and sounds which were foreign to her. Then, the nightmare would become reality as he saw over and over her sightless eyes, blood-stained face and Kimbo, trying to protect him from the sight no human should see.

A high nasal voice pierced his thoughts.

'Bloody hell, I haven't driven all this way to see him sleep. Can't you wake him up?'

A quiet murmur answered, sounding protective. He started to drift away again, but there was a strange sensation on his hand. He couldn't place the feeling, and then it tightened around his fingers.

'Uncle Jimmy?' a familiar voice said. 'Hey, Uncle Jimmy, it's me.'

Sandy. It was *Sandy*. Jimmy opened his eyes and struggled to focus. He tried to say something, but his tongue felt thick and clumsy. He hoped he'd squeezed the small fingers before the darkness claimed him again.

'Hey, Uncle Jimmy.'

Six months later Jimmy was sitting in his chair as Sandy let himself into the kitchen. He saw the boy wrinkle his nose.

'The air smells a bit stale in here. Can I open a window?'

'Do whatever you want,' Jimmy muttered, turning away. He squinted as the curtains let in the bright afternoon sunlight and he looked out to a small cement patio and high asbestos fence. He tried to remember the last time he'd shifted from his chair, but he couldn't. He wasn't sure anymore what it felt like to have the sun touch his skin.

It wouldn't have been like this if he could walk properly. If it didn't *hurt* to walk. No, the truth was that he didn't *feel* like getting out of his chair. He wanted to sit in the chair forever, to drink whisky until he didn't jump at shadows, until he no longer saw Min-Thu, dead.

As he watched Sandy move around opening windows he found himself envying the boy. So young, strong and undamaged.

Sandy came around after school every day, although Jimmy couldn't fathom why. Jimmy knew he wasn't much company, and there was nothing welcoming about the tiny council flat he was now living in. Meagrely furnished, dark and cramped, it could only be described as gloomy – which suited Jimmy's mood perfectly.

It wasn't as if he had made no effort. When he'd finally become well enough, he'd tried to look up his old mates – the ones who hadn't gone to Vietnam. But many had turned away from him, as if they blamed *him* for the unpopular war. And the others were just living their lives as if there was no war. They had neat and tidy houses, nice cars, good jobs, children even. And here he was, a crippled, broken man – and all he'd done was follow the government's bidding.

'Uncle Jimmy?'

Jimmy snapped his head up to see Sandy looking at him questioningly.

'What?'

'I asked if you'd eaten today.'

'Probably. I can't remember. But I need another drink.' He held his glass out. Sandy took it, but Jimmy could sense his reluctance. Somewhere deep down he knew he was acting just like Margo, but by hell it was easier than facing everything. Sandy would have to get used to it.

'Come on, boy. One more glass won't hurt.'

'How about I cook scrambled eggs? I saw some eggs in the fridge.'

'Just a drink, lad. Helps make the day go quicker,' he added feeling the need to justify his actions.

Jimmy watched as Sandy sloshed the amber liquid into his glass. He reached for it and raised it to his lips greedily, drinking it down in quick sharp sips. Each one burned on its way to his stomach, but it was a good feeling.

'So,' he said, trying to think of a question to ask his nephew. He knew he should make an effort. 'What'd you learn at school today?'

'Something about fractions. Did some reading, stuff. Not much.' Sandy shrugged.

'Who's your best mate these days?'

'Haven't got one.'

Oh, that hurt. If he'd asked the lad the same question two or three years ago, he would've said his Uncle Jimmy.

'Well, you gotta play with someone while you're there.'

'Nup, I just hang out by myself.' There was a long silence. 'Uncle Jimmy?' The boy's voice was soft.

'Mmm?'

'What's wrong with your leg?'

'War wounds, lad.'

'Does it hurt?'

Jimmy smiled grimly and tried to take another sip, but realised his glass was empty. How could you explain to a ten-year-old that it hurt all the time? And it wasn't the physical pain that he minded so much as the memories the wound revived.

'Sometimes. I think I'll have another drink.'

'Why are you so sad, Uncle Jimmy? Because your leg hurts? Can I help get it fixed?'

'Another drink, boy.' Jimmy's voice took on a sharp edge.

When Sandy didn't move Jimmy looked up to see a strange look of defiance and vulnerability on the boy's face.

'Do you think we'll ever drive trucks together? You promised me.'

Dimly, Jimmy recognised he was asking for reassurance. A guarantee the plans they had made would eventuate. Jimmy would come out of this dark pit he was in, full of alcohol and memories, and once more become the caring uncle he had been.

But he couldn't guarantee it. The future? He

didn't care if it never came. Why was the little idiot even asking? His hand curled around his glass, tight. His anger sudden and fierce.

'What are you waiting for, you little dipshit?' he snarled, watching with a certain amount of satisfaction as the boy recoiled from the insult. 'Do as you're bloody told and get me a drink.'

There was a choking sound and then Sandy began to cry.

The guilt he felt only made Jimmy angrier. 'Stop yer snivelling and get me a drink.'

There was no movement except for the shaking of the boy's shoulders.

'Which bit don't you understand?' Jimmy tried to stand up but pain shot through his leg and he fell back into the chair with a groan. Overcome by rage and frustration, Jimmy hurled the glass at his nephew, and there was a dull thud, then a screech as it connected with his forehead.

The wound began to swell, blood seeping from the opening above his eye and Jimmy, even in his addled state, could see the anguish on the boy's face as he backed out of the room. He held out his hand to Sandy.

'Bloody hell, lad, I'm sorry. I didn't –'

'No!' Sandy screamed at him. 'I trusted you, Uncle Jimmy. You said I could always count on you. But look at you – you're no better than Mum. You're a drunk.' Then, with a mixture of blood and tears running down his face, he stumbled to the door.

Sickened by what he had done, Jimmy rocked back and forth in shock and disbelief. 'Oh me lad, I'm so sorry,' he choked out between heaving sobs. 'I'm so sorry.'

But the boy was gone.

Chapter 23

Anna woke feeling deliciously aroused. She'd been dreaming of Sam, his fingers running down her neck, soft kisses dropped on her shoulders. In the wakefulness of sleep, she tried to slide closer to him and moaned softly. She stretched and turned over to face him, trying to mould her body to his.

Then her brain kicked into gear.

Sam! What on earth was she thinking?

She realised Matt was lying next to her; she hadn't heard him come home last night. She watched him sleeping for a moment or two, then her stomach constricted as she wondered if she had actually moaned aloud.

Horrified, she slipped out of the bed, hoping Matt wouldn't wake until she had composed herself. She padded down the hallway to the bathroom to splash her face with cold water.

Leaning over the bathroom sink, she cupped her hands under the icy water and threw it onto her face. Then she looked in the mirror.

'Great friend you are,' she muttered. 'Kate has been the only support you've had and now you're dreaming about her husband. What is *wrong* with you?'

Outside the toilet door banged and she knew Matt was up. Grabbing a towel she scrubbed at her face, trying to wipe the dreams away before she had to face him. And that's what it was, she reminded herself – a dream; not real. Don't be so ridiculous, she scolded herself. A few kind words and she'd gone weak at the knees. Pathetic!

Banging around in the kitchen, she turned the kettle on and went to check on Ella as Matt walked down the passageway.

Anna smiled. 'Hi, I didn't hear you come home last night,' she said and held out her arms for a hug, feeling like a fraud.

'You were sleeping. I didn't want to wake you.' Matt stepped past, ignoring her outstretched arms. Her smile slipped away, replaced by a mountain of guilt. Was it possible Matt could have read her thoughts?

She peered into Ella's room. Her daughter had her arm flung over her eyes as if to keep the sunlight out. This was the reason Anna was able to stay sane, she reminded herself: a gorgeous daughter who relied on her for everything. Anna knew she would do anything for Ella – no matter how exhausted and wrung out she was.

Anna shut the door and went to the kitchen. Matt was already sipping his first coffee, his head buried in a motorbike magazine.

There were five empty beer bottles on the counter, a half-empty bottle of rum and a dirty plate. That explained the mood. He must have one hell of a hangover. Not exactly the start to his holidays Anna had hoped for.

She went to the bench and saw her cup sitting next to the kettle, empty.

'You could have made me a coffee,' she said.

'Mmm?'

'I said you could've made me a coffee.'

'What?' Matt finally looked up.

'A coffee, Matt,' Anna snapped. 'Would it have been so hard to make me one while you were getting your own?'

Matt threw the magazine down, picked up his cup and walked over to the window.

Anna took a deep breath. 'So,' she said in a conciliatory tone, 'what do you think you'll do today?' There was no point starting the day off on the wrong foot.

'Don't know. I've never really had two weeks of holidays before. It was never like that on the farm. There was always work to be done.'

'Kate suggested we head out to their place today and grab some sand for Ella's sandpit. She said we could use their trailer.'

'Oh yeah.'

There was another of the long silences and Anna decided she just couldn't bear it, so she left the room.

She went outside and walked around the backyard she had put so much effort into over the past few months. She snapped the dead heads off the daisy bushes and pulled a few weeds. When she got to the back corner, she looked at the nearly finished sandpit, smiling as she admired her own handiwork.

The sleepers which she'd bought secondhand had been heavy to shift, but she'd enjoyed the burn of her muscles from the effort. As she'd belted in the steel posts to hold the sleepers together, she'd felt alive. She was *doing* something. Moping about in the house wasn't good for her. She needed to be active, out in the fresh air.

Anna lifted her head as she heard Ella begin to wimper.

'Mumma! Mumma!'

She waited for Matt to go to Ella, but the noise intensified. Running inside, Anna passed Matt, who was sitting again at the kitchen table, immersed in the magazine, oblivious to Ella's cries.

'Morning, little one,' Anna said, picking up the little girl to comfort her. 'Did you have a bad dream?'

'Mummy, you were crying.' Ella hiccuped as she snuggled into her mother's neck, her sobs subsiding.

'Crying? I haven't been crying, darling.'

'You were in my dream.'

'No, no, Ella! Mum doesn't cry. Come on, let's get you some juice.' Anna hugged her daughter, wondering what vibes she had given off the night before to make her daughter dream something so close to her own emotions.

In the kitchen, she got out a cup and filled it with orange juice. Then she turned on the TV in the lounge, placed Ella in front of it and stormed into the kitchen to confront her husband.

'Did you hear Ella just now?' Anna demanded.

'Yeah, but I don't know what to do with her,' Matt answered. 'She doesn't really want me anyway.'

'Oh, Matt, of course she wants you – she's a bit shy with you because you haven't spent any time with her lately, that's all.'

'Yeah, well, I'm busy.'

'Too busy for your own daughter? Have a think about what you just said, and see if it makes sense.' Anna slammed some bread into the toaster and stood at the counter shaking her head and watching Matt. He had yet to raise his head and look at her.

'So will you come to Sam and Kate's today?' she asked, daring him to say no.

'Yeah, might come for a drive.'

'Well, we'll leave in half an hour,' she said, glancing at the clock. She fixed Ella's breakfast and went to sit in the lounge with her.

***

Kate's kitchen smelled of baking as Anna pulled up a stool and watched Kate buzz around the room with an energy that she wished she had.

'How was your time in Adelaide?' Anna asked, horribly conscious that she was sitting in Kate's kitchen pretending to be a good friend, when she'd been dreaming about her husband.

'It was lovely. I had such a great time with Dave and his family. His girls are so beautiful. I was relieved to get home in one piece, though. I suppose Matt told you about yesterday?'

Anna snorted. 'I was asleep when he came home and he just about drank the bar dry judging by what was left on the bench this morning. I reckon he's got a bitch of a hangover – he's not talking and he's in a foul mood. Why? What happened yesterday?"

'On my way to Adelaide some idiot in a black car decided to pass when he shouldn't have and ran us both off the road. I was really lucky that I didn't clean up a tree. I couldn't believe it when Matt got out of the truck – I was in such a state; I was so glad it was him and not some stranger.'

'Bloody hell, Kate, he didn't tell me any of this,' Anna gasped. 'You poor thing!'

'All fine now, but I have to admit, it scared the hell out of me.'

Anna went around the bench to give her friend a hug. 'I can't lose you too,' she said, feeling such remorse that while she had been enjoying Sam's comfort and support her friend had almost been killed. 'I'm sorry,' she whispered in her mind.

'What's wrong, Mummy?' said Ella, appearing in the kitchen.

'Hello, darling, where have you come from? I thought you were playing on the verandah.' Anna released her friend and lifted Ella up to give her a cuddle.

Ella reached up and patted her hair. 'I thought I heard a sad voice,' she said.

'Well I didn't hear anything. Did you, Kate?'

'Nothing sad around here, Miss Ella. You need to come and sit here on the bench and help me stir this mixture. I've got to get this cake made for when your dad and Sam come back for smoko and my arms aren't strong enough. I think your help will be just what I need.'

Ella's face lit up and she quickly tried to clamber onto the bench.

'I'm going for a walk around your garden while Ella helps you. Can I grab a few of those Easter lily bulbs?' Anna asked.

'Sure, here's a bag for them.' Kate handed her a plastic bag.

Anna walked around the stone house which was decades old, stopping to smell a rose blooming out of season and brush her hand over the lavender plants Kate had planted along the side of the house. The countryside was moist and clean from the morning's fog, even though the sun was out. In the distance she could hear the front-end loader growling as Sam and Matt loaded up creek sand for the sandpit. Her gaze swung over the horizon; she was feeling despondent. She hadn't known she would miss the farm so much – and she *did*. Some of her anger with Matt probably stemmed from his refusal to see that he didn't have a monopoly on grief.

Anna shook her head. No – no wallowing, she told herself. It was worrying that Ella had been talking about crying and sadness. She had to make more of an effort to appear upbeat. She found a shovel and started to dig out some of the bulbs. It wasn't long before she heard Kate and Ella giggling behind her and she swung around. 'Boo!' she yelled.

Ella's throaty giggle became a full-blown laugh.

'Boo, Mummy!' Ella called back and ran out from behind a bougainvillea, her arms outstretched.

Anna grabbed her around the waist, and gently pushed her to the ground. She blew raspberries on her tummy, while Ella laughed and kicked her legs in the air. She'd make sure her daughter never saw her pain, Anna vowed to herself.

Anna clipped Ella into her car seat then gave Kate a hug. Matt was already behind the wheel.

'Thank you so much for having us, and for the sand,' she said.

'You're very welcome,' Kate replied.

'You know we're here for anything you need,

anything at all,' Sam added. He placed his hand on her shoulder. 'Anything at all, Anna,' he repeated.

She smiled at both of them, ignoring the flutter in her stomach, and climbed into the car.

'Hey, Matt, don't forget I want you to come to the motorbike auction with me,' Sam said, leaning down to look through the window. 'I won't take no for an answer. It's in three weeks' time.' Then he stood up and tapped the roof as Matt shoved the ute into gear.

'Catch you all later,' Matt said, and they moved off down the drive.

'Thanks for telling me about the accident yesterday,' Anna said to Matt coldly when she was sure Ella had fallen asleep in the back. 'I guess you didn't think I'd be interested in hearing that my husband and best friend were almost killed.'

'You were asleep – I didn't want to wake you. Kate said Ella had been sick and that you were really tired.'

'More like you just didn't want to talk to me.'

Anna leaned her head back against the seat and shut her eyes to discourage any further conversation. She remembered Sam's easy smile and the happiness radiating throughout the kitchen when they'd all trooped in for a break. Matt and she had been like that once. Matt had been attentive and loving the same way Sam was to Kate. She tried not to feel jealous, but sometimes it was damned hard.

Chapter 24

'I'm off then,' Matt said as he threw his rucksack over his shoulder.

Anna came out of the kitchen, wiping her hands on a tea towel, Ella following.

'Okay, well, I hope you have a good time.'

'We'll just be washing and polishing the trucks, getting them ready for the big day. Don't think there'll be much fun involved,' he said, pulling open the door.

'Will Joel be there?'

'It's his wedding, isn't it?' He looked down. 'See you later, Ella. Dad's going to the truck yard.'

Ella didn't say anything but hid her face in the crook of Anna's knee.

'C'mon, Ella,' Anna said. 'Say goodbye to Daddy.' Anna reached down to dislodge the small arms from around her legs, but Ella tightened her grip, refusing to budge. Anna glanced up at Matt to see a vulnerability in his eyes and realised Ella's reaction had upset him.

She reached out to touch his arm. 'So will you come back here before the wedding? Will we go together?'

He lifted his gaze to Anna. 'Yeah, I'll be back tomorrow. Like I said, we're only washing and polishing the trucks today and we'll probably have a few beers tonight.' He turned to leave, but stopped and squatted down to talk to Ella. 'Love you, Ella,' he said, then left.

As the front door banged behind him, Anna looked down at her daughter. 'You know your daddy loves you very much, don't you? He misses you when he's away from home. Why didn't you want to say goodbye?'

Ella ignored the question. 'Let's go see Maggie.'

Anna smiled. Ella's obsession with Maggie had developed after the shopkeeper had dropped off a toy bucket and spade, having heard about the sandpit Anna was building, then stayed to show Ella how to dig out weeds in the garden. She'd promised to come back when the sand arrived to build castles with a moat around them.

'We can call in and say hello,' she agreed, 'but then we need to get your bag packed for your sleepover at Grandma Laura's tomorrow night.'

Maggie was in the small kitchenette making a cup of tea when they walked into the corner store.

Anna breathed in the smell of pies in the bain-marie; she loved the smell of warm pastry.

Ella ran around the counter and into Maggie's arms before Anna had a chance to stop her.

'Ah, Ella! How are you today, wee lass? And where's yer ma? There she is! Would you like a cup of coffee, Anna?'

Anna nodded. 'I'd love one, thanks.'

She wandered around the shop, looking at the country art and crafts. A new batch had arrived, including an old Coke advert in a beautiful wooden frame. She studied it, thinking it would go well above her old stove. Then she saw how much it cost and screwed up her nose. It wouldn't be coming home with her today.

The bell above the door jangled as it opened, letting in a blast of cool air. Anna turned to see who had entered and her heart almost stopped as she caught sight of Alec Harper. She moved in behind a shelf, hoping Maggie wouldn't call her to take Ella. She didn't know why, but every time she saw Alec or heard his name, her pulse started to race. His sharp tongue made her so nervous. And how could she talk civily to a man who she knew was abusing an animal?

Maggie came out with Ella on her hip and set the little girl on the counter.

'How are ye this morning, Alec?' she asked in the same warm voice she would have offered to Anna.

'Fine, just fine. I'll have a pie and sauce, thanks,

Maggie,' he said. He pulled a Coke out of the fridge and put it on the counter.

'It's a lovely day, but I guess you'll be wantin' some more rain before long,' Maggie commented, ringing up the purchases.

'Anytime soon,' he answered.

Anna crept towards the window and peered out to see if Alec's ute was there. Ah, there it was and yes, there was Jasper, looking worse than the last time she had seen him. His fur was coming out in patches, and his ears and head drooped.

The bell rang and Alec was gone. She watched him get into the ute, not even acknowledging the dog sitting there.

'Anna?' said Maggie softly.

'Mmm?' she answered, her eyes still fixed on Jasper.

'Are you all right, pet?'

'Yeah.' Anna turned away from the window. 'Alec bought our dog Jasper at the clearing sale and I know he's not looking after him,' she explained. 'I tried to buy him back for Matt, but Alec was just so horrible when I asked. I was trying to see if he had Jasper with him today.'

Maggie nodded and brought out some crayons and paper from under the counter. 'Here, Ella. I've got a new desk just the right size for you. Would you like to draw?'

Ella followed Maggie to a back corner and saw the child-size table all set up and waiting. It was piled with colourful toys that Maggie put on the floor.

She sat down with an air of importance, chose a red crayon and started to scribble on the page.

Maggie handed Anna her coffee. 'Have you reported him?' she asked.

'No. I'd like to, but Matt says it's not really anything to do with us. Jasper is Alec's dog now.'

'You know, I believe that if a living creature is being mistreated, then you have to help them, no matter how you do it.' Maggie sipped her tea.

Anna said, 'Yes, that's what I think, but Matt –' She took a deep breath then, before she could stop herself, everything came pouring out.

'Oh, Maggie, I'm at my wits' end with Matt. He's so angry all the time and he hardly ever speaks to me or Ella. And she's not responding to him the way she used to – she acts like he's a stranger. Everything has changed. And so quickly.' Tears of frustration pricked at her eyes. She glanced at Ella to make sure she was engrossed in her drawing before continuing in a hoarse voice, 'I'm walking on eggshells the whole time he's home and I've started to look forward to him leaving again. Maybe it would just be easier without him.' She paused. 'Mum would be horrified to hear me say that. *I'm* horrified to say it out loud!'

Anna desperately wanted to say something about how comforting and thoughtful Sam had been, but that would be voicing her most intimate thoughts. Somehow, she feared if she spoke of them out loud, her thoughts might become more real.

At least now she could pretend she hadn't ever felt that way for Sam.

'The child needs her father, Anna,' Maggie said, but her expression was full of compassion.

'I know,' Anna groaned. 'But she picks up on my moods no matter how hard I try to hide them. I just worry about how the tension between me and Matt must be affecting her.'

'Let me tell you a story, darlin',' Maggie said, putting down her mug. 'Back in Ireland, my mam was married to a man who loved her very much and she loved him. He was my stepfather and the light of her life. He had an accident at the farm one day; a tractor brake let go on a hill. He was run over and his leg was damaged so badly that after the third infection of gangrene, the doctors said it needed to be amputated.

'This wonderful, loving man, who was mischievous and cheeky, grand fun to be around, turned into a sullen, withdrawn old man. His face turned grey with pain that was with him every waking moment. He could barely look at my mother, let alone speak to her. He resented the fact that she was still able-bodied and he was confined to crutches or a wheelchair. He turned on her.

'Then came a day me mam couldn't deal with his moods and snide comments anymore and she left. She cried and cried while she packed her bags and Daddy just sat in his wheelchair and stared at the wall. He did nothing to stop her. She didn't want to go, but she couldn't work out how to get through the barrier he'd put up.

'I stayed with him – I couldn't bear to see him left alone. He pined for my mother the whole time she was gone.

'Finally, two weeks after she'd left, he took hold of my hand so tightly I was taken by surprise; he hadn't shown any strength since the accident.

'He said to me, "Maggie, you must go and find your mother. She needs to come home."

'I said, "You know she won't, Daddy. She can't bear it anymore how you don't talk or take part in our lives."

'He started to cry – and let me tell you, my daddy never cried, not even when he had his accident and the doctors told him he would lose his leg. The anguish of Mammy leaving was worse than any he had ever experienced before. So he promised to try harder and she came back, but it was hard work. He'd kept everything shut up inside for so long. But with compromise and open communication, they did manage to work through it and have an even stronger marriage at the end.

'So what I'm asking, Anna, is how much is this marriage worth to you? Is it worth bringing your child up without her father? Of course, I'm not tellin' you what to do, pet – but your fella is a good one. He's just been hurt so very badly.'

Anna nodded, knowing Maggie was right – but she just wasn't sure if she had the strength to keep going anymore.

Chapter 25

The day of the wedding they dressed in silence, side by side, until Matt asked her if she could do his tie for him. She turned to face him and started to tie the knot.

In days gone by, she knew, Matt would have caught her hand and kissed it – and maybe that would have led to something more, if they had time – but today the silence between them was uncomfortable.

Her thoughts had been all over the place after she'd left Maggie's shop. One minute she'd made up her mind to leave Matt, and the next she knew she couldn't do it, upset with herself for even thinking about it when Matt was suffering so much. Her hands stilled as she stared at Matt's chest, willing him to show some affection, even to call her by name, but he just stood there, tense, almost as if he couldn't bear to have her near him.

'Finished?'

Snapping out of her thoughts, she quickly tightened the knot and stepped away, watching as Matt reached for his sports jacket, threw it over his shoulder and walked out of the room. 'Thanks,' he called.

Sighing sadly, she buttoned up her long dark green dress, dashed on her makeup and rummaged in her wardrobe for her shoes. She grabbed her handbag and Ella's overnight bag and walked out into the kitchen. Matt stood looking out the window and asked, 'So you'll drive tonight?' Without waiting for an answer, he walked outside and got into the passenger's seat.

Ella ran up, eyes sparkling. 'Ready, Mummy? I can't wait for sleepover!'

'Well you won't have to wait any longer – it's here!' Anna hugged her little girl then turned to Matt. 'Are you ready?'

'Yep.'

They dropped Ella off at Matt's parents' place, then set off on the drive to Adelaide.

As Anna expected, the trip was a quiet one. It seemed they had nothing to say to each other anymore.

Anna pulled up to the kerb and parked. The church grounds were filled with people but there was no one she recognised.

'Matt, am I going to know anyone here?' she asked, suddenly nervous.

He shrugged. 'You know Shane and Belinda, and Joel and Janey. And Jimmy.' He scanned the crowd. 'I probably won't know many people either. Guess some of the other blokes from the yard will be here with their wives.' Then Matt whistled and Anna turned to see a silver BMW pull in smoothly a few spaces behind their old Corolla. Its occupants were waving at them.

'Well, will you look at that?' Matt said in wonder.

'Who is it?' Anna asked.

'Shane and Belinda. I didn't know he had a BMW.'

Shane got out of the car and called, 'Hi, Matt! How are you, Anna?'

'Mate, where'd you get a car like this? You pinched it didn't you? I bet there's a report out on it this minute.' Matt went forward to shake Shane's hand.

'Look and weep, my friend, it's our new pride and joy!' He rubbed the roof lovingly then flung open the door for Matt to look inside. 'Two-litre engine, six-speed gearbox, diesel . . .'

Anna watched as Belinda got out of the car, rolling her eyes. She was relieved to see a familiar face. 'Hello, Anna,' she said warmly. 'Ignore him; he's like a kid with a new toy. We only picked it up last weekend and he's still crowing. How are you? And Ella?'

Anna smiled. 'Ella's thrilled to be having a sleepover with her grandparents. How are your boys?' Belinda had only just started to answer when there were shouts of, 'They're here! They're here!' Around the corner, came two big Mack trucks, red and blue ribbons streaming from the aerials.

Janey was sitting in the passenger's seat of the first one, waving her bouquet like a princess, while in the second one a bridesmaid sat, looking distinctly uncomfortable at the mode of transport. The flower girl alongside her was grinning broadly at the adventure she was having.

'Oh, look!' Belinda grabbed Anna's arm and they exchanged smiles. 'Only Janey,' she said.

'Only Janey,' repeated Anna, thinking of the vintage cars she and Matt had used for their wedding.

The driver pulled on the horn and the crowd cheered as Janey emerged in a figure-hugging dress. Her hair was curled and piled on top of her head, her makeup done to perfection. There wasn't a trace of the tough truckie in Janey that Anna had first met.

'Bloody hell,' said Shane. 'I never could imagine Janey in a dress, but look at her – she's gorgeous.'

Belinda smacked his arm. 'I think she's taken,' she said. 'I wish I could always look as good as I did on our wedding day. Don't you, Anna? Oh, I loved it! Floating down the aisle, the centre of attention. Lord, sometimes I don't recognise myself when I look in the mirror! Kids!'

Anna was about to agree when Shane wrapped his arms around Belinda and gave her a kiss on the cheek. 'You look that good every day!' he said. Out of the corner of her eye, Anna saw Matt shoot a glance towards her and her stomach filled with lead as he moved away slightly.

She was distracted by another honking of horns as the bridesmaid emerged and held out her hand to the flower girl, who wouldn't have been much older than Ella.

'How sweet,' she murmured.

'Just gorgeous,' Belinda agreed. 'Come on. We'd better find a seat.' She and Shane led the way into the church through a side door. Both men gave Joel a thumbs-up and he returned the gesture with a nervous smile.

As they slid into a pew towards the back of the church, Anna somehow became separated from Matt, so that she was sitting on one side of Belinda and Shane, while Matt was on the other.

As the organ started to play the 'Wedding March', Belinda leaned over to whisper, 'I can't believe how traditional this is. Except for the trucks. I thought Janey would chuck tradition out the window!'

'I wasn't sure what to expect,' Anna said and turned towards the door, where she could see Janey's figure silhouetted against the light. She took a deep breath and remembered back to when she had stood in the same spot in the small church in Spalding. She could remember the excitement of it all, her desire to run down the aisle to Matt, to shout

'Yes, yes, yes!' and to see Matt's face when he leaned over to kiss her.

'I won't cry,' she repeated softly to herself over and over as the wedding party began the walk down the aisle. Instead she concentrated on the bridesmaid, dressed in sky-blue silk with red ribbons woven into the hemline, walking slowly towards the front, holding the hand of the flower girl. The little girl's smile reminded Anna of Ella and she couldn't help glance at Matt to see his reaction. His face was expressionless. Anna wondered if behind the mask he too was remembering their own wedding.

As the ceremony started Anna couldn't help but recall their wedding service. Sam had muttered something about 'in sickness and in wealth' before they'd started their vows, making Matt snort with laughter.

The way he had held her hands so tenderly, had looked at her with love and kissed her so gently – those were her most vivid recollections. When he'd slipped the ring on her finger she had felt whole.

So different to the way she felt now.

She heard a child's cry and looked around to see where it was coming from. The formalities had finished without her realising, and the bride and groom, looking extremely pleased with themselves, were walking back down the aisle, surrounded by guests. But in the throng of people, the flower girl had been separated from the bridesmaid and was trapped in a sea of legs.

Anna moved to go to her, but Matt was closer. She watched as if from a distance as he squatted down and took out his hanky to dry the little girl's eyes, speaking to her quietly all the time. Then he hoisted her up onto his hip and looked around, trying to spot her parents. Matt seemed completely at ease as he jiggled her up and down. When they found the parents, the little girl gave him a hug before she went to her mother.

Anna felt sick. He couldn't show affection to his own child, but he could with a stranger. Well that just about summed everything up, she thought bitterly.

Finally, after many photos and congratulatory handshakes, Joel climbed into the driver's seat of one of the trucks and leaned on the horn, while Janey climbed in the passenger's side and wound down her window, flourishing her bouquet.

'Who wants it?' she yelled, then tossed it towards the crowd.

There was a smattering of laughter as a young man automatically reached out to pluck it from the air, then, realising what he had done, dropped it quickly.

'You'll be right, Dave,' Janey called, grinning widely. 'You'll have to make an honest woman of Becs now!'

As the trucks left, heading towards the reception venue, Shane wiggled his eyebrows suggestively. 'Reckon they may not make it to the reception on time.'

'Why?' Belinda asked, her brow furrowed.

'They're driving around with their own sleeper cab! Oh, the joys of early married life. They'll be getting it on and cutting it up in the sleeper cab – no stresses or strains, no kids interrupting. Not like life AK! After kids, I mean.'

Belinda slapped his arm. 'You are talking crap! It's not like you miss out often.' She smiled adoringly at Shane and Anna felt a surge of envy.

'Well, that's the serious stuff done and dusted! Would you like to come back to our place for a drink?' Shane asked. 'We're only about ten minutes from the reception and the kids are being looked after by their grandparents.'

'Yeah, we'd love a drink,' Matt answered without consulting Anna.

'Righto, follow us, then!'

Chapter 26

Matt tried to keep up with Shane but their old car didn't take the corners as smoothly or accelerate away from the traffic lights as fast, and by the time they arrived at Shane's the BMW was parked and Shane and Belinda were holding open the front door with welcoming smiles on their faces.

'How much would it cost to live here?' Anna asked as they slid to a stop. Along the way she'd seen huge houses behind fences made of stone, large expanses of lawn with long asphalt driveways. The streets were wide, tree-lined and quiet; the atmosphere spoke of wealth.

'Hundreds of thousands, if not millions,' Matt replied.

Anna was silent, then took a deep breath and opened her door. She stared for a moment at the white picket fence and the red letter box standing alongside it. The colouring of the letter box looked out of place against the faded colours of time.

Shane and Belinda's sandstone house had obviously been built around the time of Adelaide's settlement. The lawn, despite water restrictions, was a lush green, and the front yard was shaded by large trees. There seemed little sign of the four unruly boys Anna knew Shane talked about constantly.

Shane ushered them inside. 'Come on, we'll go out to the back garden. There's a bar on the terrace.'

Five minutes later they all held drinks and Shane was chatting animatedly about the drive he'd done north. Anna looked around, wondering how Belinda managed to keep the house and gardens so beautifully while raising four boys. Even the garden shed looked tidy, from where she stood. There were days in her house when Anna couldn't see the lounge room floor for the clutter – and she only had Ella!

Belinda chatted continually and despite feeling sad, Anna relaxed and laughed at the stories of the four boys. 'Now tell, Anna,' Belinda said when it seemed she had exhausted her range of stories, 'how is your babysitting business going? Last time I spoke to you, you were just starting out.'

'I love it!' Anna said simply. 'I have about eight kids who I look after. Not at any one time – I think that would kill me! It's all very casual, if a mum rings and I'm free, I'll take the child, but if Matt's home or I'm out, then I don't.'

'Well I think that's amazing! I have enough to do with my four without adding any extras into the mix. Do you think you and Matt will have more children? You obviously enjoy being around them.'

Anna squirmed uncomfortably and glanced over to see if Matt had heard, but the two men were laughing uproariously at a joke she had missed. 'We haven't talked about it recently,' she muttered, and looking for an escape she asked, 'Do you think I could use your loo?'

Belinda gave her directions and Anna went down a passageway and opened an oak door. She realised she'd gone into the wrong room when she saw the fluffy white carpet, but peeked in anyway. It seemed to be Shane's personal lounge, the walls covered in photos of trucks and speedway cars, the shelves holding Speedway trophies. There was a bar fridge in one corner and a pool table under lights in the middle of the room. The window looked out over the terrace and, even though the curtains were drawn and the window was shut, she could hear the muffled sounds of conversation. She started to back out, but noticed a photo with Matt in it and stepped forward to have a closer look.

Matt and Shane were leaning against a trailer, smiling openly at the camera. He looked so happy and relaxed – so different to how he was at home. Tears sprang to her eyes as she picked up the photo and traced the outline of his jaw. How come, she wondered, he could be like this with other people but not with his family? How had they come to this, two people who had been so in love?

The noise of Belinda's high heels walking on the polished floorboards somewhere in the house made Anna start guiltily. She shouldn't be snooping.

She took deep shuddering breaths to calm herself as she replaced the photo on the shelf, refusing to cry.

'So how's Ella doing?' Anna froze as Shane's voice became clear the closer he came to the window. She heard him pull open the fridge door, the clink of beer bottles.

'She's okay. Doesn't want to have a lot to do with me these days though. I thought it was because I was away driving so much to begin with, but now I'm wondering if her mother has something to do with it. Ella won't come to me or give me a hug. She's really off with me.'

Anna's eyes widened as a surge of anger chased away her sadness.

'Come on, Matt, mate, be real! You're only thinking that 'cos you're angry with Anna, although I can't see why. She's lovely,' Shane said. 'Why would she turn Ella against you? I mean, I know you're going through a rough spot, but Anna just doesn't strike me as the sort of person to do that.'

'Lovely?' Matt's voice was bitter. 'She's always on my case. She's always criticising, never supporting me. When we lost the farm, she just moved on like it'd never existed.' He snapped his fingers. 'It really shits me. You know, she'd actually made me believe she shared my dreams when we got married. What a load of bullshit. And now, when I'm set on finding out who stole our fertiliser and ruined us, do you think she's on my side? Ha! "Don't do it, Matt, it's over, let it go." Well I'm not letting it go. I carry this with me all the time.' Anna couldn't see what he was referring to, but she was sure it must be the little black notebook she had found in his pocket when she was doing the laundry. She'd been so shocked when she'd opened it and seen all the entries about the thefts, all his conspiracy theories and ideas; she'd pretended she'd never seen it.

'This has got all the details of every theft I know about,' Matt was saying. 'One day the bastard who did this will slip up and when he or she does, I'll be there with every skerrick of evidence to put them away.'

Anna couldn't stand to hear any more. She backed out of the room and shut the door quietly. She found the bathroom, washed her face, re-applied her makeup and then went back out to the terrace, her face rearranged into a pleasant mask though inside she was churning.

The reception was held on an expanse of lawn at the Botanical Gardens in the centre of Adelaide. The evening had turned cool and while cutlery clinked against the plates and tea lanterns swayed overhead, the laughter was growing raucous as more drinks were consumed. It reached a crescendo as Joel stood in front of the crowd to make his speech. Loud catcalls and whistles sounded from every corner.

Anna watched from the edge of the crowd, sitting quietly under one of the large Moreton Bay fig trees. She was so furious with Matt she could barely speak to him – not that they were talking anyway.

As she thought about his behaviour over the last few hours, her anger grew tenfold. Even though she'd been upset with him when they'd arrived at the reception, she had stuck close to his side. Not knowing many people made her uncomfortable and she certainly didn't want to hang around Belinda, knowing Shane had more than likely shared Matt's outburst with her on the way to the reception.

Matt had barely seemed to register her presence. He hadn't introduced her to anyone, or even bothered to get her a drink. He slipped away to talk to people she had never met before and she'd found herself alone at important parts of the night, like when she had to find their table by herself. She didn't know how long she'd sat there, alone, waiting for Matt to join her, but she had felt so abandoned and out of place she was close to despair.

When he had finally come to the table his rejection of her was humiliating. Being so pleased to see him, she'd tried to hold his hand, but he had shaken her off as if she was nothing more than a pest. The fury Anna had tried to dampen flared so strongly she'd needed to excuse herself and run for the safety of the toilets.

As soon as the main course was finished, she had left the table without speaking to him and had gone to sit at the edge of the party.

Now she observed Matt from afar. He was standing with Jimmy, a Coke in his hand, listening to the speeches as if he didn't have a care in the world. He hadn't even missed her.

In times gone by *her* Matt never would have ignored her or spoken about her as harshly as he had tonight. And try as she might, Anna could not find one little bit left of the Matt she had married. *Her* Matt was gone, she realised as she saw him grin at something Jimmy had whispered in his ear. It wasn't her imagination; he was truly gone.

Briefly she wondered if she shouldn't just take the car and leave him behind – but no, she wouldn't do that; she wouldn't be a doormat any longer. She had some things to say.

A burst of laughter at Joel's speech caught her attention and she looked around the rest of the room. She saw Belinda glance her way, sympathy in her eyes, and that just made Anna more irate. It embarrassed her that Belinda knew of their troubles and understood why she was reduced to lingering at the edge of the crowd like an outsider. Then a feeling of unease crept over her. How many other people here had Matt sounded off to? The rage inside her was building and she was powerless to stop it. It would have to be faced. Tonight.

'How dare you!' Anna's voice was low and cold, as they hit the outskirts of Adelaide and plunged into the dark countryside. 'How dare you treat me the way you did tonight!'

Out of the corner of her eye, she saw Matt glance over at her, his face impassive. She tightened her hands around the steering wheel as she stared out into the blackness, watching the white lines slip beneath the car.

'I beg your pardon?' Matt turned his expressionless face towards her.

'Listen to me, Matt – there's no point in trying anymore. You obviously don't want to be around Ella and me, and I'm sick of tiptoeing around you. You ignore your own daughter and you treat me like I'm a stranger. Well I can't do this – I *won't* do this anymore. You've changed. It's time we admitted it, don't you think? Tonight really proved it. We're finished.' Her voice cracked on the last word.

Silence filled the car until Matt said, his voice flat, 'What I'd like to know is what makes your point of view so damned right and mine not worth anything?' He turned away and looked out at the darkened landscape. He didn't utter another word for the rest of the drive home.

When they pulled up at their house Matt yanked

on the door handle even before the car had come to a complete stop and leapt out.

She watched grim-faced as Matt emerged a few moments later with a bag slung over his shoulder. Without looking at her, he got into his ute, reversed out of the drive and drove away. Where he would stay tonight, Anna didn't know.

What hurt her the most, she thought as the sobs started racking her body, was that he hadn't argued or tried to change her mind. Obviously neither of them was prepared to fight to save their marriage.

It really was over.

Chapter 27

The moon gave little light as the man adjusted his headlight. The shadows the small torch threw sometimes made it harder to see than if he didn't use it. He swore softly as he inserted the key into the padlock for the third time and twisted it from side to side. But he just couldn't seem to make the key turn.

He swore again. The thick gloves he'd worn both to keep out the bitter chill and to hide his fingerprints were hampering his efforts as well.

He glanced around the satellite depot anxiously. Even though he knew everyone would be at the wedding – making this the perfect night to act – the constant hum of traffic in the background made him nervous. He was used to doing these sorts of jobs in silence.

Going to the back of his ute, he unzipped the tarp and rummaged around until he found his toolbox.

He took out a large pair of bolt cutters and went back to the padlock. With one swift movement, the thick steel had been cut, the padlock hung uselessly from the shed's latch and the man yanked open the door.

In the stillness of the shed, he heard the scratching of a branch against the tin roof, a piece of tin banging in the wind.

He breathed in deeply and smiled. They were the noises he was used to.

He wasn't supposed to take anything from the shed except the keys for the truck he was 'borrowing', but still, he thought, it wouldn't hurt to see if there was anything else worth pinching. It's not like his accomplice could report him. Besides, he was *owed* it. Whether or not his partner agreed was beside the point.

His annoyance returned as he recalled the other man telling him there wasn't any money left. 'You took it all last time.'

'But I need it,' he'd insisted. 'I've got to pay the debt. You of all people know what the consequences are if I don't.'

'Maybe you should have thought about that before you lost the last twenty-five grand I gave you. You'll have to wait until we do another one. And I'm telling you, the next one has to be the last. I'm sick of it.' His partner had slammed the phone down.

He remembered sitting at his office desk considering his next course of action. He just needed to find a heist that would cover his debt and leave him with a bit left over.

When his partner had finally admitted there was a large load of chemicals coming in he'd seen a way out of his predicament.

He looked at dates, weather forecasts, moon phases. This was different to the sort of heists he usually pulled, so nothing could be left to chance. Like he always said, 'Perfect planning prevents piss-poor performance.'

Tonight he would live by that motto.

Walking through the shed, he ran his fingers over the crates, feeling smooth plastic. They were pallets of beer, waiting to go to a pub.

He took out his pocket knife and slit the thick plastic, hoisted two cartons onto his shoulder and carried them to the ute. He made five trips in all.

'Payment,' he muttered to himself. 'If I can't have the cash, I can take it in other ways.'

The keys for the truck were hanging on the board just inside the sliding iron door. He looked for the one with the green key tag, grabbed it and headed back to his ute. Then he drove ten minutes down the road to an all-night supermarket and parked under some lights.

His sneakers made no noise as he ran swiftly back to the depot and made his way to where the truck and flat-top trailer had been left for his use.

As he slid the key into the door, he noticed there

was a car driving slowly along the road that ran alongside the yard.

He dropped to the ground and crawled under the trailer to lie next to the large wheels.

Headlights lit up the depot as the ute swung in the open gates.

For a heart-stopping moment he wondered whether he'd been doublecrossed, but just as quickly he dismissed the thought, knowing it just wasn't possible – they both had too much at stake.

Then the ute backed out and drove away. He lay unmoving till he could no longer hear the engine, then, his heart beating fast, he made his way to the front of the truck, opened the door, and climbed into the cab.

He wound the window down a crack and waited a full ten minutes, just sitting, watching and waiting. The ute didn't return, so he hit the key and held his breath as the engine spluttered to life, sounding twice as loud as normal to his ears.

He shoved the truck into gear, drove over to where a pallet of chemical was sitting, and backed into the loading ramp. Working as quickly as he could, he started the forklift and slid the forks under the pallet. Fifteen minutes later, the truck was loaded with ten pallets. He would sell it cheaper than any retailer could and make a killing.

Sticking his head outside again, just to make sure the ute hadn't returned, the man listened hard and his gaze swept across the yard to see if anything had changed. It hadn't. He jogged to the back of the shed, pushed opened a door and entered a tiny storage room. He was only able to see a couple of feet in front of him, with the tiny headlight that was strapped to his forehead, but he knew where he was going. With his hands brushing the wall, he counted in ten steps, then five to the right and three to the left. Bending down, his fingers found the heavy iron ring on the edge of the trapdoor and he pulled firmly at it.

Down on his knees now, his fingers felt under the edge of the gap made by the door, to find a light switch. With a flick of the button, the underground room was flooded with light and the man had to blink a few times before his eyes adjusted to the brightness.

Yep, there it was. A large parcel sitting on a shelf close to the ceiling.

He reached in and grabbed it, hauling it to his chest with minimal effort. Quickly he turned off the light, pulled the hatch shut and walked towards the door, not seeing the trail he had left behind him.

He closed up the shed and, with one last glance around, jumped in the cab before driving out of the yard, stopping only to shut the gates.

Once he was on the highway going north he began to relax. He was heading back to his comfort zone of the country and there was little traffic on the road.

Two hours later, he pulled off into a parking area, let the engine cool down and turned the ignition off. Silence flooded the cab and left his ears ringing. He got out to stretch his legs.

Everything was quiet.

He unzipped his pants and took a leak, congratulating himself on the success of the operation. If his partner was so insistent that this theft was going to be his last, it was good to know he could achieve this bit, at least, by himself. There was nothing to credit his partner for except information and, of course, his partner didn't know about the business he was running on the side. That part of his life would never end. He needed it too much.

It wasn't long before he was back in the cab, and another half an hour later he was turning into his driveway. As his lights reflected off the silver tin of his shed, he could hear his dogs barking at the unfamiliar vehicle. It was a bloody good thing he lived out of town, he thought.

It took him a good two hours to unload the chemical with the front-end loader. The other goods he'd picked up on the way were easy to shift: light bags that were easily hidden. The beer he would keep for himself and unload at the house.

When he was done he threw a large, dusty tarpaulin over the lot, stood back and breathed a sigh of relief. This would well and truly cover the debt and leave him with a bit in reserve. He started to plan what he could do with the extra money – there was a really good tip on race four at Flemington and he knew it could treble his money – but he stopped; he was getting ahead of himself. It would all have to be sold first and he knew he would have to be very careful about who he offered it to.

He grinned as he looked over at a second tarpaulin. It concealed the best thing he'd ever got his hands on. It was a shame he couldn't use it more often. But even though he'd changed it pretty significantly, he couldn't take the risk. Sighing, he lifted the tarp and let his hand run over the smooth steel, then let the tarp drop.

Anyway, he mused as he checked his watch, he'd better hurry, otherwise first light would be on him before he got the truck back to the depot.

The gates were open when he arrived back at the depot and he frowned as he slowed. He was sure he'd closed them. Quickly he assessed his options, but realised there weren't any. He had to drive in.

He scanned the grounds, but seeing nothing unusual he parked the truck in the spot which had been agreed on and slid out of the cab, ever watchful.

Everything was silent except the tick of the engine cooling. Maybe he hadn't shut the gate properly and the wind had blown it open.

He walked around the corner of the shed to replace the keys, then stopped.

'Shit.'

A white ute was parked at the back of the shed and he could just make out a swag rolled out in the tray.

Quietly, he backed away, staying in the shadows, then turned and ran down the road to where he had left his ute.

As he drove home, he wondered if there was any chance the person in the ute would have heard anything. He tried to think logically, without panicking, but it was hard. That was the closest he'd ever come to being caught.

No, he decided. The walls of the shed would have blocked a lot of the noise and certainly the lights. If whoever was sleeping there had heard anything, they probably would have put it down to passing traffic.

But he was left with a burning question: why was someone sleeping in the depot tonight – and why hadn't his partner told him?

Chapter 28

Anna wrapped her hands around the cup of tea Maggie had placed in front of her. She was freezing after standing in the rain for so long, watching Matt and Ella disappear into the distance.

This was something she had never considered after Matt had left: the fact that he would still want to see his daughter. That he would take her from Anna's care – even just for a short time.

But two weeks after he'd left, Matt had arrived early this morning asking to see Ella. Anna had readily agreed, pleased he was taking an interest in her. Much to Anna's surprise, and probably Matt's, Ella, who had been unperturbed by Matt's disappearance, ran to him with her arms outstretched. They had played happily together in the backyard, despite the bitter winds and grey clouds threatening rain at any moment.

Anna had watched them through the window with a frown. She didn't understand Ella's change of heart. To be truthful, once Matt had gone she'd half expected never to see him again. She'd thought he'd just drift away into some other realm unconnected with them. But watching him with Ella, she'd understood it wasn't going to be the case. Maybe that was a good thing, she had pondered. After all, she hated waking up without him beside her and she missed him. The thought of him at least.

Still, when Matt had said he wanted to take Ella out, just the two of them, a tremor of fear had shot through her. Of course he was entitled to see his daughter, and Ella had obviously been pleased to see her dad, but to take her out? Take away her daughter who was her whole life? Anna had opened her mouth to respond but couldn't speak a word.

'I'm going to another clearing sale with Sam, so I thought it might be a good opportunity for her to come along too,' Matt had continued. 'I want to be a part of her life, Anna. You mightn't like it, but I do.'

How could she refuse?

And so, this morning, Matt had picked up Ella and they'd driven away. And Anna had stood in the drizzle, staring down the empty street, until Maggie had come and led her into the warmth of the shop. Maggie sat down at the table and placed her hands over Anna's.

Anna looked up. 'Oh, Maggie.' Anna heard her

own voice as if from very far away. It was lost and broken.

'Hush, dear heart, hush. They'll be back soon.'

Anna wiped away tears and then spoke the terrible words which she had hardly dared to consider. 'What if he doesn't bring her back? What if he takes her?' She lifted her eyes to meet Maggie's sympathetic gaze.

'He'll bring her back, Anna. He's a good man.'

Anna stood up and walked to the window, willing Matt's old ute to drive back down the road and turn into the driveway. How could she have been so stupid as to let Ella go when they didn't have any sort of agreement? Her breathing quickened and she swayed on her feet as panic threatened to overwhelm her. 'Oh no,' she moaned.

'Anna, Anna, Anna!' Maggie spoke gently. 'Shush, child. What you're thinkin' is not going to happen. He loves her too and she is his daughter. He just wants to spend time with her. Matt is hurtin', just as you are. Ella will help heal him as she will help you. Now drink your cup of tea before it gets cold.

'Then I'll need your help. I've a carton of wool which has come in and I haven't time to price it. You can do it for me so I can get it onto the shelves. Mrs Hampton will be in on Monday wantin' some wool for her granddaughter's jumper she's knittin'. But I've got stocks of broccoli and beans to put out and can't see how I'll get to doin' the wool. You'll be doin' me a favour by helpin'.'

Slowly, with another glance outside, Anna walked back to the table and sat down. She listened as the wind hurled sleet against the window and was glad for the warmth of the stove standing in the corner.

She hoped Ella was dressed warmly enough. What a miserable day for a clearing sale.

The next two hours passed agonisingly slowly, even though she was busy. Taking the wool out of the box, pricing it, sorting it by colour and arranging it on the shelf was monotonous but for a while it had taken her mind off Ella. Maggie had asked questions constantly, about her childhood and her family, studiously avoiding the subject of Ella and keeping her talking the whole time.

While she was recalling incidents from her own life or a funny anecdote about her brothers, she could forget. Then the door would open and a customer would walk in, bringing a blast of cold air. Anna would automatically glance around to make sure Ella wasn't in the way, only to be reminded that she wasn't there.

The heavy, sinking feeling would return and she would find herself struggling not to howl.

She watched the clock, painfully aware of the minutes ticking by and growing increasingly uptight. She couldn't help going constantly to the window to peer out at the street, watching, waiting ...

Maggie brought out another box of wool to distract her and Anna was just putting the last ball of wool onto the shelf when a tinkling of the brass bell above the door signalled another customer. She looked up to see who it was, but there was no one there.

Then she heard the sweet sound of her daughter's voice.

'Mummy?'

Anna jumped up and ran towards her, throwing her arms around the little girl. The relief of holding Ella swept through her and she closed her eyes, savouring the feeling of the chubby arms around her neck.

'I've missed you, darling!' Anna murmured into Ella's neck. She became aware of a coldness seeping through her clothes and Ella's hair dripping onto her skin. She pulled away and held Ella at arm's length to look at her.

The girl was wet through, her hair plastered to her head, her cheeks red from the wind.

Struggling to contain her anger, Anna asked casually, 'Where's Daddy?'

'In the car.'

Setting Ella on her feet Anna grabbed her hand firmly and started towards the door.

'Maggie, I'm off. I need to get Ella into the bath.'

'Maggie!' called Ella, struggling to get away from Anna. 'Want to say hello.' But Anna wouldn't relinquish her hold.

'Not now, sweetie. We need to get you out of those wet clothes.'

'Hello there, wee Ella!' Maggie chimed in. 'You go with your mammy. I can see you another time.'

Anna hurried out of the shop with Ella in tow, her hands covering Ella's head in a futile attempt to shield her from the freezing rain. Without stopping to acknowledge Matt, they ran across the road and into the house. Anna sat Ella in front of the fire as she started the bath, then stripped her out of her wet clothes and popped her in the bath. 'There you go, missy! You'll be nice and warm after that.' But despite her cheerful tone, inside she was seething.

What was he *thinking*?

She heard Matt open the door and come into the kitchen. She knew she was too wild to speak to him at the moment, so she busied herself soaping Ella's hair and dribbling water over her shoulders.

When she was sure Ella was warm enough, she took her out and wrapped her in a towel and took her to the lounge room to dry her in front of the fire.

Matt was sitting in his usual chair reading a magazine.

Anna dressed Ella in clothes she had laid out near the fire to warm then sent her to her room to play.

She turned to face Matt. 'You bloody idiot,' she said quietly. 'What do you think you were doing? If she gets pneumonia, it will be your fault.'

Matt looked confused.

'How could you have let her get wet through like that? Surely there was a shed or something you could have sat in while it was raining.'

'The motorbike Sam wanted to buy was up when the shower started,' Matt said defensively.

'Hell, Matt, you weren't buying. You didn't need to stand out in the rain. What sort of father are you?' Anna swiped at the magazine he was reading. 'And don't sit here in my house like you own the place. You don't live here anymore. Say goodbye to Ella and go. I'm too bloody pissed off to have you here at the moment.'

Matt sat for a moment longer, his eyes narrowed, looking like he might explode.

Anna cocked an eyebrow at him, waiting.

Finally Matt got up from the chair and stalked down the hall to Ella's room to kiss her goodbye. Anna didn't raise her head from the washing she was folding as he left. When she heard the ute drive off she sighed and dropped her chin to her chest. She couldn't believe their relationship had sunk to such depths.

She went into Ella's room and found her lying on the floor talking to her dolls, tired out. Anna touched her forehead to make sure she wasn't running a temperature, then lifted the girl into her arms and placed her on the bed. Ella reached up and put her arms around Anna's neck, hugging her close.

'Ah, Ella, I love you so much, darling.'

'I love you too, Mummy. But I had fun with Daddy.'

Oh! Out of the mouths of babes. 'I'm sure you did.' She smiled at her daughter.

Anna stretched out on the bed beside Ella to read her favourite story. As she repeated by heart the words she had read one thousand times before, her mind wandered back to Matt and the happier times. How they used to tease each other and laugh. How they had talked late into the nights, sharing their dreams and hopes. When they found out she was pregnant with Ella, the happiness and wonder they had felt at creating a new life had overtaken them both. Where had it all gone? How could it just end in fighting and anger, the only thing left between them this little girl?

Oh, she knew she couldn't stop Matt from seeing his daughter, but Ella was her arms, her legs, her heart – her whole being. Without Ella, Anna herself couldn't exist. How could she bear to be without her? She needed to look out for her daughter, to *protect* her.

Before Anna had finished the story, Ella had fallen asleep. She shut the book quietly and sat up, staring at the little girl, tracing the contours of her face, touching her eyelashes as they brushed her cheeks, and thought how heartbreaking it was that a child created in love had to be part of that love's disintegration.

Chapter 29

Matt shot out of the driveway with a squeal of tyres and a wisp of black smoke, the back end of the ute fishtailing on the wet road. As he drove out of Spalding he thumped the steering wheel angrily.

'Bloody cow.'

The rear end of the car slid out again and instinctively he eased his foot off the accelerator to reduce his speed. As if on automatic pilot, he followed the winding road back towards Adelaide, conscious of nothing but the fury bubbling inside.

Ella had loved going to the sale with him and Sam, he was sure of it – and he doubted he would have survived it without her. His clearing sale was too fresh in his memory and if it hadn't been for Sam desperately wanting his opinion on the old collector's bike being auctioned, he wouldn't have gone. Having Ella with him, seeing her wonder at everything new, hearing her giggles as Sam had sat her astride the motorbike, had made the few hours bearable and banished the memories of his own sale.

He smiled as he thought of Ella looking up at him from underneath the hood of her pink windbreaker. Her strawberry-blonde curls had been poking out and her eyes were bright with excitement. She'd loved it when Sam teased her about her purple rubber boots, pretending to be disappointed with his black ones because they weren't bright enough. When Matt had picked her up and whirled her around, she had shrieked with laughter.

With Ella alongside him, he'd felt fine. He'd exchanged jokes with a few of the locals and had even walked past Alec Harper without his usual sensation of overpowering resentment. He hadn't been able to stop himself looking for Jasper, though. He'd half expected to see him huddled in the back of the ute, out in the open. Then there had been the fleeting thought that if he was, he might just take the bloody dog back.

His heart constricted as his smile faded. Oh, how he loved his little girl – he hadn't realised how much until he'd moved out.

How much he had missed her. He missed the idea of Anna too, but he'd be damned if he would mention *that* to anyone. Ella seemed to be happy spending time with him today. He wasn't sure what had changed there, but something certainly had.

Sam had mentioned that Anna had hinted to Kate that the tension between her parents had been upsetting Ella more than anything. Maybe the little girl was feeling the benefits of a calmer atmosphere without him in the house. And was it his fault Ella had reacted to him the way she had while he had been living there? He supposed it was. A useless father as well as a farmer. Hopelessness washed over him.

He reached the outskirts of Adelaide and found himself hemmed in by the traffic – not that it mattered, since he wasn't in a hurry, nor did he have anywhere in particular to go. He drove aimlessly until darkness began to fall and his stomach rumbled. Seeing a sign for a fast food chain, he flicked on his blinker to turn in.

A young girl took his order and he found himself wondering what Ella would look like when she was this girl's age. Chewing his way through the hamburger, he was struck by a horrible thought. Would Ella even want to see him when she was old enough to look at his life and see what he really was - after all, what could he offer her? A broken man, stripped of all self-worth and confidence.

He knew there was no way Anna would let Ella come and stay with him overnight if he was still sleeping in the back of the ute as he had been since their split. Neither should she. He had to get himself together somehow, if only so he could see Ella.

***

'Matt! Come in, me lad,' said Jimmy, struggling to his feet from the depths of his lounge chair. 'What are you doing in this neck of the woods tonight?'

Matt stood awkwardly on the step of Jimmy's little cabin, hands shoved deep inside his jacket pockets. 'Sorry to bother you so late, Jimmy, I . . .' He looked around. 'I'm not really sure why I'm here!'

'No bother at all! Come in, come in, you'll freeze out there. It's well and truly winter today. Coffee? I'm afraid I haven't got anything stronger.'

'I'd love a cup of tea, if you have any.'

'Tea I can do. Make yourself comfortable.' Jimmy gestured to the other chair and limped over to the bench to turn on the kettle as Matt sunk wearily into the seat.

He rubbed his hands over his face and felt a profound tiredness come over him. He didn't think he could speak.

Jimmy passed him a cup and sat heavily in his chair. They were silent for a few minutes, then Jimmy asked, 'You all right, Matt? What can I do to help?'

Matt was embarrassed at the sudden onset of tears, but within a moment of Jimmy's quiet question his eyes had felt the familiar sensation of heat. He sat with his hands over his face for a moment and tried to gather himself.

'Sorry,' he muttered, mortified.

He felt a hand on his shoulder. 'It's all right, mate. I'll do what I can to help.'

'Anna and I've split up,' Matt choked out. 'I think I've wrecked everything.'

Jimmy said nothing.

'A while ago, I had everything I ever wanted: a farm, a wife and a baby. Now I've got nothing. I stuffed it all up. I know the truck fire wasn't avoidable; sometimes these things happen, but it was me who had told Anna not to pay the insurance. Me!' He pointed to his chest then got up and paced the small kitchen. 'Losing the farm just tipped me over the edge. It was everything to me. I didn't think anyone could feel the way I did. After all, it was my dream. No one else's. I wouldn't talk to Anna about it, I shut her out. I didn't want her sympathy or understanding because it was *me* who buggered it. I was the one who didn't manage the finances properly when it was dry. It was *me* who made the decisions, *me* who left the fertiliser in the paddock and the gate unlocked. Maybe I couldn't have stopped it.' He clenched his fists. 'But she just seemed to move on. It was like she didn't care that we'd lost the farm. She was just so wrapped up in Ella it was almost like she didn't need me at all anymore – and I didn't *want* to need her. I don't know, I've just buggered everything.'

'No, Matt,' Jimmy said gently. 'You haven't. Do you really think you are so powerful that you could bring down so many lives? Of course not! There are always second chances. You need to get your head sorted out and then go and talk to Anna. Tell her everything you've just told me. She'll understand. I've been told women deal with things differently to us blokes, that's all. She's probably still missing the farm, but wanting to make life the best she can for Ella.

'And you can't blame yourself for the way the farm was sold. The dry times were bleeding everyone, lad, and you just didn't have enough behind you to see you through. There's no shame in that. Unfortunately sometimes hard work just isn't enough.'

Matt talked on as if he hadn't heard Jimmy's words. 'I keep thinking if only the fertiliser hadn't been stolen, I could have made a real go of it that year. All the rain came at the right time and anyone who put a crop in killed the pig. There was grain everywhere that year. Except from my farm.

'I understand I've got to try and make another life now, but if I could just find out who did this to me there'd be some justice done. Oh, Anna likes to talk about "opportunistic crime" but there's more to it than that. How did they know the fertiliser was going to be in that spot that night? Nobody drives around with an empty truck hoping to steal some fertiliser. Somebody knew it was going to be there. Can you understand, Jimmy, why I need to know who and why?'

'Ah,' Jimmy said. 'So that's how it happened. I knew you'd been sold up but was never really aware of the circumstances.

'Oh, Matt, I'm sorry. Of course I can understand you needing answers – but I also know there aren't always answers for the questions you need to ask.

'I lost my business back in the eighties. Stock market crash and all that. I stewed on it for years, wondering how I'd been so stupid as to take out contracts with people who wouldn't pay the bills I sent. It never did me any good. It didn't change the fact that my customers weren't paying bills. I had to sell the majority of my business. I couldn't bring it back.'

'But surely somebody has to know something,' Matt argued. 'I mean, a farmer had to buy the fertiliser. It's no good to anyone else. Somebody somewhere knows they bought it on the cheap, so there has to be a story behind it.'

'Of course, you're right.' Jimmy paused. 'But, mate, the theft isn't your fault. I can only tell you one thing,' Jimmy pointed his finger to reiterate his point, 'you can do *nothing* about the theft.'

He was silent for a moment then Jimmy asked, 'Matt, where are you staying?'

Matt sighed. 'I've just been camping in the back of my ute over at the satellite depot. I know I should have asked, but ...'

Jimmy held up his hand. 'There's no need to apologise. Anyway, I've got a better idea. Sometime over the weekend of Joel and Janey's wedding, the depot got broken into. I've been thinking about increasing the security – and having you there would be a great deterrent. You could stay in the shed; there's a loft that's decked out with a bed and a gas cooker and a few other odds and ends. I stayed there myself when I first started having financial problems. It's not flash, but it's warm and dry.'

'Burgled? You're joking? That's terrible.'

'They didn't take too much, just a few cartons of beer. I think we got off lightly.'

'It's a wonder I didn't hear anything. Wish I had!'

Jimmy grinned. 'I wish you had too, lad! Anyway, it's over with now. The police have been, insurance company notified and as far as I'm concerned it's finished. However, having you there would mean there were lights on most nights – unless you're away, obviously – and that might just stop anyone else who is thinking about having a crack at it.'

'It might too.' Matt nodded. 'That would be great, Jimmy. I'd appreciate it.'

'You'll need to try to get somewhere a bit more comfortable as soon as you get back on your feet, though,' Jimmy advised. 'Somewhere your little girl can visit. You don't want to miss out on too much of her life.

'And you should think about going and talking to that wife of yours, too. I reckon she'd listen.'

Matt swallowed hard. Maybe Jimmy was right.

Chapter 30

Kate bounced in and grabbed a giggling Ella under her arms and threw her into the air.

'It's so bloody cold our water pipes froze this morning,' she announced.

'I know! Ours didn't freeze completely but the pipes did a fair bit of clanking and banging. I don't think they really wanted to work at all.' Anna grinned at her friend. It was great to see her. 'Did you see the frost on the lawn?'

'I saw footprints!' Kate said. 'Have you been out making footprints like a snowman, Ella?'

Ella nodded solemnly. 'Very cold and white,' she declared.

The women laughed.

'Have you finished seeding yet? Won't be long and you'll be lamb marking,' Anna commented, moving to put the kettle on. She had a sudden vision of their farm: the wooden sheep yards, the ewes drafted off into a pen by themselves, bellowing for their lambs. In her mind's eye she saw lambs running up and down the fence, not understanding why they couldn't reach their mums when they could see them through the rails. At the slightest noise they'd take fright and move as one, like a tidal wave of lambs, until they hit the other fence and couldn't go any further.

She remembered as the lambs were tipped from the cradle, one by one, each flicking its head at the unfamiliar weight of the tag in its ear, dashing around, bleating madly for its mum. Within minutes the tail would be wagging madly as it suckled from her udder.

'Your mum isn't listening, Ella,' Kate said in a singsong voice. 'She's not listening to either of us!'

'Yes, I am,' said Anna, shaking away the images. 'I was just thinking about lamb marking at home.' She smiled wistfully. 'Seems like such a long time ago. I miss it! The freedom of it all, the openness. Everything we worked for.' She sighed. 'Oh, Kate, so much has changed.'

'Yes, well, it has – but not your hair. When was the last time you had a haircut? It looks dreadful. I've booked you in for a cut and colour tomorrow. Grandma Laura is going to have you –' she tapped Ella on the nose '– and I'm taking or dragging you, whichever is easiest, to Clare for the day. Don't bother arguing.'

Anna didn't. She even smiled.

* * *

The next day, when Kate pulled into the driveway, Anna grabbed her handbag, kissed Ella goodbye, thanked Laura again and hurried out to the car.

'Hi!' she said cheerily, then noticed the expression on her friend's face. 'What's wrong?'

'We had someone at our sheds last night.'

Anna looked at her, puzzled. 'What do you mean?'

'They were in our sheds, taking things.'

'Taking things as in . . . stealing?'

Kate exhaled. 'Yep. The bastards have taken Sam's motorbike, some fungicide chemical he had just bought in Clare and a heap of tools. It's all gone.'

'When? How? Did you see them? Are you sure?'

'Oh yeah. I'm sure,' she said grimly. Kate angrily shoved the car into reverse and backed out of the driveway. Then, as they drove out of town, she recounted the events of the night before. 'We'd just finished tea and I'd let Zoom out for his nightly loo stop. He went right off, yapping like you wouldn't believe! Then he took off around the side of the house. All the work dogs started carrying on, so I thought he was around at the kennels stirring them up.

'I walked around there to get him, but then I heard him barking down near the creek – he must have taken off chasing a rabbit or a fox or something.

'We had ewes and lambs in the yards ready for marking today, and with all of their bleating I didn't work out what the noise was at first. But then it was as if my brain kicked in and I knew something weird was happening – it was a vehicle leaving the shed. They didn't have their lights on until they headed down the drive. I yelled for Sam, who came running. He saw some tail-lights and reckons it was a trailer towed by a ute.' She growled. 'Do you know how much this pisses me off?'

Anna smiled wryly. 'Actually, I do.'

'Of course you do. Sorry.'

There was silence for a while as they both stared out at the countryside. The green hills were covered in fat stock, calves running and bucking while their mums grazed peacefully nearby. Tall, waving barley crops and spindly, prickly canola had flourished during this wet year and Anna was pleased the farmers who had managed to survive the dry times were finally being rewarded.

All or nothing. One season your heart would be broken and the next it would soar as high as the clouds bringing the rain. She didn't like it but she understood it was the way of life on the land.

'I guess Sam has gone to the police?'

'Yeah, he was going this morning – but we know what they'll say, don't we?'

They looked at each other and chorused, 'It will be a bit hard to investigate. Here's your report number for the insurance,' then burst into laughter.

'Bloody hell, look at us,' said Kate. 'How cynical are we?'

'Oh, Kate, I hope they don't. I hope the police can be helpful if nothing else.' Anna knew that although she seemed to be coping well, Kate would be feeling violated, perhaps even vulnerable. Well, in time she would feel that way. At the moment she was probably still in denial.

Of all the feelings vulnerability had been the hardest for Anna to deal with at the beginning. She'd had trouble sleeping at night, worried that if someone could steal from their farm, what was to stop the thief from coming into her house?

She hadn't spoken of her fears to anyone, though. Matt had enough to worry about and, besides, her mum had often told her that the mother and wife was the glue of the family. If she came unstuck the whole family did. So Anna had done her best to repress her fear and anxiety. But her family had come unstuck anyway ...

'Are you scared?' she asked Kate now.

Kate tilted her head to the side.

'You know, I might be in a few days, but at the moment I'm just angry and maybe a bit incredulous that something like this could happen. I shouldn't be, though, should I? I mean, it happened to my best friend, didn't it?'

When they reached the hairdresser's Anna leaned across to hug her friend. 'I can't do much to help, but I can honestly say I know how you feel.'

'I know, I know. What a bugger of a thing to happen, hey?' Kate pulled back and fingered Anna's hair. 'Now we need to work out what we're going to do with your hair. It needs a good trim and maybe some layers. And I reckon we need to get some gloss into that strawberry-blonde hair of yours. Maybe some copper highlights would look good.'

'Do I get a say?'

'Nope.'

Anna lay back with her head in the basin as the hairdresser massaged her scalp. Luxury! She closed her eyes and thought of nothing else except how good it felt. She was almost asleep when a sharp voice broke through her reverie.

'Oh, I'm sure Jenny is just talking out of her arse. She wouldn't know if it was on fire. But guess what? I've just heard there's been a theft over at Sam and Kate Long's place at Spalding. They had a motorbike and some chemicals stolen last night. Tools as well.'

Anna frowned and felt annoyed. 'Bloody old gossips,' she thought. 'They can't wait to pass on the news.' Flicking one eye open, she tried to see who was talking. Hmph, that'd be right – old Mrs Harby from a farm midway between Spalding and Clare. She thought she knew everything, when she didn't really know anything at all.

'You can sit up,' the hairdresser said to Anna. For a moment she couldn't hear anything as the hairdresser rubbed her head with a towel.

Then a voice said, 'Well with the money those Longs have got they'll hardly notice the loss.'

Anna narrowed her eyes. 'Bet you wouldn't

think that if it happened to you, old busy body!' she thought, sitting there fuming as another woman added, 'Surely the police should be able to track down whoever it was.'

'Oh, I doubt it,' Mrs Harby said knowledgeably. 'Matt Butler didn't get anywhere when his fertiliser was stolen last year and neither did the bloke from Burra who had chemicals taken.'

'Oh, I remember hearing about that. Apparently Matt used to drive around the countryside at night searching for the thief. It's almost romantic in a way, isn't it?' the speaker said dreamily. 'Young man trying to avenge the loss of his dreams who finds ... Well, girls? What *did* he find? I heard he and Anna split up.'

Anna snorted as she recognised the voice: Helen Gubbins, that old windbag. Oh how she would like to punch her lights out about now. 'Anyway, I must be off,' Mrs Harby said, standing up and walking over to the counter to pay. 'I've got to pick up some chemical for Ross – he managed to get some from down south at cost price. He's good at sniffing out a bargain, my Ross is.'

'Are you sure it hasn't been stolen?' one of the other women joked.

'Of course I am, dear. The farmer has sold his farm and is offloading his excess stock. Bye now!'

Anna had been seething under the towel, but finally the hairdresser lifted it away and led her to a chair in front of the mirror. It was Helen who saw her first and Anna watched with pleasure as the other woman's eyes widened in recognition. As the other women followed Helen's gaze the salon fell quiet.

Let that be a lesson to the gossipy old bags! Anna thought.

Chapter 31

Bang, bang, bang!

The man started from his nap in front of the fire at the sound of someone pounding on the front door. With a sense of foreboding, he glanced at the clock above the fireplace.

Nine o'clock. A bit late for visitors.

He sat on the edge of the chair for a moment, toying with the idea of not answering the door, then realised he'd only be putting off the inevitable. He might as well get it over and done with.

Levering himself up he walked to the door just as the pounding sounded again. The hand was so strong against the wood he could see the door vibrate with each hit.

Bang, bang, bang!

He opened the door a crack and tried to peer into the darkness. Before he knew what was happening, the door flew open, catching him on the forehead. He felt the heel of a palm against his chest, pushing him back into the room. Stumbling backwards, he overbalanced and came crashing to the floor.

It was *those* visitors.

In a heartbeat a large man was straddling his chest, breathing beery fumes into his face and making it difficult to breathe.

'Know who I am, matey?' the visitor asked in a sarcastic voice. 'Think you prob'ly do.'

The man on the floor struggled to get away, knowing it was useless.

The big man's laugh was harsh.

'Paddy is lookin' for his money and he's gettin' a little bit annoyed it hasn't arrived yet. Got any answers for him, you lowlife?'

'I'm trying, for God's sake, I'm trying.' He lifted his head slightly to emphasise his words, but the man slammed it back into the ground.

His vision blurred with the pain, and he tasted blood from where he'd bitten his tongue.

'Settle down, boyo, and listen to me. Listen *real* good. If Paddy's money isn't in his hand by the end of this week, you mightn't like the next visit I make. You know why?'

Silence.

'Well I'm thinking you won't want to end up like my last client – Ray. Want to know what happened to him? Actually, he was a mate of yours, wasn't he?

Poor Ray!' He heaved a mock sigh. 'But I'm sure you're more interested in what I'm gonna to do to *you*. Well I might bring a big ol' forty-four-gallon drum with me. Ever got into one of them? They're pretty dark and small. Hope you're not claustrophobic. Still, probably won't matter if you are. The cement will set pretty quick. You won't be goin' anywhere. Imagine ...'

The big man implied that he might enjoy what he was planning but it filled the other with terror.

'I'm trying, please tell him I'm trying,' he begged, tears welling in his eyes. 'I'll get the money, I promise I will. I've got everything in place, I just need a bit more time.'

Holy hell, how had he got into this situation again? The first few times had been bad enough, when he'd owed nearly fifteen grand to one of the smaller loan sharks around the north-eastern suburbs of Adelaide. Paddy was different and he knew from the previous debt with him that he was in way over his head. Why did he keep going back for more?

'Boyo, you owe the man fifty big ones – you really think he's gonna let you get away with it? If you weren't such a good client, I wouldn't be talking to you. You'd be in the drum already, all set for a nice sea voyage. Get my drift?'

It took all his self-control not to move. 'I'll have it to him by the end of the week, I swear.' His voice was shaking.

'Well, then, you've got nothing to worry about.'

The man got off him and he exhaled, relieved. If that was it, he'd got away lightly. Then he felt a boot into his side and a fist to his face.

And after that he remembered nothing.

When he awoke, his jeans were wet, the house was dark and the fire had died to nothing but a glow. He could hear the dogs barking outside and groggily tried to shift himself to a corner where he couldn't be seen, in case the thug was still around. His head *hurt*! He clutched at it and felt the dried blood crusting on his scalp.

He tried to slide, but the pain in his ribs made him gasp. There was a throbbing in his chest. He'd had a good one done on him this time.

The bastard would've enjoyed it too.

The goon.

Oh, he knew the prick all right. He'd had more visits from him than he'd had from his own mother in recent years. Paddy hired him to do all the dirty work, scare the debtors.

Slowly he crawled to the kitchen and, doing his best to ignore the pain, tried to stand.

One hand, two hands, rested on the cushion of the chair just as the dogs set up another loud round of barking. He froze, fearful the thug might be lurking in the shadows, waiting for another round at him.

Without warning he felt more warm liquid soaking into his jeans and he cursed everyone he knew, especially Paddy's henchman. He stood silent and still until the dogs had settled then shuffled across to the kitchen.

Feeling around in the cupboard he found his prescription-only painkillers and popped out two pills. He reached for a beer from the fridge then swallowed them down in one gulp.

He stood by the fridge and drank the rest of the beer, waiting for the painkillers to kick in, his head swimming and every part of him throbbing. It took another two beers before he felt able to make his way to the bathroom, where he tried to strip off his urine-soaked jeans.

His head spun as he felt a sharp jab of pain. He shut his eyes, took a deep breath and launched himself into the shower. He wasn't sure how long he stood there, but the water had gone from steaming hot to lukewarm by the time he dragged himself out.

The bruising on his face had begun to swell and when he looked in the mirror his right eye had almost closed over. It would be a while before he could be seen in public again for there was no way he could give a logical explanation for the bruises on his face.

His bed was waiting and as he crawled into it, hoping that oblivion would overtake him, he wondered how he could have been so stupid as to rack up such a huge debt with a very dangerous man.

It was only then that he let himself think about Ray; the tears of self-pity started to fall. It wasn't his fault. If the horse had come in at Morphettville, he would have doubled his money and been able to pay Paddy. Then again, if the footy team he'd had a flutter on two weeks before had won, it would have been the same result. But both times, he'd lost large amounts of money.

He would have to make some visits of his own as soon as he was able, he decided. It was the only way out.

Chapter 32

Matt leaned on the horn, but the sheep refused to move. He was frustrated and annoyed. For what seemed like hours he'd been running around, yelling and waving his arms, trying to get the ewes through the gate. Finally, in desperation, he'd started beeping the horn.

Beep, beep!

'Get hold of 'em, Jasper.'

The dog ran from side to side, barking, but still the sheep just stood there.

Beep, beep!

Gradually Matt became aware that the beeping wasn't a horn – it was his mobile phone.

Beep, beep!

He fumbled for it on the floor beside his bed.

By the time he'd found it, all he saw was a missed call from a mobile number he didn't recognise. He let out an annoyed grunt. Probably a wrong number at this time of night. Two weeks ago the same thing had happened, and it had turned out to be drunk kids trying to ring one of their friends.

He lay back on his bed and lifted his arm to glance at the watch Anna had given him for their last wedding anniversary. The eerie green glow of the hands showed him it was 4.30 am.

Matt groaned and shut his eyes as the wind blew a heavy shower of rain against the tin roof. Rolling over, he tried to get comfortable, doubting he would sleep again – the alarm was set for 5.30 anyway.

The drive was taking him to Port Augusta today. The trailers were loaded full of dog food, chemicals and animal husbandry drenches, the truck refueled and ready to go. His stomach clenched at the thought of carrying things he could use on a farm. He was thinking of the farm more than ever these days; he had Jimmy to blame for that.

Matt and Jimmy had eaten dinner together the previous evening, as they had done once a week since his late-night visit to Jimmy's house four weeks ago.

Jimmy had been encouraging him to try to get back on the land, for it was obvious that farming was Matt's passion.

'No way, Jimmy,' Matt had told the older man last night. 'That part of my life is over. Oh, I'm hell-bent on finding out who stole my fertiliser, but I won't ever be a farmer again. I wouldn't be able to afford to buy land anyway.' He wouldn't admit out loud that the thought of failing was the main reason.

'I'm serious, lad.' Jimmy waved his hand in the air. 'Look around. What do you see? Lots of trucks, trailers and a good solid business. If I'd given up and focused on the wrongs done to me in the past instead of taking positive action for the future, I wouldn't have had the ability to start again.

'Matt, I'm not perfect, that I can tell you, and you already know I've been through something similar. I wasn't well when I first came back from 'Nam. I had lots of issues to work through. But when I did start to see things clearly again, I knew I had to get on with life or spend the rest of it wallowing in self-pity. So I started my business and had a few good years. Then it went guts up and I had to make a fresh start. It was bloody hard, but I did it for my nephew.

'You see I'd made a promise to the boy, many years before. I'd told him we'd go into business together. That promise meant everything to him, though probably not as much to me – but I'd given my word, I had to keep it – even when things started to go down the gurgler. If I'd let all of my thoughts and anger consume me the way you have, I wouldn't have been able to see a clear path forward.

'I would bet you made the same sort of promise to your family – to Anna and Ella – that I did to my nephew: that you wouldn't let them down; that you wouldn't let yourself down.'

They depend on me.

'It's a bit different, Jimmy,' Matt said, not looking up from the table. 'I didn't have the chance to downsize like you did. I just had everything taken away, there weren't any second chances.'

'But lad, there are, don't you see?' Jimmy leaned forward eagerly. 'Let your mind out for a wander. Use this truck driving as your second chance. Put money aside, save enough to put a deposit on a lease farm and go from there. You don't have to buy straight away. Ease back into it slowly. You'll be happier, your family will be happier and you'll be able to keep your promises.

'Then will be the time to go looking for who took your fertiliser. When you and your family are settled again.'

'I don't have a family anymore,' Matt mumbled.

'You do, me boy, you never lose your family, no matter where they are or what they are doing. That I know first hand. You? Well you're just too stubborn to see it.'

After leaving Jimmy's place Matt had had a desperate urge to talk to Anna – an urge he hadn't felt for some time. He rang her number.

'Hello?'

Suddenly tongue-tied, he couldn't think of what to say.

'Hello?' Anna's voice was wary now.

Matt opened his mouth, but no words came out. Then he hit the disconnect button.

***

Matt must have dozed off again because he awoke with a start as his phone beeped with a message.

The phone was on his bed this time, near his hand. He felt blindly for it and hit a button so he could listen to the voicemail. What he heard brought him to instant alertness.

'*Look at me,*' yelled a hoarse voice. '*Look at me! Are you happy to let them do this, when all you have to do is give me the money and they'll go away? They murdered Ray, you know.* Murdered him!'

Someone else said, '*I'm not doing this again. We're hurting people.*' The voice was muffled and Matt could only make out a few words.

'*You are a* bastard.' It was the first man again, his tone low and menacing. '*You'll let them kill me then? When it's your fault I've ended up like this?*'

'*This isn't my fault. I've redeemed myself many times over. It's yours now. I've given you enough.*'

The phone crackled and when it cleared Matt heard the second man say, '*– the last time. After this you're on your own. Don't come back here ever again.*'

A beep signalled the end of the message.

Matt sat up in bed and listened to it again. He didn't know either of the voices and he certainly didn't know the phone number. All he could think was someone had accidentally dialled his number while their phone was in their pocket. But then if he didn't recognise the voices or the number, how the hell did they know his?

He thought about ringing back but decided

against it. They were talking pretty scary stuff and he didn't want to be involved.

Should he ring the police? he wondered. No, they'd probably think it was a prank. The only clear voice was the man who sounded angry ... Or was it afraid? The other man could barely be heard and Matt wondered if he had imagined what the man was saying.

He played it again, trying to listen for background noises or anything that might sound like something he recognised.

Nothing. Or was there something? He listened to the message once more, and this time he had a vague unsettling feeling that there was something familiar about a voice or noise. But maybe that was a result of listening to it four times.

Sighing, he switched on the bedside light and threw back the covers.

The rain droplets on the window sparkled in the light of the streetlamp, and when he peered outside he could see white clouds scurrying across the sky like ghosts chasing each other.

Matt shivered, a sense of trepidation in his stomach as he thought about the phone call. He wondered about the voices, who they belonged to and what trouble they were mixed up in.

Someone wanted to kill one of them and he'd said another man had already been murdered.

He looked up at the sky again as the clouds parted to reveal a pale quarter moon. It would be a perfect night for a crime.

Chapter 33

When Matt's phone rang again unexpectedly, he looked warily at the screen, hoping it was a number he knew. Then he nodded, relieved.

'G'day, Sam,' he answered as he sipped his early morning coffee.

'How are you, Matt?' Sam asked.

Matt toyed with the idea of mentioning the weird phone call then rejected it. He was sure, or at least he hoped, that it was kids playing a joke or something similar.

'All good here, mate. Just about to jump in the truck and head to Port Augusta.' Matt waited, he could tell by Sam's tone there was something wrong, but he didn't want to pre-empt what that might be. 'What are you up to today?'

'I'm heading to the police station. Just on my way there now.'

'Okay,' Matt said slowly. Waiting.

'We've been done over just like you. They took my motorbike, all the fungicide chemical I bought and a heap of tools that I had sitting on the bench. The angle grinder and drill. That sort of stuff.'

'Bloody hell.' Matt almost dropped the phone. Why he thought it would never happen to Sam and Kate, he didn't know, but it had never crossed his mind that it would happen to someone he was close to. 'Shit, mate, I'm really sorry to hear that. Did you see anything?'

'I saw the tail-lights. I think whoever it was had a ute and trailer, but I'm only guessing. It was only luck Kate was outside. By the time she yelled and I got there, they had driven off.'

'Sam, I wish I could say something that will help, but I know there isn't anything to say. I hope the cops take you a bit more seriously when you report it than they did me.'

'Well, I'm going to tell them about you, if that's okay?'

'No worries, if you think it will make a difference. I'd like it if someone took a look at all of my notes. I'm sure they'd be interested in it if they saw them all together, not scattered over a large area like the thefts are at the moment.'

'Well, I'll let you know how I go. Anyway, I've just pulled up, so I'd better head in. I'll give you a ring later on, eh?'

'Good luck. I'll be interested to hear how you get on.'

Matt ignored his cooling coffee as he pulled out his notebook to record this latest theft. He shook his head as he re-read the notes. He couldn't understand why the police hadn't picked up that it was happening all over the mid-north. On a whim, Matt turned to a fresh page and wrote down five words: *depot theft, weird phone call.* He also wrote down the dates. Maybe there was something else happening around him.

'Anyway,' he thought, 'no point in thinking about it now. I've got deliveries to make.' As he pulled the door shut he hoped that Sam would be able to do something for them both and he felt a little ray of hope.

Five hours into his journey, Matt looked over at Shane, who had been an unexpected passenger. He had appeared just as Matt was pulling out of the depot and asked to come with him.

Shane's bloodshot eyes and tousled hair suggested he'd had a hard night or perhaps an argument with Belinda, so Matt had nodded but asked no questions. His gaze travelled past Shane to the view out the passenger window and he felt the familiar sting of regret and sadness.

In the paddock to his left, a ute was driving slowly around a mob of Angus cows, calves running at their mothers' feet. A blue heeler was leaning over the edge of the ute's tray waiting for an instruction from his owner, his tongue hanging out, mouth stretched in a smile. Even inside the cab Matt could almost smell the beautiful earthy scent of the cattle as they walked towards the yards.

'Do you still miss it? Even after all this time?' Shane asked unexpectedly.

'Oh yeah. There's nothing quite like being your own boss.' Matt returned his gaze to the road, his hands gripping the wheel.

The cattle had passed and now there were wide open paddocks of newly germinated wheat and barley. The plants were being buffeted strongly by the wind.

'Being your own boss, is that the main thing?'

Matt was quiet for a while, trying to organise the words in his head. How could he explain what he felt to someone who seemed to have everything? He had started with nothing but a dream; a dream of having his own land – a vision of lush green pastures, rolling hills and fat stock, grazing. Good yielding crops and snow-white fleeces. And he had worked tirelessly until finally he had enough money to put down a deposit on some land.

He hadn't let the days of endless sun, clear blue skies and dust storms so bad he could barely see his hand in front of his face deter him but, if he was honest, the reality hadn't always matched the dream. Reality had been bare, red paddocks, starving sheep and lack of water. For the last part of his farming life, anyway.

The day he had to drag over fifty sheep out of a muddy dam, he had almost faulted in his vision. The next day, as he'd fed hay to the starving ewes he'd kept – his core stock – he'd closed his eyes as they had tripped over each other in their haste to get to the feed. They'd left their lambs behind, the older and stronger ones trying to keep up with their mothers, the younger ones just running in confusion, forever mis-mothered and their death, nothing surer.

He had wondered at times if it was all worth it. And now, with the breakup of his marriage and the end of his dream, he continued to wonder. Life as a single bloke driving trucks, seeing his daughter on the weekend would be much easier. But something kept drawing him back to the land. The open spaces, the feeling of the sun on his skin, the life he knew and loved.

And Anna. She was part of that dream and landscape.

In the end, he couldn't work out what to say to Shane, so he just said, 'No, it's everything about it,' and reached forward to turn up Rob Thomas singing 'Mockingbird'. The chorus was about him, he was sure. Not meant for farming, not meant for Anna, not meant for Ella, not meant for this life.

That summed up everything.

Three days later he headed out to Kate and Sam's place for dinner. He was thankful that Sam had stuck by him through this whole mess, even when Matt had been rude and pushed him away. Sam had already told him they wouldn't be taking sides between Anna and him. 'We are friends with you both and that's the way it will stay,' Sam had said firmly when he'd rung to invite him for dinner.

As he turned into his friends' driveway, Matt wondered how they were coping since the theft. Now Sam had been robbed, he finally understood just a fraction of what Matt had been been through. Of course, it hadn't affected their business, but the violation was still the same.

As he added up all the people in the mid-north district who had been affected by rural crime over the past few years, he felt anger towards the police for being blind to what was happening in their own backyard. There were so many thefts.

The outside light was on and as Matt pulled up he saw the door fly open and Kate step onto the verandah to greet him. He smiled, feeling like he was coming home.

'Hi, Kate!'

'Matt, it's so good to see you.' She held open her arms and he hugged her before handing over a bottle of wine. 'Huh! My favourite. Flattery and gifts will get you everywhere!'

'What? You want flattery too? I'm not very good at that. You might have to ask your husband.'

'He's in the shower. Come in! It's so bloody cold out here. There'll probably be another frost in the morning. Oh sit down, you mad dog,' Kate said to her little Jack Russell, who was dancing on his hind legs in an effort to get noticed.

'Hey, Zoom, are you happy to see me?' Matt bent down to pick up the dog and fondled his ears as they walked towards the house. Kate held the door open and rushed him inside so as to keep the warmth in. Matt laughed as the dog tried to lick him. 'Mate, your breath hasn't got any better since I saw you last! You should do something about it, Kate.'

'Like what? Buy him a toothbrush? Do you really think he's going to sit still for that long?'

'Good point. So, what's going on here?' Matt asked as he leaned against the kitchen counter and watched Kate bustle around the kitchen. He kept Zoom in his arms, patting his head, relishing the softness of his ears.

'The usual: lamb marking, seeding ...' She was interrupted by the appearance of her husband.

'Hey there, big fella. Good to see you out here again.'

'G'day, Sam. How are you?'

The two men shook hands and Sam clapped Matt on the back. 'Got a drink?'

'Better not, mate. I'm driving.'

'Why don't you stay here tonight, Matt?' Kate asked. 'You're more than welcome.'

Before Matt could respond Zoom began to bark, struggling to be put down. When Matt gently lowered him to the floor, the dog raced to the door yapping loudly.

Sam moved swiftly to look out of the window, muttering, 'Bastards.' Kate, Matt noticed, had stiffened and paled slightly. It was a look he'd seen on Anna's face many times during the first few months after the robbery, but he'd been so caught up in his own loss he'd never troubled to identify what it was. Now he realised with a jolt what that look meant: fear. Fear! Anna had been frightened and he'd done nothing about it.

'Anything there?' Kate asked, her calm tone belying the expression on her face.

'Can't see anything,' Sam said. 'Want to go for a look, Matt?'

'I'm right with you.'

Sam pulled on his jacket and grabbed a torch by the door. 'Will you be okay here, Kate?' he asked, and Matt noted the concern in his voice and kicked himself again. He should have treated Anna that way, but he'd been caught up in too much self-pity.

'I'll be fine. I've got a hockey stick somewhere if anyone decides to come into the house,' she joked.

The two men walked as quickly as they could through the night, their boots crunching loudly on the gravel. Matt puffed a little as they strode quickly towards the darkened outline of the shed.

The farm dogs barked at the torch light and Sam switched it off as they drew closer to the outbuildings.

Matt put a hand on Sam's arm and motioned for him to stop and listen, but there was nothing but silence. 'I reckon it's just a false alarm, mate,' he said, half relieved.

Sam moved towards the shed. 'Think you're right, but Zoom doesn't usually carry on unless there's a visitor. I'll just have a quick look inside.'

He flashed the torch over the tin walls, the light throwing up sinister-looking shadows. Matt scanned the space, his eyes seeking out hiding places and dark corners.

Suddenly a shriek echoed through the darkness and Matt sensed movement in the air above him. He threw up his hands to protect his head, trying not to call out in fear.

'Shit,' he gasped as he jumped forward, his heart thumping. 'What the ... Bloody bats!'

Sam gave a weak laugh. 'Forgot to warn you about them.'

Matt heard his friend blow out a breath and turned to look at him. 'There's no one here. Let's go back to the house.'

Matt pushed his plate away and patted his stomach.

'That was beautiful, thanks, Kate. It's the first decent meal I've had since ... well, for a while.'

Kate smiled as she collected the plates. 'Coffee? Tea?'

'I'd love a tea, please. So, Sam, what's happening about finding your motorbike? What have the police said about it – anything?'

Sam pushed his chair back and stretched out his legs. 'Not a great deal. I've been in and got my insurance claim number and leaned on them fairly hard about investigating the theft, but they're just not interested. To be fair, they're busy doing so many other things that a robbery they think they're unlikely to solve isn't something they want to take on.' I did mention your case, but got fobbed off again. Too long ago to have any hope of solving it, I'm afraid. I did say it was about twelve months ago, but it didn't make any difference. Sam stopped and glanced at Kate enquiringly.

Matt looked between the two. 'What?' he asked as Kate nodded. 'What's going on?'

Sam took a piece of paper out of his pocket and unfolded it. 'You know Kate's cousin is a cop, right? Well Kate gave him a call and he suggested we compile a list of people who've been ripped off around here lately. He reckoned that one of the reasons the police haven't got on to these other cases – and yours – is because they're just seeing them as one-offs. If the thefts are all being reported to different police stations, they won't be connecting the dots. But maybe we can. This is what Kate and I have come up with. We thought you might know of others.'

Matt held out his hand for the list and scanned it, nodding as he read the familiar names. 'You're missing a few. Hang on, I've got some more info in the car.'

He went out to his ute and fetched his black notebook from the glove box, feeling a wave of excitement. Maybe Sam and Kate would help him in his search to find the thief.

As he hurried through the door, notebook in hand, he saw an odd look cross Kate's face.

'What's wrong?' he asked, as he sat back down.

'Nothing, Matt. Nothing. I just saw *you* again.'

Matt frowned, but decided not to pursue the comment. Instead, he opened the book and passed it over to Sam, who started to read with Kate looking over his shoulder.

Loneliness swept through him as he watched them. Sam and Kate shared a special bond, just as he and Anna once had. It wasn't likely they could recapture it, he thought sadly. Too much damage had been done to their relationship.

'This is great, Matt,' Sam said. 'It really gives you a sense of the radius in which the thieves have been operating – as far north as Jamestown, across to Burra, over to Snowtown and Crystal Brook.'

Matt nodded. 'I keep coming back to the fact that it must be someone living around here or Clare. The places being hit are all within a couple of hundred kilometres of here – it's almost like this area is the epicentre.'

Kate got up to put another log on the fire. The flames roared and sparks shot up the chimney as she poked at the log, trying to get it to catch.

'Okay,' Sam said, 'so we've had three burglaries

this year. Let's look at them first; they'll be freshest in everyone's minds.' He glanced down at Matt's scribbled notes. 'James Truton had some chemical stolen about four weeks ago. He lives over at Snowtown. Do you know him?'

'Nope. I know where his farm is though.'

'Then there's Gavin Knots, who lives between here and Jamestown. He had a generator taken as well as some other tools, and Lachlan Mundy had a farm ute taken.'

'There's also Mark Chambers who had bales of wool taken from his shed. So that makes four. Do you know what's similar about all those farms?' asked Matt.

Sam shrugged. 'No. Is there anything?'

'They're all on no-through roads.'

'Really?' Sam frowned. 'So you're thinking that because there isn't much passing traffic, those properties are easier targets?'

Matt nodded. 'I can't be sure, of course, but it's the only link I've been able to see.'

'Pretty interesting.' Sam mused on this for a while then said, 'I've got a suggestion. Ready to hear it?'

'Mate, I've been waiting for ages for someone to take this seriously.'

'Let's make some phone calls to these blokes who have been hit and see if they've got any more information. If we can get some solid evidence linking all of the thefts, then we'll go to Kate's cousin Dave with it. I reckon he'd be able to help us work out what to do with it. He's a bloody nice bloke.'

Matt smiled. 'Thank you, Sam,' he said quietly.

The next morning Matt left Sam and Kate's house before the sun had crept over the hills.

Once again, the morning was frosty and it took him a couple of goes to get his car started. Chugging slowly out of the drive, lights on high beam, he checked the time. He still had hours before he was due at work. Maybe he could just get one quick hug from Ella before driving back to Adelaide for his run.

Anna answered the door when he knocked, a cup of coffee in her hand.

'I wanted to say hi to Ella before I went out on the road again,' he said gruffly by way of greeting.

'She's not up yet, but you can see her if you like.' Anna opened the door wider and stood back to let him in.

Standing at the door of Ella's room, he watched his daughter sleeping. Silently he apologised for all the things he knew he could have done better since she was born. He approached the bed, bending over to kiss her cheek and ran his hand gently over her hair.

'I love you, baby girl,' he whispered and left the room, his house and his old life.

Over the road, Maggie had just flipped the sign on the door to indicate her shop was open.

'Hello, Maggie, you're up early this morning.'

'Ah, Matt, you're a sight for sore eyes, you are. And how are you?'

'I'm well. I've been in to say good morning to Ella and I'm on my way back to the depot to head off on another run later this afternoon.'

'Well, if you've got a long drive, then you'll be wantin' a coffee. Come in. And I'll fry up some bacon for a sandwich while I'm at it. Would you mind starting the potbelly for me?'

'You must be sent from heaven, Maggie. A bacon sandwich is just what I was hoping for!'

Matt crumpled some newspaper and snapped the kindling then put it all into the fire box and struck a match.

The smell of sizzling bacon filled the air and his stomach rumbled. Getting up from his crouched position, he stuck his head into the kitchen to ask if there was some more wood. Maggie directed him to an old tin tank in the backyard.

He pushed open the back door and was greeted by the smell of wood smoke. He breathed in deeply. There wasn't a better smell in the world than a wood fire burning on a cold morning. Matt found the logs and headed back across the yard. As he eased the door open with his foot, he heard Maggie talking to someone and he stopped.

He recognised the voice, but at first he couldn't think where from. Then his eyes widened with astonishment as he realised it was the voice from the phone message. At least he thought it was.

Quickly, he put down his load and dug the phone out of his jeans pocket. He had to be sure. He dialled the message bank and listened to the message again. With the voice from the shop in one ear and the message playing in the other, it was like hearing the same man in stereo.

Matt backed out of the room, his heart thumping, then he thought about Maggie's safety, and went to go back inside. Hell he wasn't sure what to do.

He listened at the door for a moment, content the conversation was normal chit-chat. Matt wondered if there might be a car in the street that he recognised and slunk around the outside of the shop. The street was empty, save for a polished white ute idling at the kerb. He saw a movement in the tray and realised there was an animal there, huddled into the corner. Poor thing, it would be freezing. Then a head was lifted into his line of vision and Matt felt himself start to shake.

It was Jasper.

Chapter 34

Anna let the curtain fall back against the window, her hand to her mouth. She wasn't sure she understood what she had just seen.

Slowly, she inched the curtain out again and looked across the road. Matt had disappeared. Her eyes swung to the tray of the ute, searching for movement, but there was none.

Had she really just seen Matt steal Jasper?

She shut her eyes and leaned back against the wall, a smile playing around her lips. The idea that he had nabbed Jasper made her very happy indeed.

'Mummy?' Ella was awake.

'In the kitchen, darling,' she called, and smiled as Ella rounded the corner, her cheeks crimson from sleep, her eyes bright. She had her favourite teddy bear tucked under her arm. Anna bent down to give her a kiss and a cuddle.

'Did you sleep well?' she asked.

'Yes, but, Mummy, I dreamed I heard Daddy talking to me.'

'You did hear him, darling. He came in to say good morning and then he left. He's got a big run to do in the truck today.'

'I wanted to see him.' Ella's voice trembled and her eyes filled with tears.

'I'm sorry, sweetheart, he's already gone.' Briskly, she grabbed Ella under the arms and swung her onto the bench. 'You need to have a good breakfast this morning. Are you ready to go and help Kate and Sam with the sheep today?'

Immediately, Ella brightened. 'Yes! The sheep. We're going to the farm.'

'That's right! We're going to help Kate with the sheep while Sam starts to put the crop in. So,' Anna said over her shoulder as she turned and began to get out the breakfast things, 'I think you'll need a *huge* breakfast.' She swept her arms out in a large arc. 'And then you'll need to get dressed in something *very* warm.' Anna pretended to put her arms into a jumper. 'Then you'll need your rubber boots!' While acting out putting the boots on she pretended to overbalance and fell onto the floor. She was rewarded by Ella's giggles.

As she drove towards Kate and Sam's farm a sense of happiness settled on Anna. Today was her first real day back at work. The babysitting was great, but she longed to be outside. It was so hard to believe she was working when surrounded by the dishes, washing and other monotonous tasks.

When Kate had approached her about helping out on their farm during seeding time, her first instinct had been to say no; she no longer felt confident that she had the necessary skills. But the more she thought about it, the more she realised she was itching to get back outside. And Kate really did need her help. She had a special mob of ewes from which she had bred prime lambs for the Producers' Markets. Sam would usually have helped mark the lambs but he was busy seeding.

Seeding! The anniversary of the theft was app-roaching fast. Anna shook her head. So much had changed in twelve months. But Kate; her support had been unwavering.

Helping Kate would be a fantastic way to thank her friend for all she'd done recently. 'There are only about one hundred and thirty ewes in the mob,' Kate had said. 'We should be able to manage them, shouldn't we? Then we can get the lambs ready for the abattoirs.'

It would also help her dwindling finances. The babysitting and small amounts from Centrelink and Matt weren't really covering everything.

Maggie had been very generous, giving her groceries in exchange for Anna looking after the shop for an hour or two so Maggie could catch up on her bookkeeping, but it never seemed to be enough. Once again she was back to trying to keep the wolf from the door.

'There's Kate,' said Ella as Anna parked the car under a large pepper tree.

'Yep, there she is. And look, Ella, she's wearing her rubber boots. I wonder if she's going to feed the chooks.'

'Chooks? Can I get the eggs?'

'You'll have to ask Kate.'

Kate opened Ella's door and gave her a big smile. 'Did I hear something about eggs?' she asked.

'Can I get the eggs?' Ella asked again, putting her arms up for a hug as Kate undid her seatbelt.

'Course you can, love. In fact, I have just the job for you: you can get all the eggs and put them in the cartons. Will you do that for me?'

'Yes!'

Kate looked at Anna. 'Fantastic. But first Mum and I need to draft the sheep and it's too early for the chooks to have finished laying, so that can be our lunchtime job. Ready, Mum?'

'Let's get going,' Anna said and they walked towards the yards.

'The mob I want to take to the abattoirs are just out there.' Anna followed Kate's pointing finger across the trickling creek to the rolling hills behind the house. There she could see a mob of about two hundred prime cross-bred lambs grazing.

'Wow,' she said. 'They look great.' She watched

as a lamb walked up and sniffed its mate, then gently bunted its head into the other's side. The second lamb took off at top speed and raced across the paddock to an outcrop of rocks and leapt to the top. The other lamb chased it and soon the whole mob were jumping and pig-rooting off the rocks. Anna looked around happily, but the sight made her ache for the farm.

'C'mon, Mummy.' Ella tugged at Anna's hand.

'Well I hope I can remember how to yell and shout at the sheep, Ella,' she said and climbed over the rails. 'You need to stay here, okay? That way the sheep can't hurt you while they're running.' She lifted the little girl into an empty pen and shot a smile at Kate. It also meant that she wouldn't get in the way.

Kate went to the head of the drafting race while Anna waded through the sheep to open the gate. She grabbed their heads, turned them towards the race, then gave a sharp, loud shout. The sheep were off and running through the draft.

Their lambs followed suit, though some baulked as they reached unfamiliar ground, and Anna had to work hard to keep the mob running. Finally the back pen was empty, the front yard full of ewes and the side one packed with small lambs bleating for their mothers. The ewes looked through the railings, trying to push their heads through the gaps, wanting to find their babies.

'It's all right, girls,' Kate told them. 'You can have them back very shortly.'

'Where's all the gear, Kate?' Anna yelled over the noise.

'In the esky next to the cradle,' Kate answered.

Anna opened the lid, took out the vaccine, guns and needles, and started to set them up. They would hang on the steel post next to the marking cradle. Anna moved on to fill the bucket with water and disinfectant and count out the tags. Finally it seemed they were ready.

They eased the lambs into a smaller pen then looked at each other.

'All good?' Kate asked.

Anna nodded. 'Okay, here we go – but I might be a bit slow at first,' she warned. She grabbed a lamb, and gently lowered it into the cradle. She certainly hadn't forgotten how to do this task. It was second nature to her as she expertly hooked the legs into the holders and thrust the needle into the cheek. 'Yep,' she said to indicate she'd finished and Kate swung the cradle around.

'I think I'm going to be sore tonight,' Anna groaned as she picked up the next lamb and it kicked out with its leg, catching her in the breast.

'I think we both will,' Kate said. 'But tell me you don't love it.'

'I don't love it,' Anna said obediently.

'Liar!'

They worked quickly, knowing there was still a lot of work to do after these lambs.

Finally Anna threw the last lamb into the cradle and bent over to ease the pain in her back.

'That was fun!' she groaned.

'Really? Doesn't sound like it!'

'Oh, Kate it was. Far out, I miss this.' She stood up and twirled around, her arms out and head back, ignoring the blisters on her hand and unfit body. Then she took Ella over to watch the ewes finding their babies. The last lamb to come out of the cradle had just found its mother and was drinking from her udder.

Ella chuckled with delight.

'Do you want to help shoo them up, Ella?' Kate asked. 'They need to go out the gate.' She pointed.

'Can I open the gate?' Ella asked.

'Yep.'

Anna watched as the little girl walked confidently through the sheep, along the edge of the yards and unhooked the chain, feeling sad this wasn't the sort of life she could offer her daughter anymore. She looked like a little farmer in her jeans, polo-neck jumper and rubber-sided boots. Her hair was pulled back in a low ponytail and the beanie Anna insisted she wear was covered by a tiny Akubra Kate had brought back from one of her trips to Adelaide.

Kate threw her arm over Anna's shoulders and gave her a little squeeze. Anna knew Kate understood what she was thinking.

'Come on,' said her friend. 'We need to get the next mob of lambs in so we can get them to the butchers. Otherwise we won't have the meat to take to the market next weekend.'

Chapter 35

It was a week before Sam and Matt could put their plan into action, but on Saturday night Matt pulled up outside Sam's house and hopped out of his ute, leaving his door open for Jasper.

Sam looked out of the window, waved and said something to Kate, who appeared silhouetted in the kitchen light, a wide grin on her face as she gave him the thumbs-up. Then, as she saw Jasper, her face changed. She ran out the door, Sam close behind her.

'You got him back!' she called delightedly. 'Jasper! Here, Jasper!'

Jasper stood back, timid, then took a tentative step forward, almost like something had jogged his memory.

'Don't be offended if he doesn't come straight away, Kate,' Matt said. 'He's really shy at the moment, but I'm hoping with a bit of love and care he'll soon get back to the way he was.'

Kate dropped to the ground and held out her hand to let Jasper smell her, all the while crooning softly to him. 'C'mon, fella, I'm not going to hurt you. Hey there, big boy, you wanna pat?'

Jasper took another tentative step towards her, then another, and she was finally rewarded with a lick to her hand. She fondled his ears, talking quietly.

Sam looked at Matt curiously. 'I don't suppose I should ask,' he said.

'Probably not,' Matt said with a grin.

Kate gave the dog a last pat then stood up. Jasper went straight back to Matt and leaned against his legs. Matt's hand strayed down to his head and stayed there.

'So how are you going to do this?' Kate asked, looking between the two men. 'The pub?'

'Yep,' Sam said. 'Where else do you go when you want information?'

'The hairdresser. Helen Gubbins and that bloody old gossip Mrs Harby seemed to have plenty to say last time Anna was there,' Kate said.

'Huh! Those old biddies wouldn't know if their arses were on fire,' Sam said. 'But honestly, I think we'll get more info from people talking to them face to face, than if we ring them. You sure you'll be okay here by yourself?'

'I'll be fine. I don't think they'll come back a second time, do you?'

'They haven't yet,' Matt reassured her.

'Lock the doors in case,' Sam said.

Kate gave him a look. 'Sam, this is a farmhouse,' she said dryly. 'Since when have we ever been able to lock the door? The bloody locks don't work!'

Sam looked sheepish and Matt clapped him on the shoulder. 'Quit while you're ahead, mate,' Matt said. 'Just keep that hockey stick close by, Kate. You'll scare anyone when you're holding it! C'mon, let's see what we can find out.'

He opened the door of the ute and, without being asked, Jasper jumped in and curled up on the passenger's seat.

'Sorry, you might have to share,' said Matt.

Sam opened the door and gently shoved the dog into the middle of the bench seat. 'I don't share my seat with anyone, let alone a dog, even if he has been rescued,' he said jokingly, until Jasper growled.

'Jasper, no,' Matt said sternly. 'You'll have to be a bit careful,' he warned Sam. 'He's not the same dog he was. I'm not sure I trust him not to bite.'

They waved goodbye to Kate and headed down the drive, the puddles reflecting the spotlights.

'So, come on, spill,' said Sam. 'How'd you get him back?'

'Well it's a bit of an odd story. I've never got around to telling you about the strange phone message I got, did I?'

Sam shook his head and Matt relayed the story, stopping only to answer Sam's questions.

'Then I worked out whose the voice was.'

'Really? How?'

'I was at Maggie's shop when I heard it. I didn't really want to meet its owner – I mean, those guys had been talking about murder and owing huge amounts of money. So I thought I'd go around to the main street and see if I could recognise a car or something, never really thinking it could be someone I knew. And there was Jasper in the back of a ute.'

There was silence and then Sam's forehead crinkled as he connected the dots, then looked down at Jasper. 'You're not telling me it was Alec Harper?'

Matt nodded.

Sam shook his head. 'Nah, mate, you've got it wrong. Old Harper has got more money than you and me and half the town put together. There's no way he's got money troubles; even though he's a bit strange, he wouldn't be involved in *murdering* someone.'

'Well that's not what he was saying in the phone message. You want to hear it?' Matt passed over his phone. 'If he's got himself into trouble then I reckon it serves him right.'

Sam raised the phone to his ear and listened attentively. 'Unbelievable,' he muttered when the message had finished. 'Are you sure? This bloke sounds a bit nasal.'

'Yep.' Matt's tone left no room for doubt.

'As does Harper some of the time. I probably

wouldn't have worked out it was him if you hadn't told me. You sure you're not just giving this bloke a hard time 'cos you're pissed off with . . . Okay, okay!' Sam raised his hands in self-defence as Matt threw him a sour look. 'Just thought I'd ask.'

Matt froze as he reached down to turn off the ignition. 'I don't suppose . . .' He gave a funny laugh and shook his head. 'No, surely not.'

'What?' asked Sam.

'We agree it's Alec's voice on the message don't we?' Matt asked.

'Well, yeah,' Sam said slowly. 'I wouldn't like to swear on it in a court of law, though.'

'I just wonder if he's having money problems. Stealing would be a good way to make some more of it.'

'Money?'

'Yeah.'

'Matt, you're off on a wild-goose chase, mate. That bloke has got more money than a bull can shit and the stuff that is going missing wouldn't pay off the farm debt. You know how much he paid for that piece of dirt.'

Matt was silent for a moment, then shrugged his shoulders. 'Yeah, you're probably right. But you have to admit it's weird.'

They pulled up at the pub and Matt shut off the engine. 'It's really too strange to contemplate,' Sam mumured.

'Ready to get out, mate?' Matt asked Jasper gently.

'C'mon then, you can come in; I'm sure Joe will find a spot for you.'

'So, we ready?' Sam asked.

'Yep,' Matt said solemnly. 'Let's go.' He tried not to look across the road at the lights from his house. He imagined Anna reading Ella a story and tucking her in for the night. He knew then she'd allow herself half an hour to relax before cleaning up the kitchen. He shook his head. He couldn't be distracted tonight. He might miss a crucial bit of information.

The warmth from the open fire, laughter and beery fumes hit them as they opened the door and walked in. At a quick glance, Matt could see at least one man he wanted to talk to, but mostly it was the normal Friday-night crowd of young blokes and their girlfriends. He peered into the restaurant area and saw that a few of the tables were full, but there wasn't anyone he knew.

'Want a beer?' asked Sam, pulling his wallet out from his back pocket.

'Yeah, thanks.'

'Hey, Matt,' called Joe from behind the bar. 'Good to see you, but you can't bring the dog in here.'

'Come on, Joe, he's hurt and just getting better. He won't be any trouble.'

'The healthies will yank my licence.'

'They here tonight?'

Matt could see Joe was wavering. 'Oh, stick him under one of the tables – but for goodness sake, don't let him roam around.'

'Cheers, mate. Thanks.' Matt walked over to a booth and slid over against the wall. 'C'mon, Jasper. Get under.' He snapped his fingers and Jasper slunk under the table, curled himself into a ball and sighed happily. Matt reached down to pat him, wondering how on earth he had survived all this time without his mate.

Matt looked up as Sam put down a schooner and saw Gavin Knots, the farmer who had a generator taken about five weeks before.

'Matt, do you know Gavin? Gavin, this is Matt Butler.'

Gavin put out his hand and said, 'I've seen you around but I don't think we've ever spoken.'

'G'day. Thanks for taking the time to talk to us.'

'I don't really know how I can help.' Gavin sat down and took a sip of his beer. 'Do you really think it's like an organised crime thing?'

'Well, I don't know about organised crime,' Matt said, 'but when you look at all the thefts, there's a lot happening in the same area. I guess we're just looking for any detail that might help us tie it all together – maybe you noticed something unusual in the days leading up to the theft of your generator?'

Gavin sat back in his chair, brow furrowed in thought.

'I don't know. I had the machine down by the dam on the road. Anyone could have just driven past, and decided they were going to take it. Gina, my wife, did see a fancy black sports car down there the day before. She remembered it because she wondered if the driver was lost, our road being a dead end and all. And it's not often you see a car like that out here! But I wouldn't think a guy driving a car like that would need a generator.'

'Nah, it sounds unlikely,' Sam agreed. He drained his beer and held up his glass. 'Anyone for another?'

Matt shook his head but Gavin held out his glass. 'A bitter, thanks.'

'Where exactly do you live on the no-through road?' Matt asked, as he shifted his drink from side to side.

'Our house and sheds are about half a k off the main road.'

'So Gina saw a sports car and you found the generator missing the next day?'

Gavin shrugged. 'Well, yeah.'

Matt wrote this in his notebook, his heart thumping. He'd had an encounter with a black sports car in that area before. Could it be the same one? Like Gavin had said, they weren't exactly common around here.

'Anything else?'

'Not really. I'm sorry I can't help more.'

'Thanks anyway.'

Sam returned with the drinks and pushed one over to Gavin. The three men chatted for a while about footy and farming, but as soon as the others had finished their drinks Matt slid out from behind the table.

'Look, I'm sorry I can't help you more,' Gavin said, following Matt's lead. 'How about I ask around a bit, see if anyone else has noticed anything strange. You never know who is on the road at night.'

'Ain't that the truth,' Sam said ruefully.

'That's dead right,' Matt said at the same time and all three men grinned. 'I'd really appreciate that, Gav. Here's my mobile.' He handed over a card with his contact details and held out his hand. 'Catch you around sometime.' He turned his attention to Sam and said, 'Let's head over to the Snowtown pub and see if Jamie Truton is there.'

Sam looked surprised until Matt said. 'There isn't anyone else here that's been affected.' After thanking Gavin again for his help, he followed Matt and Jasper out into the night.

The ute was cold and they had to wait for the engine to heat up. Matt finally gave up and looked over at his old house. All the lights were off. For a moment he wished Anna was sitting beside him, before reminding himself that she never would have agreed to help him in his investigation.

He sighed, patted Jasper and accelerated out of the car park, heading for the lonely dirt road that would take them to Snowtown.

Sam did the talking, bringing him up to date on some of the local news and for once it didn't bother Matt. He was surprised to learn that the local merchandise store had changed hands and saddened to hear a local farmer had been diagnosed with cancer, his farm now on the market. His mind leapt automatically to the idea of buying it, until reality came quickly crashing in.

As they drew closer to Snowtown, Matt noticed there were red tail-lights on the road in front of him. His heart started to beat a little faster and instinctively he pushed his foot down harder on the accelerator.

Sam stopped talking as the speedo climbed to one hundred and twenty kilometres an hour and higher. 'What are you doing, Matt?' he asked calmly. 'You're on a dirt road. Slow down.'

'Just want to catch this car.'

'Why?'

Matt stared at the red glow of the lights in front. 'Well, like you said, we're on a dirt road. Who'd be cruising along here at this time of night? It might be the sports car.'

'And it might not be – it's a bit of a long shot, mate, and if it's okay with you, I'd like to live. Slow down.'

Matt hesitated then lifted his foot a fraction, and the car began to slow. Out of the corner of his eye he saw Sam watching him, a puzzled look on his face. Matt supposed he did sound a bit obsessed, but now he was following a trail he couldn't help himself.

'It's not so late that it's strange to see a car on the road,' Sam commented quietly. After all, we're here.'

'But that's the point, isn't it?' Matt asked.

They saw the car up ahead flick on its blinkers, indicating it was going to turn into a farm driveway. Suddenly from the edge of the darkness, a large grey kangaroo jumped onto the road and froze in the headlights. Matt swung the car gently to the left. He struggled for control as the car fishtailed to the right before straightening. The kangaroo bounded off unharmed.

Matt heard Sam let out a breath.

'Okay, okay, you were right,' Matt said. 'Sorry. I just thought it might have been worth following.'

'None of this is worth your life,' was all Sam said.

Chapter 36

'So, you ready?' asked Kate as she lifted the last esky into the back of the minivan.

Anna climbed into the front of the van, smothering a yawn. Being up and about at four am wasn't her idea of fun, but at least Matt had agreed to come over early and spend the day with Ella.

'I can't believe we're up this early,' she said as Kate started the van.

'Ah, stop your whingeing,' her friend said jokingly. 'You wait, Anna – you'll love the markets. There's heaps of stuff there: meat, fresh fruit and veggies. There's even homemade sweets and jams. Cooking demonstrations. It's awesome, I love it and, don't worry, there's a man with coffee. His name is – wait for it – Tootles.'

'Tootles? Riiiight.' Anna crinkled her brow and stared out the window as the bright headlights picked up bush on the side of the road, casting strange shadows.

'Lovely bloke, but a bit like the name: odd. Hey, Anna, thanks for helping me with this. Sam just didn't have time to do it with seeding. I need someone to help me get everything inside and with the rush of customers. You should see what it's like when they first open the doors. People just swarm in. Sometimes the lines are three people deep. All the noise and bustle make it quite hard to hear what people want, so we'll have to concentrate. It's bedlam for the first couple of hours, then everything seems to settle down a bit.'

Kate took a corner a bit fast and Anna heard a thud in the back as the eskies slid around.

They followed the winding road until it opened to a long straight stretch near Adelaide and Kate pushed her foot to the floor. Still the old van wouldn't go above eighty kilometres per hour, and it vibrated like crazy. Anna was sure she'd have a headache by the time they made it to the markets.

She felt around on the floor for the thermos and cups. 'Coffee?'

'Yes please,' Kate replied.

'Why don't you buy a decent van, Kate? You've got the money!'

'Yeah, I know,' she said above the roar of the engine. 'I think Sam wanted to make sure I was going to keep going with this business before he invested in a good van. I love doing this, though. It just gives me a bit of independence – and I love knowing that people like my product enough to keep coming back. It means I'm doing a good job.'

The traffic increased the closer they got to the city, and when they reached the market grounds Anna stared in amazement. 'Bloody hell, look at all these people.' There were people blowing up balloons and setting out fresh fruit and vegetables. A lady was hauling jars of preserves out of boxes, others were setting up cooking demonstrations and firing up the barbecues to cook tasters on. There were trestle tables full of produce; one man had piled his table so high with carrots that Anna was sure that they would all fall to the ground the moment someone passed by or accidentally knocked them.

The markets seemed to buzz with their own energy and the aroma of freshly baked bread and coffee made her mouth water.

In the distance, Anna could see a busker holding a guitar. She wondered what sort of music he would play – his dreadlocks and goatee beard made her think it would be something rather alternative.

'And these are just the vendors!' Kate smiled. 'Come on, we're a bit late.'

Kate parked the van and they hurried inside. Anna followed Kate as she pushed her way through the throng of people to a storeroom. Inside she grabbed hold of an empty meat fridge. 'Let's get this out to our bay. It's over that way. She waved towards the southern end of the shed.

Once at their area Kate handed Anna a striped beach tent and some banners. 'Get as much frontage with the signage as you can without the old bloke over there getting grumpy. He'll let you know if you're out too far.'

Anna's eyes strayed to the unshaven man wearing a terry-towelling hat selling flowers and she grinned. He had a mean look in his eye. She did as she was told and then together they returned to the van and began to lug in the large eskies of meat. Kate expertly set up the lamb chops, roasts, patties, sausages and other cuts of meat she'd brought, got out her cash tin and sat down.

'Okay, we're ready. Do you want to have a quick look around? You've got about . . .' she checked her watch, 'fifteen minutes.'

'Yeah, I'd love to! Do you want me to grab you a coffee? Which way is Tootles?'

Kate pointed and settled back in her chair. 'Just follow the crowd but don't be long,' she warned. 'You'll get run over in the rush when it's opening time!'

Anna pushed her way towards the makeshift café, where she could see people lined up two deep waiting for coffee and something to eat. It was almost like a café on Rundle Street. The food was high quality and beautifully prepared and even though they were in a shed, Tootles and his staff had set up umbrellas above the outdoor seating. Anna could only imagine how gorgeous that coffee would taste.

A stall selling handmade bags caught her eye and she went over for a closer look. The lady, who wore her hair in a braid fastened with a yellow ribbon, picked up a bright pink bag with a black cat sewn onto the front and asked if she had a daughter.

'Yes, I do and she would love that,' Anna answered, fingering the stitching.

'It's yours for twenty-five dollars.'

Anna hesitated, then pulled out the money and handed it over. She would put it away for a Christmas present.

Anna thanked the lady and moved on, finding it hard not to stare at all the people. It seemed that alternative was the norm here. Young groovy uni students were beginning to make their way through the gates along with older couples, who looked like they had given up their professional lifestyle and clothing choice and branched out into the organic, grunge style of life.

Then she heard someone call her name.

'Anna! Anna Butler!'

She turned around to see Belinda Lyons walking towards her.

'Anna, how are you? I wouldn't have expected to see you here,' Belinda said, smiling.

'I could have said the same about you! I'm fine, thanks. I'm just here helping a friend. It's great to see you!'

'Ha! The same. My friend Jasmine – see the girl over there with all the braids and a nose ring? She grows herbs in the Adelaide Hills and dries them. I come every Sunday to give her a hand. Shane gets some quality time alone with the kids and I get some time just for me. It works really well. And I get to buy my meat for the week while I'm here.'

'Well, that's great,' said Anna, feeling a tightening in her chest as Belinda talked about happy families. 'Look, I'd love to stay and chat, but I was just on my way to get a coffee before opening. Kate's warned me I'm not to be late back!'

Belinda put her hand on Anna's arm. 'Of course. It can be crazy here at opening time. But listen, before you go, we were so sorry to hear about you and Matt. If there's anything we can do, please tell us.'

Anna couldn't bring herself to meet the other woman's eye, so instead she focused on Belinda's bracelet. It was gold and engraved with two entwined letters. The symbol seemed familiar, but she couldn't place it. Finally, when she felt sure her voice would be steady, she looked up and smiled tightly. 'Thanks, Belinda, but I'm doing all right. Maybe we could catch up for coffee one day? Not sure when I'll be back in Adelaide but you never know.'

Belinda smiled. 'I'd like that. Take care, hey?'

'You too!' She turned and walked back to Kate.

'Where's the coffee?' asked Kate as Anna ducked in behind the display cabinet, tears in her eyes. 'Shit, what's wrong?'

'It's nothing. I just ran into one of Matt's trucking mate's wives, Belinda. She was just saying she was sorry we'd split. She was being too nice to me, when I need to crack hardy! Although I bet she and Shane had already talked about whether it was going to happen or not. Bloody hell, she saw what Matt did that night and Shane would've told her about his little outburst!' She swiped at her cheeks.

'Anna you're going to have to get used to people offering sympathy. How else can they show they care? So many people do and you can't be tough all the time. Uh-oh, look out. Doors are open.' She stood up and handed Anna a pair of plastic gloves. 'You pack and weigh, I'll do the money.'

Several hours later, Anna and Kate collapsed into their chairs, exhausted.

'You deserve a bloody medal for doing this every Sunday, Kate!' Anna looked at the eskies and display cabinet. There was not a single piece of meat left, just the parsley Kate had decorated it with.

'Awesome isn't it? I get such a buzz out of it. I love sharing what I grow with other people – and there's a huge market for it.' Kate's eyes were glowing.

'I think you're on a winner,' Anna said. Her eyes strayed over to where Belinda was helping her friend pack up and she nudged Kate. 'That's her,' she said quietly.

Kate looked over. 'What, the chick with the dreads?' she asked, surprise in her voice.

'Nah, the other one.'

'Well they're both a bit different. I can't think of anyone I know who'd wear so much jewellery to something like this! She looks like she'd jangle every time she moved! Got a bit of money have they?'

'Oh yeah. But they've got some costs as well: four boys, to begin with!'

'Ah. Glutton for punishment.' Kate tilted her head to one side. 'I reckon I've seen her before.'

'She comes here every Sunday to help out her friend apparently. It's Shane's time with the kids.'

'Oh, that must be it. I could have sworn I'd seen her in Clare or somewhere else out our way. Well, let's get packed up and get home so you can see Ella and Matt.'

Anna replied sharply, 'I don't need to see Matt, Kate. We're not together anymore. I only need to see him when he picks Ella up and drops her off. He'd better have looked after her well. Especially after his last try.'

'Rubbish. I can't believe you've fallen out of love with him that quickly. And of course he'll look after Ella really well. You can be a bit hard on him sometimes.'

Anna shot Kate a murderous glance and started to haul the empty eskies back out to the van. Half an hour later they were on their way back to Spalding.

Anna stared out of the window at the passing countryside, thinking about Ella. She couldn't wait to get home to give her a hug. She might even give her the bag today. Of course, Ella might not be home;

Matt had been planning to take her to his parents' place – which was just as well, she reminded herself. It would be too painful to come home and find him there, even though she missed him dreadfully. Still, the thought of going home to a cold, empty house when she was tired and her back ached was depressing.

'Anna, I've got something to tell you,' Kate said in a low voice as she glanced in the rear-view mirror. 'I've been trying to work out how to talk to you about this for the last couple of weeks.'

Intrigued, Anna turned to Kate. 'That sounds interesting,' she said.

'Matt came to tea the other night and we were talking about the things which have been stolen around here. He's really put a lot of work into investigating it, Anna – and we're sure he's on to something here.'

'You are kidding me, aren't you?' Anna stared at her friend.

'No, I'm not. The amount of detail he has collected really ...'

'Oh far out, this has gone on long enough,' interrupted Anna, unexpectedly losing her temper. 'Surely he hasn't got you wrapped up in his ridiculous obsession too.'

'It's not crazy. We honestly believe there's a problem around here. Anna, we're going to help Matt find whoever did this, whether it's through active investigation or lobbying the police. I know you're not going to like the idea, but at some stage, when you're not as angry as you are now, ask me and I'll tell you all the information we have and why we believe this is important.'

'I can't believe this.' Anna crossed her arms. 'It's so stupid – you told me how hopeless it is yourself! You've seen Matt ignore Ella and I, not come home at night just to spend time investigating it. Time he could have spent with us. You know how much it's hurt me. It's the whole reason Matt and I split.'

'Yeah, I know. And I do understand, Anna!' Kate took a hand off the steering wheel and reached over to touch her arm. 'I've changed my mind because of the facts.'

'Facts? What facts? No, don't tell me.' Anna held up her hand. 'I'm not interested.'

Kate opened her mouth to speak, but Anna just shook her head. 'I don't want to hear about it, Kate.' She turned and looked out of the window, not believing what she had just heard. Her friends who had stood by her through everything had just betrayed her.

The rest of the trip back to Spalding was a very quiet one.

Chapter 37

'G'day, fellas, that your truck out there?'

Matt looked up from the steak he was eating to see a young police officer looking at them enquiringly.

Shane frowned and said, 'Yeah, why?'

'There have been a few little incidents with things going missing out of the trucks' cabs, so we're just trying to put drivers to rigs. Know who's with what company and so on.'

Matt looked at the police officer in surprise. 'Really?' he asked. He hadn't heard anything about it, and it was the sort of news which would travel quickly around the community of truckies. They were always talking on the radio as they passed each other, telling of road conditions or experiences they'd had with good or stupid drivers. Of course there had been the conversation with Jimmy, Shane and Janey, but that was months ago now and they had been talking trailers, goods, and farms not cabs and personal items.

'Yeah, it's only been happening over the last week or so, but we want to put a stop to it straight away. No need to upset you blokes or the companies you work for. You guys bring a fair bit of money into our towns when you stop here.'

'I thought you blokes were just around to make our lives difficult,' Shane said rudely. He pushed his plate away and got up from the table. 'If you want me, I'll be protecting the truck,' he said, and left the dining room.

Matt stared in bewilderment then shrugged up at the policeman. 'Sorry 'bout that. Don't know what's got into him.'

'He does have a point. We've been known to give you all curry at times. So listen, just make sure your trucks are locked up tight when you're stopping for a sleep or a feed. It's not actually the freight you're carting being taken; it's your own personal things out of the front. A bloke who drives for a stock-carrying company had his iPod, fridge and wallet taken from here a couple of days ago. Probably just young kids looking to make a quick buck, but you need to know.'

Matt frowned. 'Yeah, righto. I'll keep my eyes open and everything locked.'

'Good on you. Drive safe.' The officer raised his hand in farewell and he walked away.

Matt looked around the roadhouse and out through the windows to where Shane was pacing agitatedly around the truck. A bright yellow sign caught his eye and he realised it was new: *Keep your vehicles locked. No responsibility taken by management.*

He snorted. Bloody typical. Nobody wanted to take responsibility for anything these days. Police included, in his experience.

Matt finished up his steak and thought about what the police officer had said, then shook his head. It was just a sign of the times. Twenty years ago it probably never would have happened. Then he laughed at himself. How old are you again, Granddad?

Out in the car park, Shane was pacing around the truck, Jasper following him. Matt went over.

'What's the matter, mate?' he asked.

'Bloody cops,' Shane snarled.

'Why? They were only giving us a bit of a warning about what's happening around the place. Wouldn't be too good if we lost our fridges or stuff from the cab. He was only giving us the heads up.'

'Oh, it's the cab, is it? Well Jasper wouldn't let them in, would he? But yeah, yeah, I know. They pulled me up last week on the way to Broken Hill saying they wanted to check my tyres and paperwork. I've no problem with them doing their job, but they stuffed around, checking the rego and shit they don't usually bother with. It made me run late for a drop-off for the train. Missed the bloody thing and then Jimmy gets an irate phone call from the station owners who were expecting something really important. Cops think they own the show.'

'Yeah, well, this guy wasn't the one who did it to you. Give him a break.'

'You're one to talk. You're usually pretty cranky with cops in general too.'

'This bloke was trying to help.' Matt looked at Shane. 'Mate, you're really wound up. Is there something else the matter?'

'No,' Shane said forcefully, then he sighed. 'Not really. It's just that I'm missing Tom's birthday today.'

Matt understood. It was never easy being away from home on a special day.

'Ah, right. Well, we're on our way home now, so let's get a move on. You might be able to make it home before he goes to bed.'

Shane shot him a grateful smile and turned back towards the truck. 'You gonna take the wheel?'

'Yep, you have a camp and get rested up for seeing your family tonight.' He climbed into the driver's seat and hit the key, feeling the truck tremble beneath his hands. He waited until Shane was settled and the curtains in the sleeper cab were drawn, then turned the music on softly, shifted the gearstick and let out the clutch. They were going home. And he would be seeing Ella in a day or two.

An hour later, Matt was mesmerised by the white lines and, feeling a little sleepy, stretched out his arms, trying to get his blood circulating. He looked over to the side mirror and saw nothing. Slim Dusty's song 'Lights on the Hill' slipped into his mind and he swore. That song only ever came to him when he was too tired to be driving. It had seemed a long run this time, not helped by his constant thoughts of the investigation. Gav had rallied and unexpectedly Matt had received a few phone calls with dribs and drabs of information. He'd been trying to follow up on all of it.

Wishing he could turn the music up, but not wanting to wake Shane, he risked looking over his shoulder. The curtains were still drawn together. Perhaps he could, he thought as he leaned over to turn the volume up slightly. Just a little.

A movement in the rear-view mirror caught his eye and a rush of adrenalin shot through him.

A black car was hurtling up behind him. It had to be the same car. It was acting as erratically as the time when Kate had been run off the road.

Matt's heart started to beat faster. His hands tightened around the steering wheel and he instinctively took his foot off the accelerator, waiting to see what the car would do. 'C'mon, you bastard, pass me – I want to see who you are,' he muttered.

'What's that?' Shane's voice came from the depths of the cave.

'Oh, nothing, mate,' Matt answered. 'There's a car behind that looks a bit like the one that pushed me off the road a while back. I'm wondering if it could be the same one.'

Shane unzipped the curtains and clambered through to the front, peering into the rear-vision mirror as he slid into the passenger's seat.

'Jeez, he's going a bit quick.'

Matt took a deep breath as the car pulled out to pass. 'Here we go,' he said.

Both men watched as the car sprang forward and gained ground, overtaking them as quickly as it had appeared in the mirror.

As it passed the driver's side door, Matt looked down and his eyes widened with a mixture of amusement and disgust as he saw a young woman with her shirt open, the driver's hand down caressing her breast. The woman looked up at Matt and ran her tongue over her lips suggestively.

'Idiots! Check this out,' Matt said.

Shane leaned forward. 'What is it? I can't see.'

'He's trying to chop her up and she doesn't mind letting everyone know it.' It was the way truckies talked about sex in the cab of a truck. Chopping them up. Matt had never worked out the correlation. It sounded terrible!

The sports car wobbled over the middle white line and back over to the left-hand side of the road, pulling away from Matt and Shane quickly.

'I bet we see them in the next parking bay or

motel. Don't know why they have to put everyone else on the road at risk by doing that sort of shit while they're driving,' Matt said crossly.

'Heard a couple of blokes talking on the CB about a little business a couple of local girls have got going back there at Ceduna. Seems they think us blokes need a little bit of home comfort while we're away.' Shane shot a glance at Matt, his eyebrows raised.

'Not for me,' Matt said firmly.

'You never know. It's there if you need it.'

Matt fought down disgust at the prospect of sex with anyone other than Anna, then turned his concentration back to the sports car. It was almost out of sight.

'I wish I'd seen the driver better, but the car sure looked the same,' he said.

'Did you get the number plate of the other car?'

'Nah, he just went past so quickly,' Matt replied, then he had an idea. 'I should be recording the number plates so I know if I've seen the car more than once!' he exclaimed. 'Why didn't I think of that before now?'

'That would be one way of knowing,' Shane agreed. 'There are some wankers on the road, no two ways about it.'

They settled back into silence, watching the low, scrubby bush interspersed with farming land go by. It was dry and desolate out here and Matt had wondered more than once how the farmers out this way made any money. The crop stubbles were thin and the sheep always looked like they were struggling to find something to eat.

As they slowed down to drive through Wirrulla they saw the black car parked at the pub.

'There they are,' Shane said. 'Bet they've got themselves a room.'

Matt eased his foot off the pedal again and the road train pulled up slowly.

'What are you doing?'

'I've gotta see this bloke,' he said. 'I need to know it wasn't him.'

Shane looked over at him. 'Mate, you need to let it go. How're you gonna know anyway?'

'I don't know, but I need to eyeball him. I'll explain later, but it's really important that I do.'

With the engine still running, Matt noted the number plate, jumped down from the cab and ran across the road, flinging open the pub door. A few old-timers nursing half-empty schooners turned to look at him as he scanned the front bar and then made his way to the dining room. There was the blonde woman from the car, sitting with a large, muscly dark-haired man. Crossing the room, he walked to the toilets and looked back over his shoulder to see the man from behind.

The woman must have recognised his face because she blushed when she looked up and saw him standing there. The man turned around.

It wasn't him. Or was it? Matt really didn't know.

Disappointment flooded through him and he felt stupid. What did you expect? he asked himself. There must be heaps of black sports cars around.

He turned and almost ran into Shane, who had followed him.

'Was it him, mate?' Shane asked when they got outside.

'Can't be sure, but I don't think so.'

'Mate, you're like a dog with a bone. Once you make up your mind to do something, nothing is going to stop you.'

'You are dead right,' Matt said. 'You are *dead right*.'

'How are you going to tell when it's the right one?' Shane asked curiously. 'You don't seem to know much about the car or the driver.'

Matt thought about that and he realised that Shane was right. Did he imagine he would actually recognise the man when he saw him?

He shrugged, not really knowing the answer. The one thing he was certain of was a black car seemed to equal thefts. His fatigue forgotten, Matt climbed back into the truck. If he had to stop and check every one of them until he found the one he was looking for, he would damn well do it, he vowed.

Chapter 38

Dave Burrows stared at the whiteboard, frowning. He glanced back to the map that was lying open on his desk and once again retraced the roads to all the farms that had had items stolen from them.

There was definitely something here, but what? Briefly he thought of ringing Craig, his ex-partner, who'd lost his heart to a South Aussie girl and gave up policing to marry her, then remembered that he was away overseas, holidaying. Craig wouldn't be any use.

Neither would the new cop Dave had just been paired up with. The third one in as many years. No one seemed to want to work in the stock squad anymore. It was pretty clear the State Government didn't support the squad either. Cutbacks on spending made it difficult to operate and there were times he felt he was fighting a one-man battle and that he was a dying breed.

The phone call he'd received from Kate the day before had sent the familiar surge of adrenalin through him. Her tale of thefts and unhelpful policemen had sounded more than intriguing.

'Dave, I think we've got a problem that might be right up your alley. We reckon we've got a serial robber working over here.'

Dave had wanted to burst into fits of laughter at Kate's terminology and serious tone, but he knew better.

'Why do you say that?

'Well it all started when our mate Matt had fertiliser taken from his paddock. You've talked to my friend Anna, remember?'

'Yep, I do.'

'Since then we've found another ten farmers around the district – including us – who have had things taken, from chemicals to fencing gear, utes and generators – even bales of wool!

'We had only three thefts this year, but the more investigation and talking we do, the more we find. Most of them are small things one person can take, like the generator or the fencing gear, but you'd need two people to pinch a ute, and the chemical too. It was in big hundred-litre enviro-drums, so one bloke isn't going to be able to load them on the back of a ute by himself unless he's got a forklift – and if he did have a forklift, then surely someone would have seen lights or heard noises.

'Another couple of things that seem to tie the thefts together is that all except two blokes have seen a black sports car in the area shortly before they were robbed, and all the farms are either on no-through roads or they're quite isolated. I know you think our areas aren't remote compared to the top of WA, but when it comes to the ranges leading up to the Flinders they are. There's not a lot of traffic, unless it's local. To see a strange car is pretty unusual.'

'Have you got a list of dates and the items that were taken?' Dave asked.

'Yep, I can email it to you. Sam and Matt have been talking to all the fellas who were robbed so they've got as much info as the police. But like I told you, the cops don't seem to care. All they've done is give every one of us an incident report for insurance and leave it at that. That's why I'm calling you. Do you think you could help us?'

'Kate, I can't do anything officially – I'm not part of the South Australian police force. But look, send me your list and if I think there's something there, I'll let you know – but this is just between you and me, okay?'

'Dave, you're a legend. I'll shoot the email off straight away.'

As he went through the information Kate had sent, Dave knew there was something amiss. He tapped his fingers on the table, wondering who he should call in the South Australian police. He flicked through his files and took out a dog-eared business card, then dialled the mobile phone number, hoping Geoff Hay, the police officer he had dealt with when he'd been investigating the stock stealing in Port Pirie, was still around.

The phone was answered. 'Hay.'

'G'day, Geoff. It's Dave Burrows from the WA Stock Squad. How are you?'

There was a silence in which Geoff must have connected the name with the man he had met three or four years before, then he said, 'Well I'll be buggered! Dave Burrows. How are you, mate? And to what do I owe the pleasure?'

'Yeah, it's been a while. You still in Port Pirie?'

'No, I shifted about two years ago. I'm in Adelaide now, heading up the major crash unit.'

'Great stuff. Look I've had some good drum land on my desk and I've been throwing it around for a bit. Can you tip me into someone who can help me with it, or can you lend a hand yourself?'

'Things are a bit slow here at the moment, so give it to me and I'll see what I can do. What's it about?'

'Seems to be some goods going missing from farms in the middle of SA – not as high up as before, more around the Spalding/Clare area with a radius of about two to three hundred kilometres. With the details I've got, and the experience I've had over here, I'd say there's something going on.'

'Sounds interesting.'

'Between you and me, it's my cousin who's put me on to it – they've had a collector's motorbike taken and their mate lost a truckload of fertiliser. There's plenty of other goods been walking as well. What do you reckon – should I send it through?'

'Yeah, mate. Give us the details and I'll have a look. What's your number?'

Dave recited his number and then said, 'From what my cousin says they've no idea who's doing it but one thing that seems to be a constant is a black sports car seen in the area. No number plate, but surely there can't be too many black sports cars around there. A couple of the blokes seemed to think it might be a Mazda RX-8.'

Geoff whistled. 'Flash. All right, leave it with me. I'll get back to you.'

Dave hung up the phone and turned back to the whiteboard. Then something occurred to him, and he typed in the address of the Bureau of Meteorology's website and clicked on moon phases. He looked back at the dates that Kate had supplied him with, then checked every single one against the information on the computer. Then he nodded. Whoever was doing this was pretty organised. They only stole on moonlit nights, which would explain why no one reported seeing any lights. They wouldn't be needed. Nor would anyone take any notice if their dogs were a bit noisier than usual. Every dog barked during the full moon.

'Look out, whoever you are,' Dave murmured, excitement filling him. 'The coppers are coming and we'll find you.'

Chapter 39

Matt cleaned up his plate and frying pan from dinner and then wondered what he would do with the rest of his evening. Jimmy was busy tonight and so far he had seen nothing that interested him on TV.

He'd kept it turned on anyway, for noise and company. Jasper settled at his feet.

With the love and care Matt had showered on him since he'd grabbed him from the back of Harper's ute, Jasper's coat had become glossy and he didn't wince when he was patted. Whenever he looked at Matt, his mouth hung open in a huge doggy smile. Seeing the difference in him, Matt knew he should have listened to Anna the first time she took him.

'She tried to get me to take you, didn't she, old mate?' he said, patting Jasper's head. 'She's always been good at reading people. I should have listened to her.'

Jasper thumped his tail on the floor and grinned at Matt.

Restless, Matt picked up his mobile phone and replayed the message he had kept. He was now certain that one of the voices belonged to Alec Harper, but there was something else. The more he listened to the message, the more convinced he became there was something else in the call he recognised, but it was just beyond his reach. He was sure if he kept listening and thinking it would come to him.

He'd spoken with Jimmy about it and he had been just as bemused as Matt himself.

'I don't like the sound of that message, lad,' Jimmy had said. 'There're some tough things happening there. You'd best keep well away from it.'

'If I thought the coppers would do something, I'd take it to them.'

Jimmy shook his head. 'Steer clear of something like that. Delete it and forget about it.'

But that had been easier said than done.

The problem was he still didn't understand why the message had ended up on his phone. It haunted him during the early morning hours when he couldn't sleep and nagged at him along those long straight stretches of the highway when there was nothing but him and the road.

Why? Why him?

Man and dog sat there for a while but still restless and agitated, Matt got up again. 'This is stupid. It's not even 6.30 pm and I haven't got anything to do.

Let's see what Jimmy's got downstairs in the way of freight. We're supposed to be heading to Broken Hill next run. I wonder what we'll be carrying.'

Jasper leapt to his feet and barked.

Together they headed downstairs. As they got to the bottom, Matt heard his mobile phone ring and groaned, but realising it might be Ella calling to say goodnight, he ran up the stairs two at a time, Jasper trying to keep up. He snatched the phone off the table just as it stopped ringing.

'Bugger.'

The phone registered a missed call from Sam, so Matt called his friend's number. He'd been waiting for this call.

Sam answered on the first ring. 'G'day, Matt.'

'How're you going? Got any news?'

'Yeah, Dave's keen. He reckons you're on to something. He's waiting to hear back from someone in the police department over here to see what the next step is.'

Matt let out a breath and shut his eyes in relief. It felt like a huge weight had been lifted from his shoulders. Finally someone who had the power to do something believed him. 'Bloody brilliant,' he said quietly.

'Thought you'd be pleased. And look, there's something else. Kate found a message on the answering machine last night. Just let me swap phones so I can play it to you.'

Matt listened as Sam fumbled with the receiver then heard the long high squeal as the two phones fed into each other.

'Okay, can you hear?' asked Sam.

'Yep.'

'Right, here we go.'

'I know you're asking questions. Stop it now. Or someone will get hurt.'

Matt frowned. 'Did it say to stop asking questions?' he asked as Sam came back on to the phone.

'Yep. I think we're on the right track, don't you?'

'Well, yeah,' he said slowly, 'can you tell whether the voice is male or female?'

'Female we think,' Sam responded. 'Although it's a bit muffled.'

'I wonder how serious she is about hurting someone.' Matt mused. 'We've obviously stepped on some toes. Just makes me a bit nervous after all the talk of murder and money in the other message. I guess we should be nervous, but I'd be more inclined to think that we've annoyed someone and they're warning us off, rather than wanting to act. Does Dave know about it?'

'I'll let him know when he calls back. I guess we just keep on going as we have been, eh?'

'Yeah,' Matt said slowly, wondering if that was the right thing to do. Maybe they should just ring Dave again and tell him. Get his advice. Then he gave a snort of laughter. 'Yep, that's exactly what we should do. I mean, we're normal people. It's not like we're about to get taken down by the Mafia or something!'

Sam chuckled. 'Right you are. Talk to you when I know a bit more.'

Matt hung up, thinking about the conversation he'd already had with Jimmy and how he'd been as bemused as Matt had.

He flicked open his notebook, his hand hovering with the pen. He had no idea what to write. He wondered for a moment if the two strange messages could be related, but quickly dismissed the idea. One was male – Alec, as they knew – and the other voice was female. Plus two completely different phones. The only link was Sam and he were friends.

Matt kept pondering, but couldn't come up with anything logical, so he stuffed the mobile in his pocket and headed off downstairs again, his mind still whirling. He wandered between the pallets of washing machines and fridges, crates of smaller electrical items and parts for machinery. Finally he pushed his way right to the back of the shed and started looking at the beer and wine.

He always got a bit of a kick when it was clear he was carrying a birthday or Christmas present, but it all looked like mundane freight this time.

As he turned, a door almost hidden in the shadows caught his eye. He'd never noticed it before in the corner of the two joining back walls. Puzzled he walked in between the crates and pallets, Jasper at his heels.

When pushed the door swung open quietly and easily. He put a foot inside, his hand feeling for a light switch and, with a click, the room was bathed in light from a single naked bulb.

His eyes adjusted to the brightness and he looked around. It was just an empty storeroom.

Matt shrugged and was about to leave the room when he noticed a dip in the floor. Taking a step forward he realised it was a trapdoor. He eyed it curiously then reached down and tugged on the hefty iron ring, but it wouldn't budge.

Interesting, he thought. He considered trying again, then decided against it. His nerves were buzzing from Sam's phone call.

It was pretty rude of him to be fossicking around in Jimmy's shed when he knew he shouldn't have been here in the first place. Matt turned and walked out of the storeroom, but as he did he felt his boots crunch on something and he looked down. There was a trail of dried green leaves. They looked like tea leaves. He stooped down to get a closer look at them and Jasper nosed his way in underneath his armpit for a pat.

'Get out of the way,' Matt said quietly, still staring at the leaves on the floor. He squeezed one between his fingers then brought his hand to his nose and sniffed.

His mobile phone rang and he jumped at the shrill tone reverberating around the silent shed.

'Hello?' he said, still staring at his fingers.

'Matt, it's Shane, mate. What are you up to?'

'Not much, mate.'

'Good. I've got tomorrow off and I need to get out of the house. Kids are driving me nuts! Want to go for a beer?'

Matt looked around. That was just the thing to keep his mind off what he'd just found.

'I've got a run tomorrow, but I can catch up for an hour or so. I'll meet you at the front gate.'

'See you in thirty.'

Matt brushed his hands off and watched as Jasper sniffed the ground closely.

'Yeah, I'm a bit curious too, my friend. Anyway, we've got plans now. Let's go.'

He walked to the stairs, his mind whirling. Finally, curiosity got the better of him. He ran back up to his loft and grabbed a torch and screwdriver, then went back to the storeroom. He looked at the floor and then over at the trapdoor. He grabbed the thick circle of steel and pulled. It didn't budge. Levering the screwdriver in between the cracks he tried to loosen it. Finally the door cracked open and he found himself staring into a cellar. He flashed the torch around, and gasped at what the beam of light picked up. A motorbike. It looked like an old collector's piece. He lay on his stomach and stuck his head all the way into the underground room.

Jasper tried to squeeze in too and barked when Matt pushed him away. The woof thumped into the rammed earth walls and dirt floor and was muffled.

Matt's curiosity had just turned to fear because this room looked like it could easily be used as a cell.

Unbidden, he thought of the scream he had heard in the hills near Spalding and the tail-gating vehicle. Then he shook himself.

'Don't be bloody ridiculous.'

He flashed the torch around some more and picked up a dirt ramp that headed towards the surface. At the top of that were two iron doors big enough to get a forklift in and out of – and the room itself was definitely large enough for a forklift or ute to get into. Other than the motorbike the room was empty, but there were pallets leaning against the wall.

Matt turned his attention back to the bike. He searched for some kind of identifying feature, but he didn't really need to. He knew whose bike it was. What he didn't know was what it was doing here.

The air was like ice when Matt walked out of the shed. He zipped up his thick jacket and shoved his hands in his pockets. Glancing at the night sky, he looked for the stars even though he knew he wouldn't be able to see them for the glow of the city lights. The hum of traffic in the background was ever present.

Trying to investigate the thefts had lost all its appeal. None of what he'd seen or heard tonight made any sense. He could see it was all linked together but couldn't work out how to join the dots. He hadn't thought about the scream in ages and with the other finds tonight, it had well and truly unsettled him. Agitated, he ran his fingers through his hair and he wondered how he had reached this point. Anna had been right. He should have left it to the police. He was a farmer, not a truckie. A boring old farmer, who wanted to be working outdoors, not confined to a cab – and certainly not tangled up in investigating some sort of organised crime ring. He'd wanted to laugh when Gavin had used those words back in the pub at Spalding. Organised Crime in Spalding? Maybe it wasn't so crazy.

It wasn't his job to solve crimes. If the police had done their job in the first place, none of this would be happening, he thought angrily.

He stood at the gate waiting for Shane, thinking about what he had seen in the underground room. The warmth of Jasper against his leg was comforting. He had to be mistaken. There was no way Sam's motorbike could have ended up in that shed – not unless someone he *knew* had taken it.

That revelation more than frightened him. No, this couldn't go on. He couldn't wait for Dave any longer. He would have to make a phone call to the police. Matt nodded to himself and finally felt his inner turmoil settle. He was sure it was the right thing to do.

A bitter wind lifted his hair at the back of his collar and as he turned it up against the cold he heard something behind him. He looked searchingly out into the dull night. He was on edge, but it probably wasn't that surprising, considering what he'd just seen.

Matt bent down to pat his friend and felt Jasper tense, looking keenly to the left, his ears cocked. Then a low, angry growl sounded.

'What's up?' he asked, quickly standing up and looking around again. 'It's all right. It's only you and me here. You're probably feeling a bit nervous too. I certainly am. I can't believe we've got mixed up in some sort of . . . Jasper!' Matt screamed as pain burst through his legs, and he fell to the ground clutching at his calf.

Simultaneously Jasper let out a ferocious snarl then lunged at an outline in the darkness. Matt heard a thump, a yelp and then silence. He tried to scramble to his feet, but his knees gave way. 'Jasper? *Jasper?*' Matt's voice broke. 'Who the fuck are you?' he yelled into the night. 'What do you want?'

Silence.

Matt swung his head from side to side, trying to see. He reached out his hands, feeling for Jasper, but he didn't connect with the warm body. 'What do you want?' he asked again, quieter this time.

Slowly, Matt stood up, keeping his weight on his good leg. He wobbled for a moment then tried to take a step when an arm snaked around his throat and held him in a chokehold. Matt's hand flew to his attacker's arms, trying frantically to break the grip, but the hold couldn't be loosened.

From the darkness there was another snarl – Jasper – but his attacker kicked out and, at the same time, threw Matt to the ground and kicked him in the stomach. Groaning, he rolled himself into a ball, trying to shield himself from any further blows.

There was a flurry of movement then a cry of pain from the attacker and a heavy thump of a body falling to the ground. Matt tried to look up, thinking Jasper must have hurt the man, but he could make out Jasper lying still next to him.

The last thing he remembered was a light shining in his face and a tattooed arm reaching down to pick up the steel bar that had fallen next to the dog. 'Anna was right,' he thought. 'It is dangerous. Anna! Ella!'

Matt felt his head explode with pain and then there was nothing.

Chapter 40

Anna sat on the swing, her feet touching the ground and her head thrown back. The stars were minute twinkles in the sky but she kept staring at them, trying to make them bigger.

It was the first time in ages she'd been out to look at the sky, to see the stars and feel the night air, but tonight she'd been forced outside. The house too small, Ella too clingy and, a week later, Kate's words kept repeating in her mind.

I've changed my mind because of the facts.

What facts could she have been talking about?

Even so, why? And why, after so much time had passed, were they deciding to back Matt?

She let out a frustrated groan and got up from the swing. The lawn was wet with dew as she walked to the front yard and looked across the empty street.

Nothing ever happened on a Monday or Tuesday night in town. On Wednesday she would see the lights from the bowling green and hear the laughter from older generations while they played bowls. Thursdays she'd hear the shouts and short, sharp blasts of the whistle as the boys from the district did their footy training, but tonight, being a Tuesday, things were well and truly dead.

She looked up at the stars once again, wondering if they could tell her what had happened to change Sam and Kate's minds. Maybe she should ask Kate.

But she didn't want to. She was still too bewildered by their change of heart, still feeling so betrayed by those who had promised to support her no matter what. Was she the only sensible one, the only one who could see the search was futile? She imagined Sam and Matt driving aimlessly around the countryside stopping random vehicles, trying to solve a mystery the police couldn't solve.

But they hadn't tried, Anna suddenly remembered. The cops hadn't ever *tried* to solve the mystery. The truth of the statement took her by surprise – she hadn't ever thought about it like that before. It hadn't been solved because they didn't have all the information that Matt had, because he was watching and waiting for whoever was doing it to slip up. She shook her head and walked inside. 'Oh no! Be careful, Anna,' she told herself.

She had a shower, letting the water wash over

her, trying to forget her thoughts, then turned off all the lights and climbed into her cold bed.

It had been a long and lonely week without Kate's cheery morning phone calls. She would just have to swallow her pride and ring Kate in the morning. Yes, that's what she'd do.

'Oops, Mummy,' Ella said as she smeared her spilled orange juice across the table with her bare hands.

'Ella, don't do that . . . Oh, look at the mess you've made. It's yucky.' Tired from a night spent tossing and turning, Anna sounded crankier than she had meant to and sighed as Ella's bottom lip dropped.

'Mummy's angry.'

'A little bit, yes,' she responded as she reached for the sponge to wipe up the juice. Then she stopped and smiled, leaning over to drop a kiss on Ella's head. 'I'm sorry, Miss Ella. Mummy is just a bit weary. Sorry to be grouchy.'

She lifted Ella down from the table and wiped her hands with the sponge. 'Can you go and play out in the sandpit? I want to ring Kate and see if we can visit her today.'

'Yes! Let's go farm,' Ella said, clapping her hands.

'Come on, I'll take you out.'

She settled Ella in the sandpit then came back inside to pour herself another coffee and ring Kate. Her friend would be getting her lambs in to take to the abattoirs today so she should really ring before she started the day's work. Maybe she could offer to help mark another mob of lambs.

Reaching for the milk, she groaned as she realised the carton was empty. She glanced out of the window to check that Ella was safe then towards the other direction to see if Maggie's shop was open. It was, so she quickly ran across the road.

She pushed open the door and was welcomed by the smell of pastry and wood fire.

'Hello, Maggie,' she called, walking quickly to the fridge.

'Good mornin', lassie,' Maggie replied from the back room.

'Just got a litre of milk, money's on the counter.'

Maggie popped her head out of the door, her hands covered with flour. 'Thanks, pet. Doing anything today?'

'Hopefully going to catch up with Kate.'

'Lovely. Ah, here's my freight truck,' she said as they heard the noise of a diesel engine. 'I'd best clean up.' Maggie disappeared into the back room and Anna, her hand on the door knob, looked out.

She drew a sharp breath. 'Oh,' she said and backed away. 'I'm just going out your back door, Maggie.'

'Who's at the front?'

'Alec Harper. And he's talking to one of the blokes who drives with Matt.'

As she watched she saw Alec's face darken and his fists clench. Shane mustn't have the freight he needed. It would be just like him to get angry at something out of his control. She watched as Shane went to the cab of the truck and took out a small package in a brown box and handed it to Alec. Instantly his face cleared. Shane slapped him on the back, jumped up into the truck and started to move off, while Alec made for Maggie's door.

Anna quickly slipped out the back so she didn't have to talk to him but as she rounded the corner she came face to face with Shane, who had driven the truck to the rear of the shop and was just getting out again.

She knew she couldn't walk past without him seeing her, so she smiled, said hello and kept walking.

'Anna, good to see you. How are you?'

Reluctantly she stopped. 'Fine, Shane, just fine. And you?'

'Yeah, really well. Belinda said she saw you last week at the producers' market.'

'Yeah, I was surprised to see her.'

'Probably not as much as you surprised her. But she was pleased to see you. How's Ella?'

'Great, just as she always is. But I'm going to have to run, Shane. She's home by herself. I just popped over to get some milk. I'm hoping to catch Belinda next time I'm in Adelaide. It would be great to have a coffee with her and see the boys.'

'She would love that. I'd better keep moving myself. Take care, Anna.' He turned back to shut the door of the truck and stumbled on one of his shoelaces.

There was a tinkle as he walked away and Anna saw the flash of a silver chain hit the ground.

'Oh, Shane, your chain just fell off.' She leaned forward to pick it up and looked at it. The pendant was the same symbol that was engraved on Belinda's bracelet: two letters entwined. She held it out to him.

'Bugger,' he said, looking at it. 'Ah, the catch is broken.' He tucked it into his pocket. 'Thanks, Anna.'

With a quick wave, Anna hurried back to the house.

After checking on Ella, she poured herself a coffee and picked up the phone.

After a few rings, Kate answered.

'Hi, it's me,' Anna said.

'Ah, I was wondering when I was going to hear from you. Have you got over yourself?' Kate asked gently. 'Look, Anna, I know it's hard for you to understand, but we feel we need to do it.'

'You're right, I don't understand it – but maybe if I came over for a cuppa you could explain it?'

'I'd be happy to. It's silly to fall out over something like this when we've been friends for so long.'

'I'll be there in an hour,' Anna promised.

Ella ran to Kate, her arms outstretched, the pink hood of her windbreaker bouncing behind her.

'Helloooo, Miss Ella,' Kate called and gave her a hug. Anna reached for her friend and hugged her too; Kate planted a kiss on her cheek.

After settling Ella in the garden, the two women took their coffees out to the verandah and sat down.

'So it's like this,' Kate said. 'Matt has been keeping notes on all the thefts he's heard about – dates, locations, what was taken.'

Anna nodded. 'Yeah, I've seen his notebook.'

'Sam had started making a list too after we talked to my cousin Dave about the robberies. Then Matt came for tea one night and we compared notes. Matt had been really methodical about it. In fact, I'm sure he could get a job as a detective if he never does farming again!'

Anna grimaced.

'So here's the thing,' Kate continued. 'They decided to chat to the other farmers who've had things stolen. I spoke to Dave about it last week and he reckons we might be on to something. He said he was going to take it further, so now we're just waiting to hear back from him.

'But I think the best bit of evidence we've had that we're upsetting someone is inside. Come and have a listen.'

Anna checked on Ella quickly then followed Kate inside.

'It was left on our machine two nights ago.' Kate pushed the play button on the answering machine.

There was a scratchy noise and a squeal of feedback, then a distorted voice said, '*I know you're asking questions. Stop it now. Or someone will get hurt.*' The message ended.

Anna looked at Kate in horror then back to the machine. 'Play it again,' she said.

Kate hit the button and they both listened carefully, Anna with tingles running down her spine.

'Bloody hell,' she said as the message ended. 'Matt was right. Oh hell, he was *right*.'

Chapter 41

Dave was sitting at his desk reading an information report from the Merredin police. Five lots of twenty prime lamb had been reported missing in the past three weeks. It was hardly surprising. Lamb prices were sky high and there was always someone willing to make a quick buck at someone else's expense. What was astounding was that it wasn't happening in more areas across the state.

His phone rang and, absent-mindedly, he picked it up. 'Dave Burrows.'

'Dave, it's Geoff.'

He put down his report. 'How are you, mate? Got anything for me?'

'What I want to know is what have you put me on to?'

Surprised at the question, Dave felt a sudden zing of adrenalin course through him. He had been sure there was something to the information he'd been given.

'Why?'

'I had a phone call from the drug squad blokes today.'

'Yeah?'

'Yeah. Apparently when I went looking for a black sports car in the Spalding region I tripped a flag.'

'Did you really? Hmm, that's pretty interesting.' Dave leaned back in his chair, feigning casual, when really his body was humming with excitement.

'Yeah, they wanted to know why I was looking for it and did I have any information on it. I said I didn't really know what they were looking into, but I was investigating reports of thefts from farms with a common pattern.'

'You found something?' Dave asked.

'Yeah. I've put an information package together and I think your source was right. The problem was that all the Information Reports were made at different police stations. There were two IRs made to the Clare station, but they were twelve months apart and the officer who first took the information had been transferred by the time the second report was made. It's the government and their cutbacks which have hampered this too – the way they keep shifting blokes around.'

'You don't have to tell me,' Dave said.

'Anyway, I've got maps, pulled the IRs and, yeah,

it's got to be the same bloke. There are too many individual crimes with basically the same MO to make them one-offs.'

'I thought so too. I got all the moon phases and weather reports for the dates that the crimes occurred. Whoever's behind it is really clever and organised.'

'I agree, and they might still get away with it, too, because we have another problem.'

'Somehow I knew you were going to tell me that.' .

'We've been told to back off.'

'By who? The druggies?'

'Yep.'

'Do you know anything else?'

'Well, only what they were willing to tell me, which wasn't much. But the story goes that the car is connected to a Donald P. Hample, also known as Donnie or Paddy. I'm not going to do a search on him, because I'm pretty sure he'll be flagged too, but I know who he is. He's allegedly an underworld figure peddling drugs, but – surprise, surprise – he has a legit business: a real estate agency selling *rural* properties.

'The druggies seem to think that if they can get hold of this car, they can tie Donnie to it and a couple of crimes, but they've lost track of it.

'Now, I've been doing some thinking. What if Donnie knew the druggies had something on him – a photo of him driving it or something – and he asked someone to make the car disappear? And just suppose this someone who was meant to break it down or push it into the ocean or whatever *didn't*. Let's suppose they ghosted it instead – filed off the chassis number, put new plates on and kept it. Be tempting, wouldn't it? Brand new sports car, something to pull the chicks with.'

Dave kept silent, but he was nodding his head all the while. What Geoff was saying rang true.

'Now, if our rural thief did that, he'd have the perfect car for casing farms, wouldn't he?' Geoff continued. 'He might stand out, but a bloke driving a Mazda RX-8 wouldn't want anything from a farm, would he? He's obviously completely lost! And here's the best bit. If he has ghosted it and is using it to check out farms, he wouldn't be driving it that often. What do you think?'

'That's a pretty interesting theory, mate, and it all sounds plausible. I'm sorry if I've got you in hot water with the druggies though.' He broke off as his mobile rang. He looked at the number. 'Hey, Geoff, my cousin's calling on my mobile – just hold the line for a minute, would you? . . . Hey, Kate.'

'Oh, Dave, you'll never believe what's happened.' Her voice came in hiccups, like she'd been crying.

'What's wrong?' he asked urgently.

'We had a phone call yesterday, saying to stop meddling or something would happen to make us stop – but we didn't take it seriously. I mean, we haven't investigated *that* much, and –' She talked on, not making any sense to Dave.

'Kate, what's happened?' Dave broke in.

'It's Matt, he's been bashed. The police think he was hit with an iron bar. Dave, he's in a coma. Bloody hell, he might *die*!'

'Kate, you need to calm down. Tell me what the message said.'

Kate repeated it word for word.

'Okay, hold on.' He picked up the other phone. 'Geoff, it looks like we've definitely touched a nerve. My cousin's friend – the one who had the fertiliser stolen – has been assaulted. He's in a coma.'

Geoff swore. 'Hell, Dave, what can of worms have they opened?'

'Who only knows. I'll ring you when I've worked out what I'm going to do. Thanks, mate.'

'Talk to you then.'

Dave hung up the landline and picked up the mobile again.

'Where are you at the moment, Kate?'

'We're still at home.'

'Are you going to the hospital?'

'Yeah, we're just about to leave. Matt's wife Anna and his parents are already there.'

'Tell me what you know about the attack.'

Kate sniffed and took a shuddering breath. 'All I know is what Anna told me when she rang. His friend Shane had arranged to pick him up to go out for a drink, but when Shane arrived Matt was lying on the ground in the dark. Shane called an ambulance and now he's at Royal Adelaide Hospital. Anna didn't find out till this afternoon because Shane couldn't get hold of her – she was out at our place early this morning. Dave, I'm *scared*.'

'Of course you are. Look, just be very careful. Stay in contact with me all the time – just a text message to say things are okay. If something happens, anything unusual or strange, let me know – and make sure you tell the police who are investigating the assault about the threatening phone call you had. Have you still got it on the machine?'

'I think so.'

'Good, take the answering machine with you to the hospital and give it to the police so they can listen. Kate? Be careful. I don't know what we're up against, but it's serious shit, okay?' He hung up.

His fingers hovered over his computer, itchy to look for information on this Donald Hample and his Mazda, but he didn't dare. How else could he help look after Kate from over here?

In frustration, he turned back to the reports from Merredin, but his mind wasn't really on the job.

'Bastards,' he muttered. Desperate people had no respect for human lives when they were cornered. They would do anything not to be caught. He'd seen it time and time again when innocent people had somehow got caught up in criminal activities and had been badly hurt, sometimes physically, but mostly mentally. He didn't want that to happen to Kate. Or her friends.

He wasn't used to feeling helpless. Usually he could make a decision and act on it. Dave thought about flying to Adelaide, but he knew there was simply no point. It was out of his jurisdiction; his hands were tied.

He paced the room for a while, then shrugged. It was time to take some of his own advice. Let the cops do their job. What else could he do?

Chapter 42

Anna's eyes were red from crying. She sat next to Matt's bed, holding his hand, stroking his hair and talking to him softly.

From the time she'd received Shane's phone call, packed Ella a bag, driven to Adelaide, dropped Ella at Rob's then gone on to the hospital, six hours had passed. In that time, the doctors had assessed Matt, run their tests and worked out what they were going to do. The nurses had cleaned the blood from his head, but, surprisingly, there had been very little to see. Other than his face being incredibly pale and the various monitors he was hooked up to, he looked like he was sleeping. She still hadn't seen his doctor and had to make do with the snippets the nurses were telling her. The frustrating thing was they couldn't tell much – they weren't allowed to. 'You'll have to ask the doctor that,' they said, looking at her with sympathy.

The door opened and she looked up, hoping to see the doctor, but it was Matt's father, his face ashen. He tried to smile at Anna but couldn't seem to make his mouth work.

'Hello,' Anna said softly.

'Any change?'

'No, not yet.' Anna looked back at Matt's still body.

Ian dragged a chair over to the other side of the bed. Anna couldn't look at Ian and she hadn't been able to talk to Laura either when she had been here earlier. She'd been worried that they would ask her to leave, but she needed to be by Matt's side – she couldn't imagine being anywhere else. Their separation had been forgotten, in Anna's mind.

They sat in silence, Anna avoiding Ian's eyes, each lost in their thoughts, until Ian leaned forward and touched Anna's hand.

'Anna, love,' the older man started, 'you need to be here, okay? There's no need to feel uncomfortable around Laura and me. We know the last couple of years have been really tough for you and Matt, but we're sure this separation thing was just a temporary blip in your marriage. As far as we're concerned, you're still Matt's wife and you have a right to be here.'

Anna's eyes swam with tears. Everyone had said the breakup was just a small setback in their relationship but, until today, she hadn't believed them despite the way she'd missed him and craved his company. She had thought her marriage to Matt was truly over.

But when Shane had rung her from the hospital, the fear she had felt had taken her breath away. And now, as she sat here, holding the hand of the man she loved, she knew she could never be whole without him.

Anna felt the lump in her throat grow so large she didn't think she could talk, but somehow she managed to say, 'Thanks, Ian. I hoped you didn't think it was inappropriate for me to be here, but I couldn't be anywhere else. I love him.'

The door opened quietly and a man walked in. He held out his hand to Anna. 'I'm Doctor Grant,' he said.

Anna stood quickly and shook the doctor's hand, introducing herself and Ian.

'Is he going to be okay?' she asked desperately, all the other questions she had planned to ask suddenly forgotten. All she needed was the reassurance that Matt would be fine, that he would be himself again. Her husband, Ella's dad.

'Matt has sustained a severe brain injury as a result of his assault. There's quite a bit of swelling around the brain. So, to give him the best chance, we've put him in an induced coma. That means we've given him heavy drugs to put him in a coma – it's important you understand that we've *made* him go into it, okay?'

Anna and Ian nodded.

'Most of the swelling is at the back of the brain, where he was hit.' The doctor indicated with his hands, before continuing. 'The point of keeping him unconscious is to reduce the amount of energy needed by that part of the brain. Once the swelling starts to go down and the brain begins to heal, we're hopeful the area that has been worst affected will have been protected. If it has been, Matt should, in time, make a full recovery.

'I'm prepared to say the outlook for Matt is positive, but of course there are still plenty of variables, and we won't know for sure until he regains consciousness.'

Anna sagged against the bed in relief.

'I'm going to monitor him over the next twenty-four to forty-eight hours. That will mean some brain scans and a few other things. If the swelling has started to go down, then we'll bring him out slowly. I promise you we'll do the very best we can for him.'

'Thank you,' said Ian, his voice hoarse, tears in his eyes.

'Thank you very much, Doctor Grant.' Anna echoed his sentiments.

The doctor reviewed the chart at the bottom of the bed, then said goodbye and left.

Anna picked up her handbag. 'I'll go and call Sam and my brothers,' she said. 'I'm so thankful Ella is with Rob. She didn't really understand what was happening and why I had to leave so quickly. I just told her Daddy was sick and Mummy needed to go and see him.'

Ian nodded. 'I'll ring Laura. She was trying to get in contact with all the family before she came back in again.'

Their calls made, they sat in silence, Anna holding one of Matt's hands and Ian the other. Anna's mind was churning with questions, with things she wanted to say to Matt, but couldn't with Ian there. 'I'm sorry, Matt. I didn't believe you and I should have. I love you.' She felt an urge to talk to fill the silence, to drown out the beeping of the machines. To let Matt know they were there. She didn't want him thinking he was alone.

Finally, Anna said, 'Tell me about Matt as a baby.'

Ian shifted in the chair and cleared his throat. 'Such a long time ago, but at the same time, it seems like yesterday. He was a screamer. Used to scare us half to death in the middle of the night when he woke up wanting a feed.' He smiled sadly. 'And he was a right little monkey when he was a toddler. Had Laura running everywhere after him, much like your Ella now.' His voice broke and he looked down at the bed.

Anna saw him swallow hard and regretted her question. 'I'm sorry.'

Ian shook his head. 'No. It's okay. It's good to talk.'

They were silent again then Anna started to hum the songs she knew Matt loved. She told him stories of Ella and funny things which had happened with Kate and Sam. All the while, she was trying to connect

349

with him, willing his damaged brain to heal.

Anna didn't hear Ian get up and leave and she didn't know how long she sat there, but when she felt a hand on her shoulder, she jumped and came out of her trance.

'You need to sleep, Anna. How long have you been here?'

Anna blinked. It was Matt's boss, Jimmy.

'I don't know. I don't even know what day it is.'

'Come on, let me take you back to the yard. Or a hotel. Somewhere you can shower and sleep. You'll be no good to anyone if you collapse from exhaustion.'

'I can't leave. I need to be here.'

'What about if I ask the nurse if she can bring you a bed?'

A wave of tiredness overtook Anna as she looked into Jimmy's kind face.

'Anna, I think Matt is a top young man. I've enjoyed getting to know him over the last few months and I'm so sorry this has happened.' Anna noticed his face was creased with worry and sorrow.

'I can't leave, Jimmy, I just can't.' She turned back to look at Matt.

With a sigh, Jimmy sat in the chair Ian had vacated and he patted Matt's arm awkwardly.

'Come on, me lad, you need to come back to us. You've got a wife who's waiting to see you.'

Anna smiled sadly, and then looked around as the door opened again and a nurse entered.

'Mrs Butler? The police are here wanting to ask you some questions. Can you come and talk to them?'

'I don't want to leave Matt.'

'Well, love, it's probably best to get it out of the way so you can concentrate on getting better. I'm sure they won't take long.'

'I'll stay here, Anna. I won't move until you get back,' Jimmy promised.

Anna got up stiffly and followed the nurse down the corridor to where two police officers sat in an office.

'Hello, Mrs Butler.' The older of the two rose and held out his hand. 'I'm Sergeant Harry Jones. Could we ask you some questions about what happened to your husband?'

'I don't really know anything, we were separated,' Anna blurted out, blinking back her tears. 'I wasn't there.'

'I understand, but any tiny piece of information will help us find out who did this. Did you know he was going out last night?'

Anna shook her head. 'No. The first thing I knew was when Shane rang and told me something had happened.'

'When was the last time you saw him?'

'About a week ago. He came over to see our little girl, Ella.'

'And did he seem okay? Normal? Didn't mention he was worried about anything? Or anyone?'

'No, but he didn't really talk to me. It would be best if you talked to our friends Kate and Sam. He'd been seeing them a lot.'

'Why was that?'

'Well, they're friends.'

'Okay. So you're not aware of anything he was doing that could have put him in danger?'

Anna exhaled. It was time for her to show Matt she believed in him. Hoping it wasn't too late, she cried. 'Yes! He was trying to find out who stole our fertiliser and Sam's motorbike. But it wasn't just him, it was Sam and Kate too. There was a heap of other farmers in the mid-north who'd had things taken from their farms. Matt was convinced the same person was doing it.

'Someone left a threatening message on Sam and Kate's answering machine warning them to stop asking questions.' Anna paused, trying to catch her breath; her words were coming out so fast. 'Then this happened to Matt.'

The police officers looked somewhat stunned. Did they think this was just a random bashing? Anna thought. Well there was something going on, and it needed to be blown wide open.

There was a tapping at the door and she looked up to see Sam and Kate standing there.

'Oh, thank God,' cried Anna, then she burst into floods of tears.

Chapter 43

Jimmy left the hospital, his shoulders heavy with sorrow.

He liked Matt a great deal. He could see something in the lad he recognised from his own young self: a thirst to do what he loved. Such a shame that he'd had it all snatched away.

Oh yes, he remembered the excitement of starting his own business, of feeling complete when he was working. But he also remembered his devastation when he lost so much in the eighties. In that way, he could relate to Matt as well.

Jimmy knew Matt had been grieving since he'd started working for him and that was another emotion that he remembered. Losing the business he had built up with nothing but his own hands was like the loss of a loved one. It meant he was a failure, not only in the eyes of his wife and family, but also in the eyes of the community and to all who knew him. He'd let himself and everyone down.

Of course, Jimmy now knew this wasn't true and had tried to explain that to Matt. It was a matter of Jimmy being older and wiser. And just when he'd thought he was finally getting through to the lad, this happened.

To see him lying unresponsive in the hospital bed broke his heart.

Jimmy drove aimlessly through the city, taking turns without even noticing where he was going. Subconsciously, he must have had a destination in mind, however, because the next thing he knew he was pulling into a parking spot in front of his old home. He was back where this whole ghastly mess had started.

The large cement bricks of the public housing block were stark and grey and the paint was peeling from the windowsills. When Jimmy looked up he could see an old lady watching hopefully from the window on the second floor. Who was she waiting for? Family? Did they come often – or ever?

Litter blew down the street and a young girl with a dirty face and torn clothes sat in the gutter and stared blankly at the ground.

The hopelessness of the area filled him with despair; it was exactly as he remembered it. He was sure the bleakness of his surroundings was part of the reason he had become as desperate as he was back then. That and the war, the injury . . . and Min-Thu.

Ah, Min-Thu. He could still recall the powerful emotion of his first love. How his blood rushed when he saw her, his heart pounding and his palms sweaty. He could still see her smile and hear her quiet teasing. But then, as always, the happy memories were overlaid with others: the grenade blasts, the blood. Min-Thu's blood. Her unseeing eyes. Those memories were never far away.

He pushed up his sleeve to reveal a faded green tattoo. The initials MT, imprinted forever on his arm. He told everyone they stood for Marshall Transport. No one knew about Min-Thu so nobody could ever understand how he had loved her and how the events in Vietnam had caused him to make the biggest mistake of his life back here in Australia.

He shut his eyes and recalled his nephew as a happy, trusting child – and how he had destroyed that trust. There was no way Sandy should have borne the brunt of his uncle's anger, pain and frustration. He was back in the small room, which smelled musty and old. He saw the glass moving across the air as if in slow motion, he heard the dull thump as it hit the boy's head and smelled the blood, which came immediately.

The injury had instantly thrust him back to the grenade attack, he could hear it, smell it and feel the pain again. Min-Thu, he thought he had called out loud.

It was Jimmy's turn to have tears prick his eyes. He rarely let himself think about that day. The memories from Vietnam faded in comparison to what he had done to his own flesh and blood. How he had let Sandy down. Sandy, who had believed in his Uncle Jimmy more than any other person.

'I have to put things right,' he said aloud now. 'Somehow, I have to put things right for Sandy.'

As he was about to start the car he looked at the little girl again, dug into his pocket and pulled out a twenty-dollar note. He walked across the street and stood in front of her.

'Have you eaten today, love?' he asked.

'I dunno. Can't remember.'

'There's a shop just down the road that used to do a good fish and chips. Go and get some. Get some for the rest of your family too.' When she looked up, he could see her eyes had already taken on the dead look of the broken. He held out the money and she looked at it warily.

'Go on, I don't want anything from you. Take it and get something to eat.' Jimmy put the money down beside her and walked back to his car.

He drove off without looking back. He needed to leave this place behind. Forget it had ever played a part in his life.

Today he would make amends for the things he'd done wrong. And from today, he could move on with a clear conscience.

Chapter 44

Anna pushed her hair back from her face and rested her head on the edge of the hospital bed, still clutching Matt's hand.

'So,' she said, continuing with the one-sided conversation, 'there was Ella, dressed in a pair of rubber boots and overalls, a lamb tucked under her arm. She was the spitting image of a country kid at her best. You would have laughed if you'd seen her, Matt. She was just so gorgeous.

'Rob has had her for a little while and your mum is looking after her at the moment. Sam and Kate have been helping out too. Would you like me to bring her in to see you? I'm sure she'd love to give you a kiss.' She waited, hoping for a response – anything, even the fleeting squeeze of his fingers.

Nothing.

Anna took a breath, trying to find something else to talk about. She was sure Matt could hear her, hear everything that was said.

'I bet you're worried about Jasper. Well you don't have to be. I've asked Jimmy to take care of him until you're able to come home. It will be nice to have him back with us again. He's been to the vet and seems to be fine. His ribs are a bit sore where he was hit, but luckily nothing was broken. Maggie is looking after Bindy over at the shop. I bet she's sleeping in front of the potbelly and being fed tidbits by anyone who walks in. I hope no one reports her being there!'

The door opened and Kate peered in. She waved and motioned for Anna to step outside.

'Kate's just popped in, Matt. She wants me for something. I won't be long.'

Anna gently released Matt's hand and left the room.

'Anna, love, how are you going? No, don't answer that. Stupid question.' Kate pulled her into a hug then stood back to look at her. 'Anna, you've got to get some sleep. Those bags under your eyes would take you to America for a year!'

'Oh, thanks, Kate. You've made me feel so much better,' Anna said.

'Sorry, sorry. Bloody hell, I'm making an impression today. Any change?'

'No, nothing. I keep talking but the doctor said he wouldn't respond in any way. I'm sure he can hear me, though. I remember reading some article in the paper about a woman who was in a coma for a year and she heard everything – including when her parents and husband had a huge argument in her hospital room. I know he can hear me, Kate, so I just keep talking.'

'Of course he can hear you. Keep telling him how much you love him and how you need to be together to make your lives whole and he'll remember every bit of it when he wakes up. Have you eaten? Can I get you a coffee or something?' Kate reached over and put her hand on Anna's shoulder. 'I don't suppose I could convince you to come to the hotel and have a shower? You need to have a rest.'

'But I've got to be here, Kate. I can't leave. The doctors might want to bring him out of the coma. I need to be here when he wakes up.'

'Of course you do. But I'm sure the doctors won't bring him out without telling you. And they'll bring him out slowly so you'll have time to get here. Why don't you check with the nurses and I'll take you back to the room for a shower and a decent meal.'

Anna hesitated for a moment, running her fingers through her hair. It felt greasy and she realised she felt dirty and rumpled. A shower would freshen her up and maybe some time away from the hospital would give her something else to talk to Matt about. She'd exhausted her list of topics.

'Okay,' she agreed. 'But we can't be long.'

'Excellent. Come on then.' She pushed Anna gently towards the exit.

'And I'm only coming if you help me do something,' Anna said.

'Sure! Anything,' Kate answered.

Anna was holding a large blanket over the top of Jasper and he was wriggling.

'For goodness sake stop it, Jasper,' she whispered to him.

He whined then stopped moving.

'How are we going to get past the ladies out the front?' wondered Kate aloud.

'They're always so busy, I'm sure we can get by without anyone noticing. If we can get to the stairs, we'll be fine. He can run up them and hopefully we shouldn't see any of the staff. Okay, ready?' Anna asked as she hoisted the heavy dog further up into her arms.

'Ready.' Kate pulled her most determined face and walked casually through the door, making a beeline for the stairs.

'Excuse me?' Anna's heart dropped as she heard a lady's voice, but she kept walking.

'Excuse me?' the lady's voice called louder.

'I got it,' Kate muttered, 'you keep going.' She spun around, a brilliant smile plastered on her face. 'Hello!' she said loudly.

'We're raising money for the hospital. I wonder if you'd be interested in making a donation?' asked the lady.

As Anna disappeared through the heavy fire escape doors to the safety of the fire escape stairs, she heard Kate exclaim, 'Well of course I am! Show me how.'

Anna's heart was pounding as she put Jasper down, but her face was determined. 'Matt's been feeding you too well, Jasp. You're nothing but a great big, heavy lump!'

They started up the stairs, but had only gone one flight up when they heard the door slam and echo through the stairwell. 'Shit,' Anna swore and quickly shook out the blanket.

Jasper saw what she was doing and ran on further, not letting her throw the blanket over him.

'Jasper,' she whispered. 'Jasper, come here!'

A familiar voice floated up the stairwell. 'It's okay, it's only me.' Kate's footsteps could be heard clattering loudly up the stairs and Anna let out a sigh of relief.

'You gave me a heart attack!' she said.

Kate appeared around the corner. 'Thought I would. C'mon, only another flight to go.' She looked over her shoulder, then up the stairwell.

Quickly they ran on until they came to the entry to the ward. Kate opened the door first and peeped out. Gently she shut it again, holding her fingers to her lips. 'Nurse alert,' she said softly.

Jasper looked up and whined, then thumped to the floor with a great sigh.

Kate glanced down. 'Yeah, we're a funny lot

aren't we, Jasper? First of all we throw you under a blanket and nearly suffocate you and now here you are running up stairs, with not a sheep in sight. Don't worry, you'll like where we're going.' She opened the door a crack and looked out again.

'Let's go.'

Anna dropped the blanket onto a surprised Jasper, scooping him up as he let out a yelp.

'Shh,' the girls said in unison. Edging into the corridor, they ran towards Matt's room and pushed open the door.

Laura smiled at the girls, then saw Jasper. Her face changed and a frown settled on her forehead.

'Should he be in here?' she asked.

'Probably not,' Anna said, 'but you know how much Matt loves him.'

Jasper sniffed the air and took a tentative step towards the bed, then backed away. He looked at Anna questioningly.

'It's okay, he's just sleeping. C'mon, Jasper. Get up.' She patted the bed. Jasper didn't move. 'Get up, mate. You can get on the bed this one time.' Still no movement. Finally she dragged him by the collar, lifted him up and placed him next to Matt. 'Honey, I've brought Jasper for you. Can you pat him?'

Anna took Matt's hand and placed it on Jasper's head. The dog licked his master's hand and without another glance at Anna, settled in alongside Matt, sighed, shut his eyes and went to sleep.

Anna looked at Laura, who smiled weakly at her.

'Thank you, Anna,' she said in a low voice. 'This is all just so hard.' Her voice broke.

Walking over, Anna put her arms around Laura as her mother-in-law hugged her back. That's all they could do in this situation: hug.

A nurse bustled in and, without looking at Matt, pulled his chart from the holder at the end of the bed. A wet tongue licked her hand. 'What?' She gazed at Jasper in surprise.

The girls looked at each other and all their pent-up emotions suddenly erupted in nervous giggles. The nurse raced for the door, calling for another nurse.

'C'mon, Jasper,' Anna said. 'Back to Jimmy with you.'

Laura put her hand on Anna's arm. 'Thank you,' Anna whispered.

A few hours later, Anna was back by Matt's bedside. She picked up his hand and stroked it gently with her thumb. She had something she needed to say.

'Matt, I was so against you looking for whoever stole the fertiliser,' she began. 'I guess at first I just thought there wasn't any point. I couldn't see how finding out who the perpetrator was would make a difference. Then it was because I really wanted you to focus on something else. I felt that you were destroying yourself by obsessing over it. And to a point, I was right, Matt, because you shut us out, me and Ella. But I was wrong not to support you.

'I hate what has happened – I hate that you've been hurt – but I'm also very proud of you for sticking up for what you believe in. I'm sorry I didn't believe in you. I miss you, honey. So much! I miss the farm too, more than you've ever realised, I think. But I miss you more. I wish we could have talked and worked through it. Oh, Matt, I want to start again, don't you? Ella needs you, I need you – we belong together and I've always believed that. You used to believe it too. Seeing you like this has made me realise how much I do love you. I've never stopped.'

A nurse bustled in, ignoring Anna's tear-stained cheeks, took Matt's vitals and left again. Ten minutes later the doctor arrived.

'Anna,' he said, 'I'd like to try to bring Matt out of the coma tomorrow.'

Anna, overcome with emotion, put her hands to her face. But she was smiling. It was going to be onwards and upwards from here.

Chapter 45

Matt's eyes flickered open and he blinked at the bright light.

'Hi, Matt,' an unfamiliar voice said. 'I'm Dr Grant. It's great to have you back.'

He tried to form words, but his mouth was dry. Someone held a straw to his lips and he drank gratefully. He focused on the person holding the straw and saw it was Anna. She was smiling at him.

'Hi, gorgeous,' she said.

He licked his lips and tried to say something.

His mind was spinning. Surely Anna shouldn't be here - she wasn't part of his life anymore. But he wanted her here, needed her. He wished he could feel her arms around him. Hear her laugh. He knew she could make everything feel right.

'What? Where?' He wasn't sure why he was here. He tried to move but his body hurt.

'You're going to be sore, Matt,' said Dr Grant. 'Do you remember what happened?'

'No ... yes – someone hit me,' he said as the memory came flooding back. 'Waiting for Shane. But someone hit me.'

The doctor nodded. 'Good, Matt. I've had you in an induced coma for five days, but you've been doing really well and it was time to bring you out.'

Matt felt his eyes closing as he tried to take in the doctor's words. What did he say his name was again?

Blindly he reached out his hand for Anna. When he felt her soft hand in his a warmth spread through his body and he left himself drift back into the darkness, knowing she would be there when he woke again.

He didn't know how long he was asleep for but the next time he woke he could feel a pressure on his hand and heard weeping. He frowned as he opened his eyes.

'Mum.'

'Matt.' She stopped crying for a moment, then a fresh round of tears began as she said his name again. 'Oh, Matt.'

Matt looked for Anna to help him, but she wasn't in the room. Where was she?

'Anna?' he asked.

His mother wiped her eyes and smiled. 'She's

gone to pick up Ella, so she can see you. And your dad is on his way. He's been here every day, as has Anna. Oh, Matt, I'm sorry, I just couldn't sit here, seeing you like that, but they did. Anna was just a tower of strength. She barely left your side. She loves you so much, Matt.'

She was interrupted by a nurse coming in to check his blood pressure and temperature.

'Doctor will be in to see you again shortly,' she said. 'But there are some police officers who asked me to let them know when you woke up. They're quite anxious to talk to you.'

'Oh, surely that can wait?' Laura said indignantly.

'It's okay, Mum,' Matt interrupted.

'But, darling . . .'

'It's okay, Mum,' Matt repeated. 'I think I'm feeling better.' He didn't know why, but he knew he needed to talk to the police. There was something bothering him but he couldn't put his finger on it. Talking to them might help.

The door flew open and Ian strode in. 'Matt. Oh, thank God you're okay.' He drew Matt's head to his chest, which was heaving with emotion.

'Steady on, Dad. I'm a bit sore.'

Half laughing, his father released him. 'It's good to see you, son,' he said, then he turned to the nurse. 'No police until tomorrow,' he said so firmly that no one dared contradict him.

There was a steady stream of nurses checking on him over the next two hours. Matt dozed off and on, and talked quietly with his parents. They had just decided to leave for the night when Anna and Ella walked through the door.

'Daddy!' Ella cried.

'Hello, sweetheart.' He held out his arms and Ella clambered onto the bed and plonked herself firmly in his lap.

'Where have you been?' she asked.

Matt opened his mouth to answer, then stopped. Where had he been? He could remember snatches. A noise behind him, Jasper snarling furiously and the pain.

He remembered soft voices, pressure on his hands, quiet words.

'I've been asleep,' he said at last. 'Daddy has been very tired.'

'That's what Mummy said. What's it feel like to sleep for five days?' Ella looked at him enquiringly.

Matt tried to laugh, but everything still hurt. 'It's very tiring.'

After a few moments more, Anna said, 'Come on, Ella, it's time for you to go now.' Then to Matt she said, 'Kate is waiting outside. We didn't want to tire you too much the first day.'

'But you'll come back?' he asked.

Anna's face broke into a huge smile. 'Sweetheart, I'll be here all night.'

Matt's sleep was full of broken dreams. A man's arm, a phone ringing. Messages that made no sense and threats that were bone-chilling.

He woke to a cool hand on his, soothing words and a warm body lying beside him.

'Shh, it's a bad dream.'

Matt struggled to sit up. 'His arm,' he said.

'What?' Anna fumbled for the switch to turn on the light.

'The bloke who hit me had something on his arm.'

'What sort of something?'

'A tattoo, I think. I'm not sure, but I remember he leaned down to pick up something. He had a torch and I saw it in the light.'

'Okay.' Anna rubbed her head and Matt could tell her eyes hurt. She was obviously tired. 'Do you want to talk to the police now? I'm sure they'd come. It was only because your dad said they had to wait another day that they haven't been yet.'

Matt slumped back on the pillow, frustrated at his weakened state.

'Guess we can leave it until tomorrow,' he said.

Anna snuggled against him and he lay still, enjoying the feel of her. She felt like she had when he'd first touched her all those years ago, and for a moment he wondered why he'd ever left her. But from somewhere deep inside the feelings of loss, betrayal and failure rose again. He should push Anna away, he thought, but he didn't have the energy – and anyway, he didn't want to.

'We belong together and I've always believed that.' He wasn't sure where those words had come from or why they were foremost in his mind, but he knew they were true. And now here she was, curled up next to him on a single hospital bed. A bloke couldn't be more lucky, he thought, as he stroked her arm.

Anna twisted around to face him. 'I love you,' she said. 'I always have and always will.'

Matt looked at her seriously and ran his fingers over her face. 'I love you too,' he said softly. 'And I'm sorry.'

'So am I.' Anna leaned forward and pressed her lips to his.

'So, Matt, let me make sure I've got it all straight. He kicked you and then he shone the torch in your eyes while he leaned down to pick up something. We're assuming it's the assault weapon. That's when you saw this tattoo?' Sergeant Jones, one of the two detectives who were standing at the end of his bed, looked up from his notes.

'Yeah, that's right.'

'Can you describe the tattoo?'

'I can't really remember it, I just know there was something on his arm. It was green and maybe about the size of an apple. I think I'd know it again if I saw it, but it seemed like squiggles all linking together. It was only a quick glance. I was concentrating on other things.'

'Righto. So is there anything else you can remember that might help us?'

'Well, it's not really to do with the attack, but I've got a strange message on my phone. Anna, do you know where my phone is? The last thing I remember it was in my pocket.'

'I think it's in the drawer of your bedside table.' She opened the drawer and rummaged through Matt's personal effects. Finally she held it up.

'Here.' Matt took the phone from her and dialled his message bank, then held it out for the police officers to listen.

'I'm pretty sure the bloke who's doing most of the talking – the one needing money – is a guy called Alec Harper. He lives in Spalding. But none of it makes sense. He shouldn't need money – he's supposed to have heaps. A while ago I did have a stupid thought he might be trying to steal to get some cash, but he'd never be able to pay the farm off with the small amounts he'd be making.' I don't know who made the call, but there's something familiar in the background. That crackling noise, it sounds like something I've heard before, but I can't put my finger on it.'

Sergeant Jones held it to his ear and listened. 'Yeah, I know what you mean. Almost like a radio in the background. Look, we can break this message down and isolate the background noises ...'

Matt interrupted. 'What did you just say?'

'We can fade out the foreground noises ...'

'No, before that. You think it sounds like a radio?'

'Well, yeah, it sounds like a CB radio – like truckies talking.'

Matt went pale and held out his hand for the phone again.

Anna was looking frightened.

'Truckies?' she whispered.

'You're right – that's what it is,' Matt said, holding the phone to his ear. 'I'm sure of it. Like the radio in Jimmy's office and our cabs.'

'But it couldn't be Jimmy,' Anna gasped.

'Of course it's not Jimmy, honey,' Matt reassured her. 'How would Alec Harper know Jimmy? All trucking companies have CB radios.'

Detective Gorry looked interested. 'Who's Jimmy?' he asked.

'Jimmy Marshall, my boss. He owns East-West Haulage.'

The detective scribbled a note. 'Right, and how do you know that the man in conversation here is Alec Harper?'

Matt related how he'd heard Alec Harper's voice in Maggie's store.

Gorry nodded. 'Okay, we'll check it out. Now are you sure there's nothing else you can remember that might help us identify your attacker?'

Matt thought for a minute. 'I'm not sure, but it's possible Jasper bit him. I can sort of remember this howl of pain, but I'm not sure if it was him or me. Jasper was definitely snarling.' Matt stopped and shut his eyes, then opened them again suddenly. 'Sam's motorbike! Geez, there has to be a link here somehow. It was in the shed. In an underground storage room. Like a cellar.'

'What?' Anna looked confused. 'Matt, are you *sure* you're feeling okay? The bike was stolen from Sam's shed.'

'I know, I know, but I saw it – at least I think I did. There's a room under the storage shed. I found a trapdoor leading to it just before I went outside to meet Shane. And there's something else ...' He frowned. 'Oh yeah. There were green leaves on the ground. Just a few. I wondered if it might have been marijuana.'

'Marijuana and a stolen motorbike?' Sergeant Jones asked, clearly perplexed. 'Is there any chance you could explain this from the beginning?'

A couple of hours later the door opened and a stranger walked into Matt's room carrying a folder. When Matt looked at him quizzically the man introduced himself as Detective Ringo. 'I'm with the drug squad,' he explained. 'I'd like you to have a look at some of these photos and tell me if you recognise any of the tattoos.'

Matt heaved himself into a sitting position. 'I'll give it a go,' he said. 'I'm not sure how much I actually remember though.'

'No worries,' said Ringo, opening the folder and

putting the photos out in front of him. 'Take your time.'

Matt picked up the photos one by one and looked at them carefully. He discarded the tattoos of naked women, wolves and swords instantly, but kept returning to two, which were symbols.

'I think it was sort of like these two,' he said slowly. 'I just remember it all being tangled together. Sort of like a spider's web, but not one.'

Ringo didn't respond; he just sat and let Matt think things through.

Finally Matt shook his head. 'I can't do any better than that, I'm sorry. Those two look about right, but I can't distinguish between them.'

'That's fine, Matt. You've given us something to work with so it's a start.' He'd begun to gather up the photos when Anna walked in.

'Oh, hello, Detective. Am I interrupting something?' she asked.

'Nah, just looking at some tattoos to see if I recognise any of them. I picked these two.' Matt held out the photos and Anna took them.

She considered them for a moment. 'I've seen something like this one before,' she said. 'Belinda's got a bracelet like it.'

'Really?' Matt frowned and took the photo, studying it closely. 'But they're not exactly the same, are they?'

She looked at the symbol again. 'I don't think so, but I've only seen it once before. They look sort of the same. How bizarre. Why would this bloke have a tatt that's the same as Belinda's bracelet?'

Detective Ringo cleared his throat and asked, 'And Belinda would be . . .?'

'Oh, she's Shane's wife, he drives with me. He's the one who found me and called the ambulance when I was attacked.'

Something glittered in Ringo's eyes. 'So you're saying that the symbol in this picture is the same as one on Belinda's bracelet?'

'Well it's similar,' Anna said. 'It would be a pretty strange coincidence, wouldn't it?' She shook her head. 'It can't be the same.'

'Well, leave it with me,' Ringo said. 'I agree that it's pretty unlikely, but I'll look into it.'

Chapter 46

Matt's release from hospital was a special occasion. Anna picked him up in her beat-up old dual cab, with Ella and Jasper along for the ride. This time, the grumpy nurse who had discovered Jasper on Matt's bed and given Anna a severe dressing down turned a blind eye to the dog, who tried to lick every nurse in sight.

Matt walked slowly down the hall, focusing on making his legs walk as far as the ute.

On the drive home, Matt didn't take his hands from Anna's knee.

As they neared Clare, three police cars passed in convoy, heading towards Adelaide. Matt followed their journey in the rear-view mirror.

'Wonder where they're going?' he said.

'Who knows? But we're heading home!' Anna said happily.

When they pulled into their driveway Matt's parents were waiting, along with Sam and Kate, Maggie and Anna's two brothers.

Matt opened the door of the ute and climbed out slowly. There was a cheer and Matt raised his fist above his head in victory. 'I'm home!' he called.

Sam raised his glass. 'Here's to Matt,' he said. 'And Anna, of course.'

'To Matt and Anna,' the crowd around the barbecue chorused.

Matt slipped his arm around Anna's shoulders and kissed her on the lips. A shout of approval went up from the group and Anna blushed.

As Anna went inside to fetch some more napkins Sam came over and sat next to Matt. 'How're you holding up, mate?' he asked.

'Really well. Man, it's great to be home.' Matt looked up at the clear blue sky and breathed deeply.

'How'd the interview with the cops go? They quizzed us fairly thoroughly.'

Matt laughed. 'You should have seen their faces when I started to talk about your motorbike. They must've thought the drugs the docs were giving me were affecting my brain! But when I went back and explained everything from the start, including the fertiliser and everything else, the cops got a bit of a picture of what's been going on. It was a relief to tell someone.'

'Yeah, I can imagine.'

'You know what, though, Sam? I'm not worried about it anymore. I know the police are on the case now and I feel confident they'll find the culprit.'

As if on cue Anna came out of the house, holding the phone in her hand.

'Matt,' she called. 'Matt, it's Sergeant Jones for you.'

Chapter 47

'Matt, it's Sergeant Harry Jones here.'

'G'day. Anna's here too. I've got you on speaker phone.'

'Good. Look, I wanted to be the first to tell you that we've arrested someone for the theft of your fertiliser and all the other thefts in your area.'

Matt licked his lips, his mouth suddenly dry. 'Who?'

'Alec Harper. He's been charged with stealing, among other offences.'

'It was him!' Matt hissed. 'I thought it must have been. But why? The bloody bastard! He sent me broke and then he bought my *farm*. My dog.'

Anna had her hand over her mouth, her face ghostly pale.

'This is going to be all over the papers tomorrow, so let me quickly give you an outline of what's happened. There's still an investigation in progress, though, so I can't tell you everything. Matt, someone came forward and told us that Alec was the one who bashed you and a great deal more information.'

'Who came forward?' Matt asked immediately.

'I'm afraid I can't reveal that at the moment – but I can tell you Harper was probably concerned not just about you discovering it was him who was stealing everything, but also that you might inadvertently bust open the drug ring run by his daughter.'

'His *daughter*?' gasped Anna. 'Alec Harper has a daughter? He's never even had a girlfriend for as long as we've known him.'

'We put it together when you identified the tattoo. That's how the people in this ring identify each other – they all wear that symbol. If you look closely, you can see the letters MT.'

Anna and Matt stared at each other, then Anna asked, 'Who is the daughter?'

'Belinda Lyons.'

'Shane has got one!' Anna said suddenly. 'He has a chain with that symbol on it – and it's on their letter box too! I saw it when we went there the night of the wedding!'

'Letter box?' Matt asked.

'Yes, Anna, you're right,' Jones said. 'Shane Lyons was involved too. He was the delivery man for interstate clients while Belinda sold hundreds of kilos through the producers' markets in Adelaide. She and her friend were growing marijuana in the

Adelaide Hills and using her dried herbs stall as a front. We've also linked them to Donald Hample, who is also known as Paddy. Anyway, you can sleep soundly – they're all in custody. And yes all the houses have these symbols to mark where the drop-off points are. The Lyons' was their letter box.'

'Shane?' cried Matt in disbelief. 'Are you sure? I mean . . . he's my mate.'

'I think you'll find that dealing drugs was how they funded their lifestyle, Matt,' Jones said sympathetically. 'But back to the rural crime, I can't tell you why Harper stole these things – like I said, that's still under investigation – but it was a separate operation to the drugs.

'Their drug operation had been under investigation for a long time and that's why the guy your policeman friend in WA contacted was warned off. The drug squad wanted Paddy Hample more than anyone else, and they didn't want the investigation of the theft to get in the way.'

Long after they'd rung off, Matt sat staring off into the distance, trying to absorb what the detective had told him.

The party had dispersed quickly when they had heard Matt's cry of disbelief and seen Anna's shocked face. Ian and Laura had bundled a crying Ella into the car and taken her with them to give Anna and Matt some space.

As Anna handed Matt a cup of tea, lights swung into their driveway; a minute or so later there was a knock at the door.

Anna opened it and Jimmy stood there, looking uncomfortable, twisting a felt hat in his hands.

'Can I come in?' he asked.

Anna nodded.

He followed her into the lounge where Matt was and sat down.

'I need to tell you something,' Jimmy began haltingly, putting down the hat. He nervously played with the sleeves of his jumper and pushed up the cuffs to mid-arm. 'I've made so many mistakes in my life but Sandy was the biggest. He's my nephew and I love him dearly, but he has a problem. Jimmy rubbed his nose. 'I'll explain from the beginning.

'His childhood was unhappy. His mother was completely irresponsible; she drank, had man after man through the house and Sandy was exposed to all of this. He looked to me as the one stable person in his life, and for a long time I was. I was there for him as much as I could be. I loved that boy like he was my own.

'Then I was drafted. Went to Vietnam, twice.' Jimmy's voice wobbled but neither Matt nor Anna noticed – they were staring at the tattoo on Jimmy's arm: MT. Matt's brain went into overdrive; the marked trailers! Anna shifted closer to Matt.

'Just before I went the second time, I promised Sandy that when I came back we'd go into business together. I was trying to get him to stay in school.

'But so many awful things happened in 'Nam – the most terrible of all being the death of Min-Thu, the woman I loved.' Jimmy's eyes watered, but he continued on, staring into the fire. He touched his tattoo. 'When Sandy and I started the business, I designed this logo. I tell everyone it stands for Marshall Transport but really it's for Min-Thu.'

He sighed. 'Matt, lad, I'm sorry. This whole thing has been my fault. I kept giving in to Sandy. Didn't try and get him to stop. You see, I felt I owed him, because when I came back from 'Nam, all cut up over Min-Thu's death, he was the one I lashed out at. He ran away and I lost him for six years. *Six years.*

'It took me almost that long to sort myself out. I was sick – malaria. Plus my leg had been infected where the shrapnel from the blast had got me. And I was an alcoholic to boot.

'When I finally did pull myself together, I went looking for Sandy and found him on the streets. We did go into business together, and it was fine for a little while.' Jimmy allowed himself a small smile, obviously thinking of the good times.

'But one night Sandy disappeared. I knew he was taking money from me, but I couldn't work out what he was doing with it. So I followed him and watched as he blew nearly two hundred bucks. That was a lot of money back then. Gambling. He was addicted. Then he told me it was my fault he was the way he was. I had let him down.' Despair filled Jimmy's face. 'My fault,' he whispered. There was a long silence.

Matt and Anna didn't know what to do, so they sat without moving, poised, ready to run if they needed to.

'It was my fault and I let him keep telling me that. I just wanted to make everything right again, so when he said he owed money to loan sharks I found something for him to steal; I encouraged it. I'd set it all up and he'd just have to go and take it. Often I found buyers for the goods he'd taken.

'That way, Sandy could pay off his debts and he'd be okay. Nothing would happen to him. I tried to keep him out of trouble – I bought him a farm, a way to make a good honest living, but he kept going back to gambling. I stood by and watched him crumble and I still couldn't do anything, so I kept finding ways to get money for him.

'I tried to get him to make an honest living through farming. I knew a little about it from when I was a kid and thought I could guide him. That wasn't to be. I could never work out how he kept the farms looking so good when he didn't have very much money. There were always new things; a silo or a bull that had cost the earth. Even with all the goods he was stealing and I was organising for him to take, the money factor never added up.

'Then, the last year or so, I couldn't abide it any longer. Matt, I'd come to know you, I'd seen what our handiwork had done to you, to your family – people that I care about. Then I started to think about the other people we might've hurt. I tried to give you hints, lad. The message on your mobile, and it was me who went to the police. I had to make amends somehow. That's why I kept encouraging you to talk to Anna. I didn't want your marriage breakup on my conscience as well.'

Matt held up his hand. 'I don't want to hear any more. You *arsehole*! Get the fuck out of my house. I never, ever want to see you again. You ruined me! Do you hear? You ruined my life and nearly destroyed my family. How dare you apologise now, as if that could make it right. Well it can't. Get out!'

'Wait, Matt,' Anna said. 'There's just one thing I don't understand. Who's Sandy? The police never mentioned a Sandy.'

Jimmy looked up, his face shattered. 'He's been Sandy since he was a child but when he came off the streets he wanted to leave it all behind. He now goes by Alec – short for Alexander – Alec Harper.'

Matt sprang from the couch in such a rage that Anna cried out.

'*You* bought my farm? You weren't content with sending me broke, but you went and bought my farm too? You bloody bastard! Was it you who hit me too?'

But Jimmy shook his head violently. 'No, lad, no! It wasn't me. It was Sandy, he's got a tattoo in the exact same spot. They were all so worried you were about to blow their whole operation open. All the drugs. Belinda, Shane, Sandy. I had no idea the drug running was going on. Not until Belinda came and threatened me.

She needed the money to keep raising those boys. Sandy needed the money to keep up his appearances and pay off his debts. Shane just seemed to go along with Belinda.'

Jimmy's face was pale and defeated as he fumbled in his jacket for a yellow envelope, which he laid on the chair. 'I am so sorry. That's all I can say: I'm sorry. I tried to tell you by letting you hear our conversation on the phone, but you didn't realise who it was. By then Belinda had come to see me. I don't have much left in my life, Matt, but the business. She would have made Shane resign and dobbed me in for organising thefts. When you didn't pick up on the hint, I wasn't going to push it any further.' He backed away, towards the front door. 'One day I hope you'll be able to see just how sorry I am.'

Epilogue

The yellow envelope from Jimmy had sat in the lounge for weeks before Matt and Anna felt the desire to open it.

They'd followed the case in the paper, had been interviewed by the police and called as witnesses many times, but telling the story never became any easier. Matt was devastated by the final blow Jimmy had delivered. He'd been certain Jimmy was as good a friend as Sam.

There was still an ordeal to get through: a court case, sentencing and a lot more. Today Anna decided it was time to celebrate the closing of that chapter of their lives.

Ella had eaten early and gone to bed by the time Anna lit the candles, set the roses on the table and cooked Matt's favourite meal. When he walked through the door after a day in the sheep yards with Sam, she greeted him with open arms.

'Good day?' she asked.

'Not bad, but better now I'm home.' He wrapped his arms around her and she moved into them, lifting her head for a kiss. Matt moved to go and wash his hands, sniffing at the same time. 'Yum, that smells delicious.'

'Special treat,' Anna said and ran through to the kitchen. 'You go and have a shower and I'll bring you a beer.'

Anna smiled as she heard the water running and looked over at the yellow envelope that she'd been fingering all day. Opening the envelope would bring closure to this whole mess. Today was the day to do it and put the last two years behind them.

After they'd chatted over a drink, Anna served dinner, then dessert. She reached over and picked up the envelope from the bench, saying, 'Don't you think today is a good day to open this?'

Matt looked at it in silence, then took a deep breath. 'We could, I guess. You do it.'

But Anna passed it across to him. 'No, he brought it for you.'

Matt hesitated, then tore the flap open. Inside were three sheets of paper. At first Matt stared at them, uncomprehending, then a smile began to spread across his face.

'Far out,' he said quietly. Then, 'Far out!' He looked at Anna, his face alive. 'He's given us our Manna back, Anna. Our farm!'

Anna grabbed at the papers and looked. Sure

enough, there was Jimmy's signature on each page. All they had to do was sign too and the farm would be theirs once again.

Matt whooped and jumped to his feet, pulling Anna with him. They embraced, laughing and crying, as they saw their future open up once more.

Later, when their excitement had settled and Anna was doing the dishes, Matt flicked through the CD collection until he found the one he was looking for.

'Anna,' he called. 'Come here.'

She appeared in the doorway wiping her hands on a teatowel. 'What's up?' she asked and let out a little squeal as Matt grabbed her around the waist and swirled her around.

'Can I have this dance?' he asked, just as The Police started to sing 'Every Breath You Take'.

'Yes,' Anna replied, looking into his eyes. 'Yes, you can.'

And they danced.

Author's Note

Slim Dusty sang a song called *My Dad was a Road Train Man*. My sister and I used to love singing it together in the car and we always thought of our dad because *he* was a road train man. Together we saw a lot of this wonderful country from the cab of a truck.

Dad, along with a few others, was a pioneer in the trucking world. His achievements include designing and manufacturing the first skeletal trailers with fuel tanks front and back and with a tray in the centre. He was also involved in a practical research project from which the requirements of the operations of triple road trains were developed. This work saw him inducted into the Shell Rimula X Hall of Fame in Alice Springs in 2010.

I am so proud of all that Mum and Dad have achieved together and that's why *Purple Roads* is based around trucks. It's also a thankyou for everything they've done for 'us three kids'. We love you, Mum and Dad.

The Vietnam War was a terrible time. My character Jimmy was conscripted. In real life, he would have had a one-year posting, but for the purposes of this story, he has two. Any other mistakes are my own.

Acknowledgements

To Myles Williamson, for showing me over the trucks, talking the language and helping me with the details. Thanks also for reading the appropriate chapters. So many things have changed since I was a kid hanging out in trucks!

Jeff Ogilvy, the first ever triple road train driver in Australia and friend of the Parnells, thanks for all your stories and help.

Karin Bridle for the offer of help, the reading, and to Alan Bridle for talking about a time that I'm sure he would rather forget: the Vietnam War.

Dave Byrne for once again helping me with plot points and the crime side of things.

Louise Collins, who won the 'naming' competition and changed Cam to Shane (for her brother).

My heartfelt thanks and love go to my family, without whom I am nothing: Anthony, Rochelle, Hayden, Mum and Dad, Nicholas, Ellie, Suz, Nathan, Ned, Mrs McD, Sharon and Ron.

Carolyn Middleton: you know why. You know everything! Love you to pieces.

Margareta Osborn-Kerby: new friends can become like old ones.

My Condy mates: Amanda, Gill, Lynda, Mandy, Tiff, Marie, Sue and Nev.

To my mates away: Mrs Mackay, Kate Biggins and

Robyn Lane. I miss you all so very much and am thankful for the phone!

My wordsmith mates, who love words and books as much as I do: Nicole Alexander, Lisa Heidke, Fiona Palmer, Sara Foster and Wendy Orr, I love talking shop with you all. Thanks for your friendship! And the Queensland Writers Centre, all of you simply rock.

Maggie Mackellar, meeting you has been one of the highlights of writing. You are an inspiration.

Angela Slatter, for your keen eye and friendship. Kim Wilkins, for your advice and teachings.

My agent, Gaby Naher, who is so good at guiding me calmly through the process when I am so highly strung.

Belle Baker, who has grabbed my dream and run with it, displaying as much passion as I could have hoped for.

Siobhán Cantrill, I love working with you. Louise Thurtell and all behind the scenes at Allen and Unwin, I can think of no better hands to be in. Kate Hyde, the book tours won't ever be the same. Will miss you.

Ali Lavau, I do love your edits!

Psalm 139: v 1–18.

To all who read my books, thank you for investing your time in *Purple Roads*. I hope you enjoyed it.